CN00691347

Will Tripp buys
a lifestyle

HETTIE ASHWIN

Published by Slipperygrip 2020

Copyright © Hettie Ashwin
All rights reserved

The moral right of the author has been asserted.
This book is sold subject to the condition that
it shall not, by way of trade or otherwise, be lent,
re-sold, hired out, or otherwise circulated without
the author's proper consent in any form other than
that in which it is published and without a similar
condition including this condition being imposed
on the subsequent purchaser.

PAPERBACK
 ISBN 978-1494998912 published 2014
POCKET EDITION
ISBN: 9782491490027

www.hettieashwin.blogspot.com
facebook.com/alacrity.vivacity

Cartoon by Brooker Studio
www.thebrookerstudio.com

Books by Hettie Ashwin

<u>Humour</u>
Literary Licence
The Reluctant Messiah
Mr Tripp buys a lifestyle
Barney's Test
The Truffle War
Fat Bits
Boat to Baguette
Murder! Mayhem! and lesser cuts of meat.
I'd rather glue me nut sack to a bullet train

<u>Thriller</u>
The Crowing of the Beast

<u>Speculative fiction</u>
The Mask of Deceit
Pi - trilogy

<u>Short Stories</u>
After the Rains & other Stories
A shilling on the Bar

<u>Novellas</u>
A Strange kind of Paradise (series)

He who would go to sea for pleasure,
would go to hell for a pastime

French Proverb.

CHAPTER 1

Mr. Colin Tripp stood back and admired her elegant lines. The words of the agent once again floated through his dream like state. Sound, solid, elegant lady of the sea and a steal. He roused himself and blinked in the bright sunlight. The birds were singing, the fish were jumping, and if there was cotton, it would be high. Mrs Tripp took a look at her husband's glassy eyes and saw the unmistakable signs of love.

'Isn't she a beauty?' he purred to his wife. A real lady of the sea.'

Mrs Vivian Tripp answered in her reserved manner, 'Mmmm.'

'What do you think? I mean *really* think darling.' Mr Tripp looked at the 38' Sloop rigged ferro called Moonlighting which was moored at Hope Springs Marina.

'Is it s'pose to lean like that?' Mrs. Tripp put her head to one side to get the full effect, but Colin Tripp had already resumed his dreams of sailing the seas; the wind in his face, the spray joyfully playing on the bow of the boat and his hat at a jaunty angle.

Mr Avery Lightfoot had wandered off, because

1

as most boat brokers know, you can plant the seed, but you can't make it grow. He had been trying unsuccessfully, on and off, for about eight months to sell Moonlighting; a 38-foot sloop with a sturdy pedigree, an experienced sail boat just waiting for the right mug er- buyer to come along. Some wag had suggested, when he first posted the ad in his office window, that the only way it would sell was if he chucked a mail order bride in the deal, because only a single bloke who had been done over by a divorce would contemplate living in such 'salubrious' surroundings. But Mr Lightfoot was quietly confident he would off-load Moonlighting after an afternoon of photo shopping and a few palm trees, plus two bikini clad lasses were strategically placed in the picture.

'It's not just a boat,' Mr Lightfoot sidled up to Mr Tripp, 'You're buying a lifestyle.' Mr Tripp smiled the smile of one who completely understands the subtleties of such a profound statement.

'A lifestyle,' he murmured, imagining his little peaked cap which was now accompanying a beard and a pipe.

'Er...Mr Lightfoot,' Vivian Tripp interrupted her husband's bonding moment.

'Yeees?' Mr Lightfoot said, knowing a thing or two about the female psyche and boats.

'Can we go onboard?'

'Certainly M' Lady. Certainly.' If there was one rule Mr Lightfoot adhered to in his professional life it was that women have the last word and usually the one after that. Mr. Tripp looked at his wife and then to Mr Lightfoot shrugging his shoulders as if to remind the men, that women really have no idea about boats. It was a condescending look that Mrs Tripp had seen on more than one occasion as Colin dragged her around to lumber yards for the rumpus room that was still in progress, to the metal fabrication shop for the half-built caravan that was to be their retirement excitement and the roadster spare parts department for the fun of restoring a true classic, which stood in the shed covered in an old painting drape.

'Er, would you mind taking off your shoes, the decks you see.' Vivian pursed her lips and slipped off her Hush Puppies and the Tripps followed Avery Lightfoot like lambs to the slaughter. The men stepped off the dock and the boat heeled with their combined weight, groaning and rubbing its oyster encrusted side on the dock. Mr Tripp scampered after the broker into the cockpit and took the wheel. His vision blurred and now the beard and pipe were keeping company with a casually tied kerchief about his neck and a blue and white striped t-shirt.

'Colin,' Vivian snapped and brought her husband into the real world. He smiled and let out a small giggle.

'Darling?' Viv called.

'Sorry honey, here let me help you,' Colin took Vivian's hand and heaved. Once on board she ducked under the bimini, which as an awning had seen better days. It's press studs had given up any hope of holding together sometime after the battle of Waterloo and loose threads hung like spider webs all over the seams. Vivian pulled a pesky thread that fell over her face and set a chain reaction in motion that saw the whole thing unravel in less time than it takes to say 'my goodness'.

3

'They are cheap as chips to replace. People do it regularly up here; it's the tropical sun you know.'

'Oh.' Vivian moved to the side as the awning sagged over her shoulder. Colin once again took the wheel and began to dream.

'Mr. Lightfoot, why are we leaning so dramatically?'

'Well it's not too difficult to understand Mrs Tripp.' Vivian had heard those words more than once. Men thought that just because she wore a skirt and carried a handbag she left her brain at home.

'Understand what darling?' Colin re-joined the tour.

'Mr. Lightfoot was telling me about the lean.'

'Oh the lean,' Colin repeated, pushing up his glasses. Mr Lightfoot slipped into the conversation like an eel into a plate of jelly.

'Why yes. The lean is only because of the blow on berth. The prevailing winds you see. Always blows like this at this time of year. We call the them trades.'

'Trades,' Mr Tripp reiterated breathing deeply.

'Well, what do you want to see first?' Mr Lightfoot knew if he let the client dictate the tour he could quickly gauge what they did and didn't know. Some ask about gudgeon pins and gear box ratios and fractional rigs. Others about fridge capacity and cupboard space and drinks cabinets and then there were those, like the Tripps, who Avery classed as virgins.

'Well I guess we should start at the front,' Mrs Tripp said.

'Bow darling,' Mr Tripp corrected his wife. Colin had been boning up on *Nautical terms for*

4

beginners by Percy Landers, a pocket book he bought at a garage sale while looking for roadster spare parts.

'Right,' Mr Lightfoot concurred and led them along the deck to the bow.

'Watch the lowers as you pass,' he cautioned. The Tripps immediately ducked. 'And be mindful of the dorades. They are virtually irreplaceable at this age.' Mr Tripp trod gingerly looking out for a stray dorade (whatever that might be as Percy Landers hadn't covered that particular subject,) lest it bite his ankle or lasso his wife's handbag.

'Right. Here we are.' Mr Lightfoot stood off to one side. Someone in Moonlighting's past had had the foresight, or the stupidity, to add a bow sprit of enormous proportions. It jutted out like an accusing finger.

'Go on Mrs Tripp. It's quite safe.' Mrs Tripp padded down the plank to the very end in her stocking feet.

'Now you Sir,' Mr Lightfoot thanked the power of the cinema, and the Tripps enacted the scene from Titanic as he pressed his mobile phone to ring, the tone fortuitously being the theme tune.

'Excuse me a minute please.' Mr Lightfoot backed down the foredeck and let the moment wash over his 5% commission. After a decent interval he re-joined the honeymooners. 'Shall we carry on? I've got another person to show through in the afternoon.' This small snippet of information galvanised Mr Tripp. He backed down the plank and rubbed his hands together.

'Right. Let's get on then.' The Tripps were shown the windlass, a real workhorse from a different era when things were made to last and the rigging, which has survived many a storm. Mr. Tripp gave it a satisfactory twang. Mrs Tripp caught her skirt on a small strand of wire poking out which Mr Lightfoot affectionately called a meat hook. The couple nodded and looked at the dorades, as Mr Lightfoot described their ingenious efficiency to swing to the prevailing wind and flood below decks with fresh air.

'Dorades darling,' Mr Tripp pointed as if initiating his wife into an elite club that only talked in nautical terms.

'Are they supposed to whizz about like that in such a light breeze?' Mrs Tripp asked. Colin practiced his look again and Vivian heard him click his tongue.

'All in the design,' Mr Lightfoot commented. 'Now the winches are for the traditionalist you understand.' The broker quickly moved on to the more substantial parts of the boat.

'Of course,' Mr Tripp answered spinning the headsail winch.

'No tailing or 2:1 gearing here, pure muscle.'

'Yes.' Colin fingered the bronze.

'I thought they had removable handles?' Mrs Tripp asked. Colin conceded her the question and looked to Mr Lightfoot.

'Strictly speaking, yes, but these are fixed. No worries about losing it overboard.'

'But wouldn't it be a little...inconvenient?'

'Ma'am?'

'Well it seems to me,' Vivian began, 'that if you have this handle sticking out at that angle it's bound to poke you in the thigh or ribs or knee at some point.' Mr Lightfoot smiled. A sort of condescending smarmy grin that set Vivian's teeth on edge. He drew a pontificating breath.

'A boat has...a different mindset. Things that happen on a boat, Mrs Tripp never happen in a house. You will be surprised how nimble, lithe and athletic you will become at sliding, dodging, ducking and weaving. It will, in time, become second nature.' Mr Lightfoot looked down on the innocents as a Holy Father looks at his flock. 'Shall we go below?' They moved off, Colin's trouser pocket momentarily catching on the winch handle and delivering a small split in his pants.

'The doors are solid wood.' Mr Lightfoot said as he tried the padlock. They sprang open and he pushed the companionway hatch back. A foul musty smell flew out and the Tripps staggered from the odour. Oblivious, Mr Lightfoot pressed on.

'Mind your head,' he said as Colin ducked, but not nearly enough, and a loud crack reverberated through the saloon.

'This is the saloon,' Mr Lightfoot squeezed to one side of the central table as Mrs Tripp slipped into the other, their legs bent ready to sit.

'Sit,' Mr Lightfoot said and Mrs. Tripp plopped onto the bench seat. She tried to lean back, but as the bench seating was made for someone with nine-foot-long legs she more or less slumped like a drunk after a rather boisterous office party.

'Roomy and plenty of space to have a nap,' the broker patted the seating which had as much give as an Indian bed of nails. Colin stood in the doorway and held onto the elaborately turned handhold that fell from the cabin roof to the floor.

'That's teak,' Mr Lightfoot said. Colin stroked the pole and smiled.

'Teak.' Colin mouthed the word.

The broker led them to the V berth. They each took their turn to step into the master bedroom. It had an insert that made the two skinny mattresses into one and took up all the floor space.

'Do you mean we have to dress in the dining area?' Mrs Tripp could see the woman's point of view straight away.

'There's always the bathroom dear.'

'And here it is,' Mr Lightfoot opened a small door that only someone with the hips of a nine-year-old boy could fit through.

Colin and Vivian took turns to poke their heads in the head. The room had various cupboards and boasted a manual toilet that had a permanent snarl. It's out-stretched arm, used for flushing, had a patina of green mould and when Viv lifted the lid she let out a yelp as a crab scuttled down into its bowels.

'What was that?' Colin craned his neck to see.

'I'm not sure, but it was alive.' Vivian stepped back into the saloon setting a chain reaction in motion as the two men moved out the way, ending up with Colin sitting on Avery's lap who was slumped on the saloon seat.

'Well of course the toilet will have to be replaced, new regulations and all that.' Avery attempted to slide sideways out of a difficult situation in more ways than one.

'What do you mean?' Colin, in a well-practiced nervous action, pushed his glasses up his nose.

'Well Mr Tripp, Colin,' Mr. Lightfoot began, 'The new regulations stipulate that you need a holding tank, and as this head goes straight out to the sea,' he arched his eye brows, 'there is no macerator.' Avery let the words sink in. 'The new modern electric heads have a macerator and then the waste is deposited in a tank which is pumped out at a more convenient time.'

'Oh.' Colin nodded as things were as clear as mud. Viv had more of a handle on the situation.

'So, we need a new toilet and a holding tank and something to pump it out?'

'Well that's about the jist of it.' Avery nodded.

'And where do we pump?'

'Well there is talk of a pumping station being built in the near future, at the yacht club.' Even Colin could see the next question.

'And what do we do in the meantime Mr Lightfoot?' Vivian asked with more than a bit of sarcasm.

'Well madam, you have to go beyond the green zones and well....' Avery politely coughed and left it up to their imagination as the conversation was becoming decidedly off. The three stood in the musty boat and entered a quiet zone thinking of exactly what would happen beyond the green zones. After a decent interval Mr Lightfoot coughed again and continued the tour. He crab walked to the galley and turned to Vivian.

'You will appreciate this Mrs Tripp.' Avery hooked his finger into a latch set in the cupboard top and pulled. The lid lifted on the fridge and Viv peered into the dark depths.

'What is it?'

'The fridge M'lady.' Vivian scrunched up her nose and took a good look. The lining was streaked in mould, there was the odd piece of something that she assumed used to be food on the shelf and the copper piping hung like gallows with a plastic bag slung over it like a criminal. Vivian shot a look at Colin,

'The fridge,' she said and stepped back.

'And the stove is a classic.' Avery pulled a filthy tea towel off the burners. The two-burner stove was covered in black although it was supposed to be stainless steel. 'Just needs a bit of elbow grease. Nothing a bit of hard work and a woman's touch won't fix.' Viv pursed her lips at the demarcation line concerning jobs. Avery went into overdrive, 'And these sorts of things are worth a fortune on eBay if you had a mind to sell it. People love the traditional.'

'Traditional,' Colin reiterated, nodding his head in agreement.

'Just look at the storage Mrs Tripp.' Avery Lightfoot shuffled out of the way and the Tripps moved in turn to fit into the tight space.

'Now the engine?' Colin asked. Mr Lightfoot smiled and rubbed his hands, then massaged Colin's perceived weak spot.

'Ah, I can see you are a man who knows a thing or two.' Colin puffed up his chest while Vivian narrowed her eyes at Mr Lightfoot, not being fooled for an instant. Avery moved to the table and began the Chinese puzzle that was needed to see the engine. He unlatched the table wings, slid the middle panel forward, clipped the two sections to the mast, which went through to the keel, knocked back the pin holding the sliding bolt and the table folded away. Then he unhooked the box over the engine from the floor latches and flicked up its removable sides leaning them on the seats. Finally, he slid the rest of the box off the engine and with a nifty piece of rope to stop it falling, he trussed it to the cabin roof.

'Easy.' he said and smiled. Colin looked at the workhorse as Mr Lightfoot described the Lister two cylinder 'dunga'.

'Why dunga?' Colin asked.

'It's an affectionate term for the noise it makes. Dunga, dunga.' They all looked down at the dirty, grease encrusted, monster with a life support system of hoses that stretched back into the dark recesses of the boat.

'Reliable?'

'Made to last.'

'Easy to service?'

'Solid.'

'Low hours?'

'Classic.' The way Avery sidestepped every question he should have been a politician.

'Should there be water down there, Mr Lightfoot?' Vivian watched the black swill slop from side to side. Avery put on his condescending look, 'for women who just don't understand the mechanical things' and smiled.

'Most boats have,' and here he slowed his speech as if talking to an idiot, 'bilge water.'

'Bilge water darling,' Colin relayed the information. Vivian pursed her lips as tight as a clam about to be prised off a rock.

'Hmmmm. They moved over while Avery re-assembled the table like he was on a game show and the clock was ticking.

'Right. Shall we?' He steered the Tripps to the cockpit and fresh air, then went into his spiel. He pointed out the merits of Moonlighting, the camaraderie, the almost free holidays, the various anchorages within spitting distance and the family fun that could be had for the modest price. Then he took it up a notch extolling the virtues of yachting and its green credentials with solar power, wind power, battery banks and 12-volt bliss.

'Your carbon footprint is about a size 5,' he ended smiling. If Colin had been given a pen the deal would have been done, but Vivian steered him away from the hard sell and said they would think about it.

'I understand completely. But I must tell you others are interested and I'm bound to show them through.'

'Oh, we understand completely Mr. Lightfoot. Absolutely.' Colin grinned and followed his wife off the boat.

'Absolutely.' Vivian added, as she slipped on her Hush Puppies.

'Uncle Frank would have loved it.' Colin drove home along the highway and tried to reason with his wife.

'Oh, I'm sure he would Colin, but he left that money in his will with the stipulation to have some fun, not do up an old boat and get rid of unmentionables beyond the green zone.' Vivian picked at the pulled thread on her skirt.

'But just think of the fun we could have. And all free Viv. All free. That's got to count for something.' Vivian thought of the holiday brochures she had gathered when they first heard of Uncle Frank's money. Tasmania – 4-star hotels, spa baths, and all the extras. New Zealand – 10 days of luxury travel, Paris by train, Rio at mardi gras. It was all possible with dear old Uncle Frank and his last wish.

'But how long has it been since we had a real holiday Col? Or even a honeymoon?' Colin mused on the question. Their honeymoon was cut short when he was called back to work after the partner at the accountancy firm died unexpectedly. They tried to have a holiday a few years later, but their first child decided he wanted to be there too and arrived three weeks early and it seemed something was always in the way. Now he could see endless holidays, family trips, and all in the comfort of their own boat.

'Now we can go on as many holidays as we want Viv. Just imagine it. No packing, just hop on board and throw the lines off and we are away. He drove up their driveway and cut the engine. 'Viv, I really want this, and I think Uncle Frank would have approved.' Vivian gathered her hat and bag and looked at the hang dog expression sitting next to her.

'Well...how about we go for that trial sail Mr Lightfoot talked about. Then we can decide if we really like it.' Colin shut the door of the Commodore and smiled. *It was a start*, he thought. They walked around the back of the house passed the half-built rumpus room that was to be for the kids, who had now all left home and went to open the back door, but it was already open.

'Rodney? Mike? Sandra?' Vivian yelled out to discover which one of the kids was visiting home.

'It's me, Mum,' Sandra yelled back from the lounge. Vivian dumped her handbag on the kitchen counter and put the kettle on.

'Where have you two been?' Sandra asked. She came into the kitchen and busied herself with the coffee machine.

'Oh, we went to see a boat.'

'It's a yacht darling, not a boat.'

'A yacht then,' Vivian corrected herself with just a hint of sarcasm.

'A yacht. I don't understand?' Sandra poured the coffee.

'Well, it's like this...' and Colin explained everything from the free holidays to the family trips, to the hours of endless fun.

'What Dad has left out is that Uncle Frank said to do something *we* would enjoy. I really don't think he meant buy a boat. I thought he, more or less, meant go on a holiday.'

'But it will be a holiday. An endless holiday Viv. Nothing to do but enjoy ourselves.' Vivian had heard those words more than once. She wanted to remind Colin of the camping adventures they planned. She packed, she cooked, she cleaned, she unpacked, she washed, she cleaned and Colin carried the car keys.

'Well we haven't decided just yet Sandy. The broker,' and here Vivian qualified what she actually thought of Avery Lightfoot. 'Who is as slippery as a greasy pole, said we could go on a test run. A sort of little sail to see if we like the boat...yacht' Viv

14

finished looking over to Colin.

'Sounds interesting.' Sandra had a fair idea of her father's brain buster ideas. She still bore the scars from his attempt to build a tandem bicycle that saw her brother cruise around the corner of the house while she went straight ahead into the garage door.

'What brings you home anyway Sandy?' Vivian asked.

'As it happens I'm going to a fancy dress and I wanted to borrow that striped jumper you have Mum. It's a nautical theme party. Todd needs the Captain's hat. He has the beard and pipe. I'm a crew member.'

'No worries Luv, I'm sure we can find it and something else besides.' While the women busied themselves, Colin stepped outside to finish his coffee and spied his next-door neighbour, Ted Gunn.

'G'day Ted.' Colin said as he sauntered over to the dividing fence.

'Howdy.' Ted stopped his gardening labours and came over for a chat. It didn't take long for Colin to slip his boating excursion into the conversation and even less time for Ted to step in with,

'Boats! I know everything about boats Col. In the blood you see. My relative was a sea Cap't'n from way back. I can tell you everything you need to know. Don't you worry about that!' Colin nodded. Very early on in their relationship Colin realised that Ted knew everything about everything and this accumulated knowledge was about as much use as a chocolate teapot. If pressed for a few examples Colin would show the rumpus room windows that weren't square (on Ted's expert eye for these things), the redundant plumbing pipes that cost a small fortune to install (on Ted's expertise in these matters,) that had to be pulled up and relayed and the electrical fire which nearly gutted the caravan because Ted installed a small exhaust fan over the cooker. All these forays into DIY came with Ted's unequivocal 'Don't you worry about that!' Why he became embroiled in Ted's handyman misadventures Colin couldn't quite say. His wife on the other hand *could* say and did so, on numerous occasions. So, it was with a small sigh and some misgivings that Colin nodded his head and tried not to invite Ted to take a look at his mooted purchase. He sipped his coffee, looked at his feet, ran his tongue over his front teeth, but pride is a funny thing. Before Colin could say poop deck, somehow Ted was invited to come down to the marina and have a look at Moonlighting, just to see if it was a good deal. All Colin had to do now was tell Vivian. He wished he could say 'don't you worry about that!'

Colin slipped his impending visit to the boat into the conversation as Vivian was serving up tea. He hoped she might not hear straight, or not hear at all, but he had no such luck.

'Not Ted, Colin. What does he know?'

'Well actually, he knows quite a bit. He said...' and here Colin went on to extol the virtues of Ted's maritime history and his depth of knowledge ending with,

'And his uncle, or something, was a Captain, or something.' Vivian served the tea and bit her lip. She didn't want to press the point with Colin as she had hoped to work on him, starting with his favourite food, to see the sense of a holiday in luxury and excess, lots or excess.

'Well if you think it is a good idea darling. Pork chops and apple sauce?' for Colin, life didn't get any better than this.

It was in bed when Colin did his best brainstorming. There were endless possibilities when he was lying flat on his back and using Viv as his sounding board. Now he lay down and threaded his hands behind his head, crossed his legs, stretched out and closed his eyes. The vision he saw brought a smile to his lips.

'You know they say boating is the family thing to do,' he played the woman's sentimental card. 'And you always said we should do things as a family.' Vivian sat down and rubbed her hand cream over her elbows.

'Oh Col, don't you think after all these years I know what you are trying to do. You'll have to try harder than that.'

'Well, Uncle Frank's money shouldn't just be frittered away Viv. I don't think your holiday is what he had in mind. I think he would want a lasting epitaph.' In a blinding moment of inspiration Colin suggested they re-name the boat Frank.

'Well, we don't really know what he had in mind at all, do we? He was such an eccentric type of man.' Vivian swung her legs onto the bed and snuggled up to her husband, threading her legs

17

through his. Colin began.

'Remember when we went for that beach holiday? Uncle Frank always wanted to hire that boat. He even bought that Captain's cap. The one that Sandy took for her fancy dress.' Col opened his eyes and looked at his wife. 'And he had that anchor in the front yard.'

'Only because someone left it there and he never bothered to move it. Remember Col, he swapped his wheelbarrow for it and then he had no way of moving it. Must have been on the front lawn for 5 years or more.' Colin frowned at the memory. Uncle Frank had asked him to help move it once and Colin had spent a week in a back brace after he did something to a disc. It was a reoccurring niggly pain that now could lay him up for at least a week.

'I remember. But just think of the fun Viv. The free things we could do.' Here Colin closed his eyes and a smile played over his mouth. 'I would be on the deck; you could be sunbaking on the front deck, the kids fishing, the sun warming our backs. We could eat fresh caught fish; anchor up at night, the waves gently rocking us to sleep in our own home. The morning sun waking us and the smell of the sea.' He sighed. 'Then sailing with the sails out, the crack of the wind. The crew all pulling together. I could use Uncle Frank's cap with the braid and we could have such fun. Imagine it Viv. Fun for free. We could go anywhere we wanted.' He sighed again and let his mind wander for a minute. 'You know I read that boating and marriage go together. You gain a lifetime companion. You realise your strengths together, your weaknesses.'

Colin knew all this soppy talk was a bit much,

18

but he knew his wife even better.

'But Col,' Viv began, 'Uncle Frank did tell me that we needed to relax. Right after you started the extensions. He said, 'Viv you need to go somewhere and relax. If I had the money right now I'd say you need to have a holiday',' Vivian played with Colin's chest hair twirling it about. 'Can't you see us in a nice hotel with a spa and champagne, soaps, candles, music, then dressing for dinner? Steaks and seafood cocktails. We could take a cruise. That's on a boat. Imagine all the things we could do Col. We could just relax for 10 days.' Viv reached over and brought out the travel agents' brochure from under her pillow. 'It says you can eat at over 6 different restaurants. 40 different specialty shops and look, they have a different movie every night. I could wear my new shoes and that dress I saw the other day for $60. You could be in Chino's and a polo top with one of those sweaters over your shoulders. We would stroll along the deck, the light breeze playing on our tanned faces, music wafting over the calm sea, gin fizz in our hand...' Viv imagined her wardrobe and dinner at the Captain's table.

'Huh, sorry luv, I dropped off. What were you saying?'

 CHAPTER 2

Colin looked out of the kitchen window – it was going to be a glorious day for sailing. He waved a tea towel at Ted, who looked up from his lawn mower. Colin opened the window and in a fit of enthusiasm yelled that it was a fine day for sailing. A rip snorter.

Ted licked his index finger and thrust the digit in the air, much like a bidder at auction and looked skyward.

'From the south east Col. A bit rough by the arvo,' he pontificated on Colin's big day. Colin knew the forecast as he had been up half the night on the internet watching the isobars as someone studies the stock market, looking for that window of opportunity. It came at 3:27 with the forecast of light winds, 5 to 10 knots.

'Colin, is that Ted?' Vivian walked to the window and peered into the yard.

'Just telling him we're going out sailing.'

'He's not coming, is he?' Vivian grabbed Colin's arm steadying herself for the answer. She remembered all too vividly their last outing with Ted and vowed then never to repeat the experience.

Colin's broken glasses, a black eye and they still had to pay the parking fine after Ted put up a fight with the sticker licker and Colin was in the way.

'No, no. Not this time. I was just telling him our plans that's all,' Colin tried to dispel anything that could spoil his day. He knew from bitter experience Vivian could stick her heels in and you couldn't change her opinion, not even if the bribe came with diamonds. He was aware that the boating life for the Tripps needed to be introduced in small steps, each one carefully managed to afford the maximum fun and stress-less experience. Once again, he assured his wife Ted was definitely not coming.

'Not on your Nelly Viv, this time it's just us. I plan a glass of champagne, fish lunch and well...' he patted her bottom, 'who knows what else besides. Vivian smiled and made a mental note not to pack her bathers.

The drive to the marina was occupied for the most part with lists.

'Did you bring the sunscreen?'

'Yes.'

'Have you got the keys?'

'Yep.'

Did you pack, what about the, should we have brought and the list went on.

'I rang Mr Lightfoot,' Viv began, 'and he said we needed jackets, and hats and could we get hold of an EPIRB?'

'A what?'

'That's what I thought. I didn't want him to think I was a complete fool, so I said I would see what we could do. He said we could buy one from him, if necessary. What is it?'

'Beats me.' Colin shrugged his shoulders.

'Perhaps we could go to the shop at the marina? They should have it.'

'Good thinking.' Colin patted his wife's leg.

'Excuse me, could we have an EPIRB? A large size if you don't mind.' Colin went into imagining the exchange. 'Oh, and one for my wife, the green if you have it.' Viv laughed adding,

'Does it come with a salad, or is it extra, I'm not sure I could manage an EPIRB and salad.' They both giggled at the idea.

'Sir, take your hand off my wife's EPIRB, you cad.'

'Oo darling, you have got a big EPIRB, let me help you with that.' The joke ended and they laughed as Colin pulled into the marina car park.

Hope Springs Marina lay in a basin of water that the tide seemed to have forgotten. The turgid soup carried flotsam and jetsam around the boats as if someone was going into recycling and had decided to have a weekend off. Plastic P.E.T bottles, plastic bags, the odd banana peel and a brown scum which hung off the mooring ropes and looked quite nasty greeted the Tripps as they walked down to Moonlighting for a quick look. She was tied up to the dock with some blue and yellow rope that had seen better days.

'We should replace that,' Colin pointed to the twine.

'Well, let's just get our EPIRB first.' Vivian said. They walked back up to the small set of shops nestled in the corner of the complex and Colin pointed,

'Look a Chandlery.' The sign indicating the Hope Springs Chandlery hung on one lone screw and swung in the light breeze. The Tripps walked inside and took a step back as the merchandise crowded every spare space and seemed to be racing for the door.

'Hey ho,' a voice shouted from the depths.

'Hello?' Colin answered. The Tripps peered around a mountain of cables and wire.

'Hang on, won't be long.' the voice shouted. Colin and Vivian waited at the door and then a squat, barrel-chested, sun pocked, dishevelled man poked his head around a stand of hats and grinned.

'Rowdy Rawlinson,' the man introduced himself with a booming voice and squeeze his fat body past the hat stand and held out his hand.

'Colin Tripp and this is my wife, Vivian.'

'T'rific. Now what you after?' Rowdy shouted. Viv looked at Colin and he began.

'Well...we are going out sailing today and Mr Lightfoot...you do know the broker, Mr Lightfoot?' Rowdy nodded and Viv winced in anticipation of another shouting match. Colin continued, 'Well. Mr. Lightfoot suggested we get an ...' Col looked sheepishly at Rowdy, 'An EPIRB?'

'Bollocks.' Rowdy roared.

'Pardon.'

'Bloody bollocks,' Rowdy boomed. 'You're the couple,' he shouted at Viv, 'What's gonna buy Moonlightin' yeah?' Colin nodded and smiled.

'Well, ya only goin' on a short haul yeah?' Colin nodded again and began to feel like one of those little dogs on the parcel shelf of a car.

'Well,' Rowdy shouted, 'ya don't really need

23

one. Lightfoot will have one.'

'But,' Colin began and Rowdy held up his hand.

'Look,' he put his arm around Colin's shoulder and shouted in his ear. 'Lightfoot is just trying it on, ya know ... he's probably getting a kick back or some'in.' Colin nodded again.

'So, Mr Rawlinson, you are telling us we don't need one?'

'Yeah,' Rowdy shouted at Viv. Vivian shot a look at Col and mimed slippery eel. Colin let his eyes wander over the shop.

'Could you think of anything we might need Mr Rawlinson?' Rowdy smiled and thought the Tripps a gift from heaven.

When Colin and Vivian finally left the chandlery, they had several shopping bags and an ear ache.

'I'm not sure we really needed that hat,' Viv looked at Col sporting his Captain's hat.

'And I think you could do without those things on your sunglasses and that extra strap,' he pointed at Vivian's toggle glasses straps and matching hat strap that anchors your hat to your shirt collar. Vivian fished about in one of the bags and brought out the brass key ring in the shape of a ships wheel.

'I bought this for you darling,' she handed over the present. Colin looked at his wife and smiled.

'This is going to be fun, and we got out of it for under $150. How good is that?'

They walked to the Commodore and started to assemble their gear for the trip.

'These coats are great,' Colin slipped his windbreaker on and admired himself in the car window.

'Mr Rawlinson...Rowdy said they will breathe,

and if we don't decide to buy Moonlighting then we'll still have very serviceable jackets for a holiday, or something.' Vivian put her matching jacket on and they gathered the esky and their picnic and went in search of Avery Lightfoot.

Mr Lightfoot hailed the Tripps from the dock and watched as they made their way to the pontoon.

'Morning all,' he said and held out his hand. 'Any luck with the EPIRB?'

'Well,' Colin began. 'Rowdy said...' Avery made a face like he had been sucking on sour plums at the mention of Rowdy and his advice.

'Oh, never mind about that. I managed to get one.' He fished about in his bag and produced the device. Viv and Col came in close and looked at the Emergency Positioning Indicator Radio Beacon.

'No salad,' Vivian dug Colin in the ribs with her elbow and giggled.

'Eh?' Avery said over his shoulder.

'Nothing,' Viv trilled and smiled at Colin. They followed Avery down the ramp and trotted up to C15 where Moonlighting was moored.

'I've been over things this morning and she's ready to go.' Avery smiled and Vivian shivered. *A rat with a gold tooth,* she thought to herself. 'Need a hand?' Avery went to put his hand on Viv's bottom.

'No thanks,' Viv side stepped the contact. 'I wore my slacks this time. No meat hooks today. All that ducking and weaving Mr Lightfoot.' Avery watched Vivian get onboard and Colin followed.

'Now we need to understand what is happening here,' Avery said and then gave the Tripps the lowdown on what and how and when to get the boat under way. Aside from his lascivious manner he knew his stuff and Vivian and Colin listened, nodding in all the right places.

'So, are we ready?' The Tripps nodded. Avery went below and opened the seacock for the engine, then turned the key. The Lister coughed. He was about to give it another go when there was a commotion on the dock.

'Hey, hey,' someone was shouting. Avery came up the companionway steps to see a large man running for the boat.

'Ted,' Colin said, his eyes as big as all-round anchor lights. Col looked over to his wife who was fiddling with the bimini cover so it didn't impede the view. Vivian whipped around and if looks could kill, Ted would have been in Davy Jones's locker before he took another step.

'I,' Ted puffed, 'Just,' he huffed, 'made it.' he took a deep breath and held onto the teak gunwale.

'I...' Colin began and then thought better of it and shut up.

'Gloria said I could come at the last minute.' Ted smiled. Vivian narrowed her gaze and made a mental note to strike her next-door neighbour off the Christmas card list. Ted heaved himself onto the boat and lumbered down the side deck to the cockpit. He caught the winch handle in the groin on the way and let out a yelp.

'Watch that,' Viv said stifling a giggle, 'Boats can be a bit tricky sometimes.' Avery came into the crowded cockpit and Colin introduced Ted.

'My neighbour, Ted Gunn.' Mr Lightfoot held out his hand.

'All set then?'

26

'Absolutely,' Ted said and took his place behind the steering station. Avery beckoned Viv downstairs and proceeded to show her what to do.

'When I shout, just turn the key, just like starting a car. Then when she is ticking over, dunga, dunga, your job is done.' Viv nodded. Avery went back outside and gave Ted a steely glare. Ted moved over.

'Right, Colin,' he began, and then explained the gear lever, the throttle and reiterated the rope sequence. Colin nodded some more.

'OK people, let's go.' Mr Lightfoot knew a thing or two about boats - and people. He had Colin casting off the lines, he told Ted to bring in the fenders, and Vivian starting the engine.

Moonlighting gradually reversed out into the channel and then Avery put her into forward gear and she gently gathered speed, one dunga at a time.

At high tide the channel to the open sea can look quite inviting. It is only on low tide that the jagged rocks are displayed to frighten sailors. Colin looked at the hazard and thought the best course of action was to close his eyes.

'Do you feel alright?' Viv asked seeing her husband with his eyes shut tight.

'Fine, just...thinking.' As Moonlighting made her way down to the breakwater's end Colin opened his eyes and began to smile. He took a deep breath and put on his jaunty hat and stood next to Lightfoot itching to take the wheel.

'Can I...have a go?' he asked Lightfoot in the manner of school boy asking to light the bunsen burner. Avery stood firm and gave Colin a withering stare, as if to say - you must be on drugs. He gently steered the boat around the last marker and then Lightfoot turned to starboard and headed for the shipping channel, when there was a loud splash. Viv came sprinting up the stairs and Colin stood on the cockpit seats.

'What was that?' he yelled. Ted popped up from the side deck.

'It just rolled off - not my fault.' Avery, Colin and Viv watched as one of the fenders bobbed in their wake.

'We'll have to go back Mr. Lightfoot?' Colin asked.

'Not possible I'm afraid. On a schedule here.'

'Oh.' Colin nodded and looked for Ted who had ducked down and seemed to be out of sight.

'Er Mr. Lightfoot,' Vivian began, 'I was just noticing the instrument panel down there,' she pointed into the saloon. 'Should the needles be jumping about like that? One actually says it's 195 degrees in the red.' Colin listened in and silently cursed he didn't ask the first intelligent question. Mr Lightfoot gave one of his condescending smiles and Viv ground her teeth and narrowed her gaze for what was to come.

'Calibration my dear. It's a concept.' Colin nodded and looked at his wife,

'A concept Viv.' He adjusted his hat, pushed his glasses up his nose and with slightly splayed footing he put his hands on his hips and looked ahead. His pose wouldn't have been out of place on the jacket of a seafaring novel except for the price tag still attached to his hat and waving in the wind.

'Not bad,' he said to no-one in particular, 'making good time.' Ted reappeared in the cockpit and hung on.

'Right - what about the mainsheet?' Avery looked at the men. Colin nodded and grinned.

'Boy-' Avery pointed to Ted, 'get f'w'd.' Ted began to squeal that he knew a thing or two about boats when Avery barked, 'NOW.' A pig running from the butcher's knife couldn't have moved quicker.

'You,' Colin flinched, 'play out the sheet rope.'

'Er, Mr Lightfoot,' Viv began. 'Could you just explain that for my benefit?' She played the helpless female and the men hung on Captain Bligh's every word.

'It's quite simple Mrs. Tripp. He...' and Avery pointed to Ted, 'is going to the mast and start to wind the sail up. Your husband...' and Avery pointed to Colin, whose ears were flapping as if they were employing semaphore to signal the passing island ferry they had an idiot on board, 'is going to hold the rope when it comes off the winch because it isn't self-tailing.' Avery grinned and raised his eye brows which made him look a bit simple.

'Thank you,' Viv said and winked at Col.

'Right,' Colin said and he scampered to the mast. 'Ted, come on.' he yelled back to his neighbour. Ted's knuckles were white as he hung onto the life rail. He blew out a large breath and then wiped his brow.

'I just...' he started and then his stomach gave a heave. Whatever he had had for breakfast it didn't present well at elevensees. Ted lent over the rail and let rip. Viv and Avery looked away, not so much out of politeness, but to stop that awful thing called a chain reaction.

'I have kwells,' Viv offered, trying to hide her smirk.

'No good now. Should have taken 'em hours ago.' Avery tutted and stood firm.

'What should I get him then?' Viv asked.

'Ginger beer.'

'I have orange cordial.' Viv went below and returned with a bottle of orange and a straw. Ted grabbed at the offering and sucked like a mosquito at a carotid artery.

'Looks like you're the crew now Mrs T.' Avery grinned and Viv made her way to the mast feeling Lightfoot's gaze on her backside most of the way.

'Colin, Ted's sick.'

'Oh.' Colin gave a sly grin. 'Too bad,' he smiled.

'Colin!' Viv began to admonish her husband. Colin shrugged his shoulders,

'Bad luck eh?' and they began to giggle.

'OK,' Avery yelled, 'I'm rounding up.'

The Tripps waited for his signal and then, when the boat was facing into the wind, they began to inch the mainsail up the mast. It was half way when it jammed.

'It's stuck,' Colin yelled. The canvas flapped about.

'Take a look at the slugs,' Avery yelled back.

'What?' Colin shouted.

'He said to look at the slugs,' Viv explained.

'Slugs?'

'I think he means these,' Viv pointed to the sail slugs, the small runners that slide into the track up the mast.

'How did you know that?'

'Well, when we were in the shop and you were looking at those boots and...' Viv was cut short.

'For the love of...' Avery started, 'we'll be in New Guinea if you don't get on with it.' Colin found the problem and repositioned the offending slug and they continued to hoist the sail. It travelled all the way to the top then he cleated off the halyard and looked up. The canvas was an off white with quite a few patches, one particularly catching their eye.

'Southside tractor parts?' Viv read the patch. 'Should we ask for a signage fee?' Colin counted thirteen patches including the one made from an advertising banner.

'I think it's still ok Viv. Just needs a bit of this and that.' Vivian had heard those words on more than one occasion. The 'this and that' usually ended with a shed full of redundant parts, cheap Chinese tools for every eventuality 'because if you want the job done, you must have the right tools' and a depleted bank balance.

'Hang on,' Avery cautioned and brought Viv back to the present. Moonlighting turned to catch the wind on a beam reach and she picked up her pace. The sail caught the wind and filled then Avery beckoned Viv to the steering station.

'Cut the engine.' he ordered. She trotted downstairs and pushed the stop button. Suddenly the world was quiet except for the odd belch from Ted. Colin and Viv sat in the cockpit and couldn't stop smiling. Avery looked at the beaming faces and knew Moonlighting was sold. He tapped Colin on the shoulder,

'You're the Captain.' Colin stood up, gave his hat a final pull and positioned himself behind the wheel.

'Just keep her on this course. The wind is doing all the work.' Avery sat back and began to count his commission plus GST. Colin put all his concentration into steering and held the boat on course. He smiled at Vivian and his chest swelled,

'Isn't it grand?'

'Yes,' Vivian replied looking at her husband having the time of his life. She put her dreams of a luxury cruise away in the back of her mind and started to think of boat shoes and ships bells, when her musings were rudely interrupted by Ted and a belch that sounded as if a bath plug had lodged in his epiglottis.

'Sorry.' Ted winced and tried to concentrate on the horizon.

'Would you like something to eat? A dry biscuit perhaps?' Viv could see Ted was suffering. He shook his head and swallowed hard, the plug refusing to do its duty and stop the flow, and retched over the side.

'He needs something in his stomach.' Lightfoot sat back and watched the sail. Vivian popped downstairs and returned with some of their picnic lunch.

'Chicken salad roll?' She passed over the wrapped roll and Ted grasped the offering as a dying atheist grabs at confession. When he had finished he perked up and looked skyward.

'That looks a bit iffy.' Ted pointed to a cloud on the horizon.

'Iffy?' Lightfoot asked following the

pointed finger.

'Yup, iffy.' They all looked to the bank of cloud on the horizon.

'It's moving away. Nothing to worry about.' Lightfoot resumed his seat.

'Er, Mr Lightfoot,' Vivian stood up. 'Can you just run through the toilet one more time. I ...' Avery smiled and licked his lips. Vivian shuddered at the lascivious lech. The pair disappeared below and Ted slid over to Colin.

'I'd go in that direction if I was you.'

'Where?'

''There,' Ted pointed to the outcrop of rocks at the end of Magnetic Island.

'Why? Mr Lightfoot said keep on this course.'

'Don't you worry about that Col, I know these waters, and there is a reef just beyond that marker.'

Ted stood up and tried to wrestle the wheel from Colin's grip.

'Hey.' Colin gripped the wheel a little tighter and looked his neighbour in the eye.

'Boat coming Colin.' Ted pointed to the Maggie Island Ferry heading in their direction and as Colin turned to look Ted slipped into the prime position.

'What the?' Colin stood to one side.

'Ted look,' Col pointed to the ferry which could travel at 22 knots rather than Moonlighting's 4. Ted, not to be fooled by the same ploy, took on the stance of Captain and only a sharp bread and butter knife would have prised the limpet off his rock.

'Ted, I really think we need to manoeuvrer - that ferry...' Colin stared at the power cat looming large on the horizon.

'No worries.'

'Mr. Lightfoot,' Colin shouted down the companionway into the saloon.

'Just a minute,' Avery replied. 'We are having a bit of trouble with the door.' His understatement was just enough to get him some time as Vivian was locked in the bathroom and the door jammed shut. Colin fished about for the quick reference guide he purchased from Rowdy. It denoted the bag size for crabs, flags for quarantine, the telephone number in case you found yourself rescuing a dozen boat refugees and needed an interpreter and the mixture ratio for 2 stroke outboards, but nothing in the way of road rules at sea. He racked his brain to remember what Rowdy had said when he regaled them with a frightening tale of shipwreck.

'I think we pass on the right,' Colin offered, adding, 'motor gives way to sail.'

Ted smiled, 'Don't you worry about that,' and resolutely stuck to his heading which would lead Moonlighting straight across the path of the Magnetic Island Ferry and if they didn't clip that one there would be another in half an hour.

'Mr. Lightfoot,' Colin sounded frantic.

'Right, just a tick.'

'NOW.' Colin barked. Avery scooted upstairs and saw Colin's eyes, which reminded him of that overdue Alfred Hitchcock movie he had at home.

'What is it?' Colin pointed to the ferry and as Avery turned the wave piercing power cat blew its horn five times.

'Arrgh,' Avery let out a yelp and flung himself like a bargain shopper at the January sales after a 36' flat screen T.V. at Ted and the wheel and the boat began to turn.

The ferry passed in a spray of water, the tourists training their cameras, iphones and video recorders on Moonlighting and the near miss, including Avery's rugby tackle, and probably uploaded the whole thing on Utube within 20 minutes.

'Jeez.' Ted lay on the cockpit floor. 'Someone should do something about those ferries. Maniacs on the high seas.' He picked himself up as the boat rocked in the ferry's wake and sat down. 'Any more of those sandwiches?'

Avery settled down and breathed a sigh of relief.

'Do you have any qualifications?' he shook his head in disbelief and glared at Ted.

'Well I did have a boat licence once.' Ted said. Avery cocked an eyebrow.

'I...well...it...' Ted stammered then fell back on the tried and true, 'don't you worry about that.' He turned, 'Oh look, a seagull.' he pointed and hoped to change the subject. The three men in the boat looked at the gull when they heard a loud knocking from below.

'Oh, my Lord, Mrs T,' Avery jumped up and began to go downstairs then took a long hard look at Ted.

'Colin, could you just go? The latch has broken.'

Colin went inside and yelled to his wife, 'Coming darling.'

He surveyed the door and quickly ascertained that the handle was on upside down and the tongue had fallen in on itself. *If nothing else*, Viv thought as she heard scrabbling on the other side of the door, *Colin was an expert at pulling things apart*.

'Hang on Viv.' Colin found a screwdriver in

the cutlery draw and was soon at work and in the time it takes to say 'open the seacock and pump vigorously' Viv was free.

'Heavens. I thought I'd be in there forever.' Vivian kissed her husband and smiled.

'So, what was happening up there?'

'Well, it seems our neighbour...'

Viv held up her hand, 'Stop right there Colin Tripp. If it involves Ted I really don't want to know. That man infuriates me. Why did he come along anyway? He is such a...'

It was Colin's turn to hold up his hand. 'Viv, he's here now.' Colin pulled his wife close, 'so we will just have to grin and bear it I guess.' Vivian gritted her teeth.

'Hhummpp.'

'Ahoy there.' Mr Lightfoot yelled below. 'Alright down there?' Colin and Viv emerged blinking in the bright sunlight,

'Er...that door seems to be on upside down or something.' Colin began.

'Well, a minor detail Colin. Minor,' and here Mr Lightfoot shot a withering stare at Ted Gunn who was hovering in the cockpit itching to get his hands on the wheel.

'Er...Vivian, you have anything else to settle my stomach? Must have had a dodgy egg this morning for breakfast. I told Gloria not to buy that free-range stuff.

'Viv?' Colin asked his wife.

'I've another sandwich if you'd like,' Vivian tried to be civil.

'Great.' The three men looked to Viv in the

expectation she would jump at the request and scuttle downstairs. The pregnant pause lasted for an uncomfortable half a minute and then Ted coughed,

'I'll go shall I?'

'What a good idea.' Vivian said a little too sarcastically.

Ted disappeared down the companionway and Avery filled the void with the merits of sailing versus the motor. He waxed lyrical about a feeling for the sea. He talked of the wind in your face, the smell of the ocean and if he'd been conversant with Forrester and Hornblower he'd have thrown in a few quotes for good measure. As it was, he ended with a small pracie of Capt Ahab's monologue, sans wooden leg and the call of the ocean on a man's soul. It was a mighty effort, but well rewarded. Colin bit his bottom lip and grabbed his wife's arm.

'Viv,' he managed to croak out, his emotions welling up in his throat like an extra-large boiled egg. Vivian looked up at the sail, the seagulls, the sunlight playing on the waves and nodded at her husband. It was all just perfect. The three drank in the moment when there was a loud bang and crash heard from below and Ted bolted up the steps and made a bee line for the rail. He leaned over and heaved. Avery, Colin and Viv politely looked the other way as Ted squandered their cut lunch, feeding the fish. The noises he made would try the hardiest of constitutions and it was with more than a modicum of self-control that the three kept their stomachs in check. When Ted had finished, he stood up.

'I feel better now.' Colin swallowed hard and tried to keep his mind on Avery's words, but it didn't look good as the mal de mare tightened its grip on his stomach.

'Col?' Viv looked at her husband as his face resembled an open-mouthed clown at the showgrounds and then his lips pursed so tight an Egyptian would have had a hard time putting a cigarette paper between them.

'Col?' Vivian took his arm. Colin shook his head and pleaded with his eyes not to answer. He swallowed once more then puffed out his cheeks and sucked them back in again. It was a spectacular show as he scrunched his face, squeezed his eyes tight then let out an enormous burp. As he gradually turned white, then a pale green, those present knew the inevitable was about to happen.

'I'll just go and check those fenders,' Vivian scooted up to the bow of the boat.

'I think I need to check the engine.' Avery left the wheel on lock and jumped two at a time down the steps to the cabin. Colin stole a glance at Ted and if looks could kill the police might have been looking for a double murder with only one victim.

'Nothing to it,' Ted said as he poked his straw in a fruit drink and smiled. Colin, now in the grip, lunged for the stern rail and opened his mouth. He waited, dribble the only outcome. He closed his eyes and wished he were dead. He toyed with the idea of suicide, a noose, blunt force trauma, anything to get going.

He listened as Ted sucked the last of the juice and wished he could shove that box right down his neighbour's neck. He thought it a grand idea and was just about to return to the cockpit when his breakfast once again saw the light of day.

38

Vivian screwed up her face and looked out to sea. She had never been any good with sick. Nappies were a doddle, cuts and sores easy peasy, but sick had a checkered history and now she fished about in her slacks for the possibility of a stale boiled sweet or a refresher sachet from KFC, anything to get past the moment. After a small interval and a quick check for noise she popped her head up and saw Colin sitting opposite Ted looking like something dragged up from a long-forgotten crab pot.

'Darling,' She trilled from the bow, 'alright now?' Colin nodded and polished his glasses while cutting daggers at Ted who smiled as a simpleton smiles at a lump of gravel in the road. Vivian joined the men and Avery reappeared.

'Everything fine is it?' The assembled group nodded. 'Right. Well. We will just shoot over to Picnic bay for a bit. I can show you the anchoring system if you like, we can have a spot of ...' Avery looked at Colin, 're-fresh-ments.' he said very slowly so as not to upset the uneasy truce between Colin, his stomach and the inevitable chain reaction. The group nodded again.

The boat enjoyed the light breeze and as they headed for the bay on Magnetic Island the Tripps began to perk up. Vivian watched as they slowly but surely inched their way close to shore. Colin took an interest in the depth sounder and fish finder and Ted fiddled with the VHF radio getting ready to relay some inane jabber across the air waves.

'Just a bit more then if you wouldn't mind,' Avery looked at the Tripps, 'We need to get the sail down.'

'Oh.' Colin and Vivian scampered to the foredeck and at Avery's shout the sail was hauled down. Moonlighting began to slow down and then Avery scampered to the bow and let the anchor down. It hit the water and the chain rattled over the gypsy.

'That's it then,' he looked at the chain as it continued to play out then with one deft movement hit the windlass break and the whole contraption gave a groan and the anchor chain went tight. 'Easy.' Colin nodded and smiled, a sort of 'I don't understand, but I'm not going to let you know that and I'll find out later' sort of smile.

'Lunch anyone?' Avery asked and they all looked at Ted who was eating the last piece of fruit from the esky and Avery Lightfoot joined the long list of people who would strangle Colin's neighbour if given five minutes alone with him in a dark alley.

'Well we could go to the pub if you like. I haven't anything pressing for the rest of the day.'

'I thought you were on a schedule Mr. Lightfoot?' Viv inquired.

'It's malleable. Fluid.' he replied. Mr Lightfoot licked his lips in anticipation of a schooner or two of cold refreshment. 'And you can see how the dinghy performs.' he added quickly, changing the subject.

'Right.' Colin looked at his wife and hoped his decision was the right one. Vivian smiled and Col breathed a sigh of relief. He knew if his wife was happy everything would be ok.

The tender was hanging at the back of the boat on two outstretched arms known as davits and it was with some trepidation that Avery began to winch the dinghy down to the water.

'Bit stiff,' he said, trying to underplay the screeching, the flakes of rust falling off and the jerking movement. 'Nothing a bit of WD won't fix,' he gave the rope one almighty tug and the small inflatable dinghy hit the water outboard first. Vivian looked over the side at the small boat,

'Will we all fit Mr Lightfoot?'

'Not a problem.' Vivian took one look at Ted who could pass as a rugby goal post fender and frowned.

Vivian's climb down the rope ladder to the little boat was undertaken with everyone giving encouragement and advice. She sat at the bow and watched Ted come next. The rope ladder groaned and strained as he started to climb only to stop three rungs down.

'What is it?' Avery leaned over the side.

'I'm stuck.'

'Ah.' Avery said as if his annunciation explained everything. Ted began to fish about for the next rung when his predicament became clear. His shirt had caught on a cleat and was riding up as he descended. The sight was not a pretty one and reminded Vivian of her father's butcher shop and pork belly.

'Go up Ted.' Vivian encouraged.

'Go down Ted.' Colin pointed.

'Stay there.' Avery said and he bent down. He began to undo Ted's buttons. There was a renting and the shirt gave way and Ted, now free, slipped the rest of the way into the waiting dinghy below catching the folding anchor in his back.

'Jeeez,' he exclaimed and winced.

Colin came next and trod on Ted as he tried to manoeuvre about. The little tender rocked as the three positioned themselves to distribute the weight, but as the two men, plus the outboard were about three of Viv she was sitting high on the bow and the transom was precariously close to being swamped. Avery stood on the ladder and tried to direct traffic.

'Mrs Tripp, if you could just,' he pointed and soon the occupants of the dinghy were playing twister without the advertised fun. Eventually they settled down on the seats and waited for Mr Lightfoot. He swung into the boat and they looked expectantly for him to get things moving. The outboard had other ideas. As much as he pulled, throttled, fiddled and cursed the two stroke would not work. It spluttered once, coughed a couple of times and that was it.

'Mr Lightfoot...' Vivian began, 'perhaps you need to just pump that little bobble for the fuel. She helpfully pointed to the priming bulb and smiled. Avery gritted his teeth and took the bulb in his hand and squeezed. He hated a smart arse. Vivian looked out to sea and covered her smirk with her hand.

The short trip to the beach was covered in three minutes flat as Avery rung every rev from the little 6 hp engine. The occupants bounced, jiggled and jangled about on the small seats and hung on as they were ferried to the island.

'Right,' Avery said as they trudged up the sand to the pub, 'lunch.'

It was only after their hamburgers and chips arrived that Ted and Avery remembered they had forgotten their wallets. Vivian's curdled glare did nothing to shame the thick-skinned freeloaders.

The journey back to the boat was in silence as Vivian glared and Colin avoided her gaze. He was feeling this boating life was rather exhilarating and needed Vivian to feel the same way.

'Darling,' he began as they climbed aboard, 'would you like to take the wheel back to the marina? If that is alright with you Mr Lightfoot? Avery nodded and ran his tongue over his front teeth. He could see a sale and knew Vivian was the key.

Ted and Colin manned the winches and unfurled the headsail for the trip back while Avery slipped in behind Viv at the wheel and gave her a few pointers. The breeze was slight, the scattered clouds afforded some relief from the sun and Vivian seemed to be a natural. She listened, learned and took control. Avery found her a star pupil and so decided to encourage her to dock the boat.

'Oh, I couldn't, really.' Viv protested.

'You're a natural Mrs Tripp. Nothing to it. Just do as I say.' Viv nodded and smiled. From the foredeck Colin saw the smile and began to think on Moonlighting as *their* boat.

'She's a beauty isn't she Ted?' Ted nodded and then headed for the rail. Colin felt he was needed elsewhere, and pretty quick, so scooted up to the cockpit away from any thoughts of wasting a good lunch. Ted squandered his in a spectacular fashion.

'Now we just have to go slow. No hurry at all,' Avery told Viv as she throttled back. Colin had wound in the sail and under Avery's instruction made the fenders and lines ready.

'Steady Mrs T.' Viv nodded. 'Easy turn now.'

Viv nodded some more. Moonlighting swung in a leisurely arc and pointed into the berth.

'Now a bit of reverse.' Viv kept nodding. Colin jumped off the boat and made her fast listening to Avery's directions and the sloop came to a stop.

'Fantastic.' Avery smiled at Viv who smiled at Colin who smiled at Avery. It seemed to Colin the world had stopped spinning for just a moment and he caught his breath. Ted re-emerged and staggered off the boat.

'Well I'll see you at home. Gloria will wonder where I am.' He hot footed it up the dock leaving the Tripps to clean up and talk turkey.

The Tripps were still smiling as they pulled into their driveway.

'Wasn't it wonderful the way it felt under sail?'

'And you did a wonderful job of docking darling.'

'And you were wonderful winding the winch Colin.'

'And it was wonderful sailing back, wasn't it?'

They both agreed that Uncle Frank was wonderful too and it would only be a matter of an out of water survey and Moonlighting would be theirs.

Everything was just wonderful.

CHAPTER 3

'Next Wednesday. Right.' Colin hung up and relayed the message to Viv who was cooking tea.

'Mr Lightfoot says we are booked in next Wednesday for the lift and survey. He said something about bringing a Dutch how.' Col shrugged his shoulders at his wife's questioning face.

'I dunno.' He went in search of *Nautical terms for beginners* by Percy Landers as Viv busied herself with mash potatoes.

Throughout the meal they talked about boats, ruminated on boats and thought about boats.

'Why don't you just ring and ask Col? Just say, oh by the way, where would I get a Dutch how.' Colin shook his head. It wasn't as simple as that when pride takes a hand. On more than one occasion Colin had fetched the wrong end of the stick because of his reticence to ask the obvious. He, if pressed, and had a good number of beers to soften the humiliation, would recount the time he was arrested waiting outside the women's toilets on a transit stopover in Bahrain because he couldn't read the Arabic signs and didn't want to ask.

'I know just the man who will know.' Colin

smiled, 'Rowdy Rawlinson' he raised his voice in imitation. 'You can ask him Viv,' he looked at his wife and thought the whole matter settled.

Wednesday morning dawned bright and hot. The summer seemed to be having one last ditch effort and blazed away oblivious that it was supposed to be getting cooler for the wind down to the dry season in the Tropics. Mr Lightfoot had suggested Colin and he take Moonlighting around to the boat yard and Viv could meet them there with the car. They followed the plan and after Viv had dropped her husband off at the dock she went in search of the elusive Dutch how. The Chandlery was open early and Viv stepped inside to be greeted by Rowdy.

'Hello there,' he boomed looming large from the counter.

'Er hello,' Viv smiled then came straight to the point. 'Look Mr Rawlinson, I need a Dutch how.'

'Eh?'

'A Dutch how.' Rowdy scratched his head, then his belly, which was having a hard time staying covered by his t-shirt.

Rowdy leaned in close and shouted. 'What's this all about young lady?' Viv took a deep breath and explained the situation. They were going on the hard for a slip for a survey or something or other and Mr Lightfoot...' At the mention of Avery, Rowdy made a face and shook his head.

'You'd be wantin' a Dutch hoe then.' he yelled. Viv nodded. Rowdy led her to the back of the shop and a collection of gardening implements. He rattled around in the 44-gallon drum and came up with the said tool.

'For scrapin'.' Viv shrugged her shoulders. 'Take it, use it and bring it back. You'll soon see.'

'Thank you.' She left the shop and after buying morning tea headed for the boat yard. Avery had given her directions and for anyone approaching by sea the yard could be found with just the pointing of a finger. To get to the water's edge by vehicle was a different matter. There were laneways, one ways and no ways. She felt hopelessly lost and so back tracked and decided to ask Rowdy.

'Which one?' he shouted at her.

A quick phone call to Avery's office decided the destination and with a map drawn on the back of a greasy pie bag Vivian once again set off.

She arrived just in time to see Moonlighting rounding the breakwater and heading for the boatyard dock. Anyone new to boating has an expectation that things get done and that is that. Vivian surmised that if she started to pour the flask of coffee and set out the buns they would be snacking in 10 minutes or so. After all, she could see the buttons on Col's shirt. The Tripp's first lesson is boating was just beginning as the travel lift made its slow, snail like progress towards the lifting pen. Moonlighting crawled into position and then the men in the boat yard debated the state of the ropes, the length of the rigging, the feel of the wind and the Gross national product of the Ukraine before they decided things could progress to the next level. The straps that lift the boat were positioned under the hull and moved forward. Then they were moved backwards, then forward again. All seemed well and Vivian waved at Colin and gave the thumbs up when a hooter went off in the yard. The workmen turned as one and walked away.

'Excuse me, what was that?' Viv asked a young lad who was following the crowd.

'Smoko, the van won't wait. You want anything?' and he hot-footed it to the euphemistically called roach coach.

Viv gingerly made her way along the finger of dock that took the enormous travel lift wheels.

'They have gone to smoko darling.' Colin shrugged his shoulders. Then Vivian had a bright idea and raced to the car and bundled everything up in a shopping bag and when she was in position Colin held out a boat hook and took the offering. The hooter sounded again after 15 minutes and Vivian stood up ready for action.

The travel lift driver sauntered over and after a good scratch, a bit of a rummage and a spit he resumed his position. The rope men stood their ground and debated the whole thing over again, this time postulating on whether the Pope mobile had bullet proof glass and if there were cheap flights to Fiji in June and then finally with a lot of shouting and gesticulating Moonlighting slowly began to rise from the water. The bottom of the boat was a mini reef. Long tendrils of weed hung from the rudder and the whole thing seem to be wriggling. The boat rose and cleared the wharf then began moving at geriatric walking frame hip replacement pace to the pad and stopped over a large drain.

'All yours,' the travel lift driver said as he shut the engine off and climbed down. He took one look at the boat and then quickly produced a small knife and prised off an oyster and ate it. Viv shuddered at the thought.

'Can you find a ladder?' Colin called from the deck. Vivian hunted about and found a steel ladder which seemed to be made of lead. She dragged it, heaved it and sweated it to the boat, then walked it upright to finish leaning on the railing.

When Colin was on the ground he looked at the hull. It was covered in primordial ooze and began to smell.

'Oh, I have our 'how'. It is a hoe. A Dutch hoe.' Vivian fetched it from the car and carried it back triumphantly. 'Rowdy said we could borrow it,' she smiled.

'Right,' Avery grabbed the tool. 'Like this,' and he began to scrape the hull of its marine life. He handed the hoe back to Colin. 'Just going to the office, won't be long,' and he strode away.

'We really need two of these don't we,' Viv said. 'You start and I'll see what I can find.' She left Colin at it and went hunting.

Scraping a hull can be a messy job. It wasn't long before Colin had mussels in his hair, the odd slime splat on his shoulder and something gelatinous and stringy hanging off his elbow. Vivian came back with another homemade scraper fashioned from the remains of a paint tin and a broom handle and they got to work. Avery had made it look easy, but as every whelk hunter or limpet picker knows, you need more than a hunger and a bread and butter knife to shift a mollusc. Colin and Viv laboured in the hot sun scraping at least 4 years of growth and as the pile of marine life grew so did the stink.

Avery appeared sucking on an ice block and informed them that the surveyor would be about an hour. Then said he had to pop off for a bit and left the Tripps looking like seafood chowder and smelling like a barrel of putrefying fish.

The 'hour' turned into two and a half as the Tripps waited watching the boat yard go about its business. Nothing was done in a hurry, nothing was attempted without a conference first and time took on a surreal feeling as the Tripps slowly wound down. By the time the surveyor finally arrived they were slumped at the side of a building wondering about the tyre pressure on the travel lift and the major exports of Hong Kong in 1960.

Mr Petrokovitch or Pedro, as he was known on the dock, was a short squat fellow with more body than legs. He wore a shirt with most of the buttons missing and pair of shorts that had given their all about ten years ago, but refused to retire. He held out a meaty hand to Colin and smiled.

'Well?'

Colin smiled. 'Yes, well indeed.'

'So.' Pedro stood back and put his hands on his hips or thereabouts, as he had lost his hips in his mid 40's and around the 90kg mark.

'Er, Mr Petrokovitch?' Vivian began, 'Do we need to do anything?'

'Ah.' Pedro said sucking on his teeth and then began to walk around the boat. Avery sidled up to the surveyor and hovered.

'All good so far.' he flashed his 'rat with a gold tooth' smile at Pedro.

'Hmmmm.' Pedro brought out a notebook and then licked the stub of a pencil that had materialised from nowhere. He shot a glance at the Tripps and bared his teeth making a sucking noise and shaking his head. Colin swallowed and picked a starfish from his shirt front and tried to avoid the stare.

'Look, I think we need to clean up a bit,' Vivian pulled on her husband's arm. 'Let's leave them to it, shall we? I'm thirsty and well, I think it may be a while.' She pulled her anxious husband away and they went in search of a toilet, or at the very least, a hose to clean themselves up.

'So?' Colin asked the surveyor as they walked up to the boat after a decent interval. Mr Petrokovich scrunched up his face and sort of tried to smile, but it looked like he had only read about it and forgotten the instructions. He bared his teeth and stuck out his tongue.

'So.' Pedro said. Colin looked to Avery who was hovering at a distance.

'He said he will post the report.' Avery interpreted.

'Oh.' Colin nodded.

'Hmmmm.' Pedro nodded.

'He likes to get paid in cash.' Avery said and looked at Vivian.

'Well I'd like an invoice please.' Vivian stepped into the circle of men. She hated it when they acted like it was a secret club and she wasn't invited. Pedro produced his pencil and licked the end. He fished about in his shorts pocket and found a small note book and scribbled his fee. Then with a flourish he handed it over to Vivian.

'Oh.' Vivian read the figure and looked at Colin, trying to get him to confer away from the others. She pulled her head to one side and swung her eyes to indicate the car.

'We just need to go to the car.' She pulled Colin away and when they were out of ear shot showed him the scrawled note.

'$550. Is that good or bad?'

Colin shrugged his shoulders. 'Beats me.'

Once the bill was paid in full Colin and Vivian were assured Moonlighting would be painted with antifoul and would await their decision. Avery would oversee everything. They left the boat yard thinking they had paid their money and it was a done deal. The drive home was in silence with the windows wound down, each thinking on their own boating experiences so far, cost versus lifestyle. They had seen quite a bit of the former and precious little of the latter.

It was an anxious wait for the report and when it arrived in the post Vivian postponed opening it until Colin came home from work. The checklist was long and exhaustive and everything seemed to be fair to middling, condition wise.

'Nothing a bit of this and that won't fix.' Colin looked at his wife with that excited puppy look that she couldn't refuse.

'Well darling. I guess we have bought ourselves a boat.' Vivian smiled. 'But Col, it will be *our* boat. I want a say in what goes in and what gets chucked out.'

'Of course darling, of course.' Colin kissed his first mate.

Moonlighting was sitting in the pen at the boat yard waiting for the Tripps to take charge. Avery coached Vivian on the procedure and Colin took care of the ropes. They slowly moved out into the river and then down to the bay.

'You won't be disappointed Mrs Tripp.'

'I hope not.' Vivian helmed the boat around the commercial wharf to the marina. She had remembered her lesson in docking and as the men busied themselves with fenders and ropes Viv slid the boat into its berth. It was only when she had relaxed that she noticed a small crowd watching.

'Very well done.' A man came up to Viv and smiled.

'Thank you; it is only my second time.'

'Really.' He turned to his companions, 'It is only her second time,' he shouted. There was a murmur amongst the crowd. Colin sprang into the mix,

'We just bought it.' He beamed at the boat.

'Really.' The man relayed the information to the others, 'They just bought it.' Once again the crowd digested the information. Avery stepped up to the group and handed over the keys to Colin.

'She's all yours.'

The weekend was, Colin declared, going to be a cleaning weekend. They would tidy up the boat and get things ship shape. All that week Colin had been talking in nautical terms and the novelty was wearing thin.

'Ahoy there,' Colin hailed Ted from the back door. Ted waved and came to the fence. 'We bought the boat.' Colin said.

'So, you'll be going out then?'

'Well, we have to get things ship shape first. A bit of spit and polish on the navy bronze, not much really.'

'Don't you worry about that Col. I've got just the thing. Never fails.' Ted nipped inside and came back to the fence holding his miracle worker aloft.

'Don't you worry about that.' Ted beamed. 'This'll do the trick.'

'Thanks, and well...when she's ship shape you and Gloria should come down for sundowners.' Colin knew he should consult Viv first, but as he was caught up in the moment of boat ownership his invitation just slipped out.

'Great. That'll be great Col. Er...you won't be taking her out will you?'

'Not for sundowners Ted.'

'Right. Right.' Ted said. 'See ya then Col. Look forward to it.'

'Yes.'

The men stood at the fence and shuffled their feet.

'Well...I...'

'Yes.'

'So, I better get on.'

'Ok.' They parted company and Colin took Ted's jam jar of evil looking goo inside and put it with the cleaning things they had started to collect for the weekend.

CHAPTER 4

Moonlighting had more than a lived-in look. The previous owner had sort of just stopped doing any maintenance about 4 years ago and it showed. The woodwork inside was covered in a grey grime and every fingerprint he left had developed into mouldy smudge that a classroom of forensic scientists could spend hours on. The Tripps knuckled down and began the laborious job of cleaning up someone else's mess. They found all manner of surprises, from a bullet to a stash of Russian Rubbles.

Vivian took charge of the galley while Col took a look at the engine. Demarcation was alright up to a point, but the kitchen was her preserve.

Vivian went to turn on the sink water and there was a great deal of knocking and then the water spat out of the tap and bounced right out of the sink ending all over her shirt.

'Colin,' she called from the galley. 'Can you come and take a look at this?' She tried again gently coaxing the tap open, but it produced the same result. All the water ended up over her and nothing in the sink. Colin popped his head up from the engine bay,

'I'll be there in a minute. I seem to be stuck down here.' He wriggled his left leg which had gone to sleep, scrunched up under him and over a nasty sharp jutting piece of metal. The engine had a myriad of sticky-out bits that were only put there to make life difficult and catch your clothing. Colin tried to back out, but became stuck on a ragged hose clamp and a bit of fencing wire.

'Viv,' he yelled, 'Can you help.' It was a brain teaser, but Viv managed to extricate Colin and he crawled out and rubbed his dead leg.

'I think we need to employ a very small child.' He looked at the spot where he had been mopping up the bilge water.

'I have just the thing.' Viv shot back to the galley and came up with a soup ladle. It was taped to a pair of tongs and now Colin could reach those hard to get at places without needing a chiropractor and Panadol forte. Colin looked at Viv's problem. He tried the tap and the water blew out of the tap, bounced out of the sink and soaked his shirt. He tried once more and the pipes began to moan. There was a small groan, a rising thumping and then the chorus ended with a howl that could have been straight out of an Alien movie.

'We need to look at that.' They listened as the pipes ticked over once or twice.

'Oh Colin,' Viv exclaimed and screwed up her nose.

'It wasn't me.'

Viv sniffed the air and then it dawned on her that the hideous stink was coming from the plug hole. The water must have re-activated the grey water holding tank and now it was taking on a life

56

of its own. She bent down to confirm her suspicions and quickly stuffed a tea towel down the pipe and coughed.

'How do we get rid of that?' Vivian pointed at the sink. They traced the pipe to a holding tank under the floor with a screw inspection plate.

'Are you game?' Colin asked. Vivian put a hanky over her nose and gathered her heavy-duty rubber gloves, a bucket and the bleach. She nodded.

Colin began unscrewing the lid and the putrid stink escaped, making him gag. Whatever had been in the tank was now taking a second stab at life. Vivian shone a torch into the dark depths, then gingerly put her gloved hand inside. She scooped a large handful of sludge and thwacked it in the bucket.

'There is a bit of grunge on the walls,' she said understating the problem of about six years of e coli habitation and what looked like the remains of a failed soap factory. She scooped a second handful and threw it in the bucket. Long tendrils of hair, soap scum and what used to be food made up the black mix. Colin backed away.

'I'll just get you another bucket.' He ran outside to get some air.

When it was finished Viv had collected three 9 litre buckets of sludge and the holding tank breathed easy after what seemed like a lifetime of blocked arteries.

It took all morning with Bleach, Houdini's home help, Scrub-o-matic and Three Minute Miracle, but the Tripps couldn't get rid of the peculiar odour.

'I think we should go to the Chandlery, Rowdy,'

and here Colin shouted in imitation, 'should have something.' Vivian giggled and carried on the joke. She stood back and scratched her head and yelled,

'I used to 'ave one of those.' They began to laugh and soon Colin was lying on the settee holding his stomach from laughing too much.

'Come on Col. Let's take a break and go to the shop.'

'Hang on.' Colin said, 'I think I have something.' He fetched the goo Ted had given to him.

'It is supposed to clean things, or something.' He held the jar to the light looking at its gungy green.

'What is it?' Viv asked. Colin shrugged his shoulders not wanting the conversation to take a nasty turn towards his neighbour.

'S'pose to be great for everything.' He unscrewed the lid and poured the contents down the drain and waited. There was a minute silence, then bubbles began to appear in the sink and Viv took a look at the holding tank. It was foaming at the mouth.

'Col, we better do something.' She stood back. 'Colin.' Her husband, usually a 'can do' man couldn't think of anything, so she took control and found the pump switch.

'Pump.' she said by way of explanation. The mechanism began to chug over and then get going. There was a gigantic sucking noise and the heady brew blew outside through a skin fitting. Viv raced upstairs and looked over the side. A milky scum spread across the water and then a fish popped up. It took a last gasp and floated along with the poison.

'Colin,' Viv called. They watched as the wildlife took exception to their holding tank contents and up and died. It was only with a colander that they were able to scoop up the evidence and tie it good and tight in a rubbish bag to be taken home at a later hour.

'I think we need to go to the shop,' Vivian took her husband's hand and they walked away, knowing some things are better left unsaid.

Rowdy Rawlinson stood behind the counter and absently picked a scab on his forearm. He looked up as the Tripps entered and threaded their way to the front of the shop and smelt the air. He held his nose up to the prevailing waft and then frowned.

'A bit of blow back,' he yelled. Colin nodded and smiled and rubbed his neck.

'What can I do for you?' Rowdy shouted and took a step back from the stink.

'We wanted to know if you have anything for drains?' Vivian pulled on her shirt and picked off a nubbule of something grey and looking remarkably like Rowdy's scab.

'Drains,' Rowdy shouted and screwed up his nose.

'Yes, drains Mr Rawlinson. We seem to have a bit of a problem.'

'Problem.'

'Yes.' Viv answered thinking the conversation wasn't getting anywhere.

'Right.' Rowdy squeezed past the end of the counter narrowly missing a stand full of lurid fishing lures and beckoned the Tripps to follow. They made a conga line and eventually ended up at the back of the shop.

'Blockage or stink?' Rowdy inquired. Vivian looked at Colin and bit her lip to stop a smirk.

'Stink.' Colin said settling the problem.

'I used to 'ave one of those.' Rowdy yelled and Vivian had to turn away to stifle a laugh. 'This'll fix it.' Rowdy rummaged about in a cardboard box and produced a 2-litre bottle of Bilge Blast-Off. He read from the label, 'guaranteed to extinguish bilge odour.' He wiped his nose on his t-shirt sleeve and sucked his teeth.

Vivian regained her composure and queried, 'guaranteed?'

'Viv,' Colin began, 'I think Mr. Rawlinson knows a bit about it.' Rowdy stood there like a spectator who had paid for front row seats at the Colosseum and seen the best of the action already. He absently picked at his scab and waited.

'I'm just saying, because they all *say* guaranteed, but ...well it's just a marketing ploy and it's $25.00 for 2 litres which seems quite a lot to me.' Vivian looked at Colin and Colin knew that look. She had the same look when he came home with a set of tools that came with a lifetime guarantee and they didn't last a gnat's lifetime. 'That's all I'm saying.' Viv put her hands in her pockets and looked at the floor.

'Mr. Rawlinson, are you sure?' Colin tried to placate his wife and still hold some sort of control over the situation.

'Take a whiff of this.' Rowdy cracked open the bottle and passed the brew under the Tripps noses. The aroma that burnt the hairs in their nostrils had the flavour of school toilet disinfectant mixed with plasticine.

60

That sort of rubbery, playdough, lino floor smell.

'Well?' Rowdy replaced the cap.

'We'll take it.' Colin said. They retraced their steps through the crowded shop only taking one wrong turn at shackles and aerials to arrive at the counter and handed over their bank card.

'Want to start an account? I send 'em out once a month.' It seemed like a sensible choice and so the Tripps signed up, not knowing that a chandlery account was the easiest way in the world to spend $100 before ten o'clock on a Saturday morning without even trying.

Now with their Bilge Blast-Off they headed back to the boat to begin the process of making it liveable.

'You didn't get that rubbish?' A man on the next dock looked at their purchase.

'It's guaranteed.' Colin suggested.

'Useless,' the bloke countered Colin's logic.

'Mr. Rawlinson assured us it would work,' Viv chipped in.

'Rowdy? He wouldn't know a smell if his nose was in his armpit.' The man held out his hand. 'Arnold Burkitt,' he said, then a little woman peeked out from behind the large barrel-chested Arnold, 'and this is Connie.' Connie smiled and held out a very small white dog.

'And this is Chester. Say hewwwo Chester to the wubbly people.' She smoodled up to the dog and then went to hand him over to Vivian. Chester took offence at the smell and snapped at Vivian's outstretched hand.

'Oh, Chester, naughty boy,' Connie cooed.

'We are in a bit of a rush just now,' Vivian

backed away. 'We can catch up some other time.' Colin grabbed his wife's arm and they waved as they ducked into Moonlighting and took the companionway stairs two at a time.

'Did you see those matching jackets with the boat name on them?'

'And wittle wittle Chester.'

'And their peaked caps.' Vivian rolled her eyes and Colin giggled.

'Stop it Col. They're probably really nice people.'

'Ok. It takes all sorts.'

'Exactly. Now let's have a go at Blast-Off.

With three more trips to the chandlery for a new pump, $50.99, a length of electrical wire, $23.87 and 4 hose clamps, $18.66 ea (are you sure that is *each* Mr. Rawlinson?) the Tripps managed to get the bilge pump working for the sink overflow that had been laying low in the bowels of the boat long enough to qualify as a primordial swamp with its own fungal life forms. Blast-Off scoured the sump and doubled as a paint stripper, but the smell was gone.

With a few other small jobs, the day came to a close and the boat was beginning to take on a homelier appearance. The mould had been scrubbed, the bench tops revealed their true colours, the stove wasn't matt black after all and the bilge pump had spat its last artery choking globule over the side. Things were looking up. As the Tripps meandered down the dock chatting about their plans for the boat, Colin stopped his wife,

'Are you happy darling?' Vivian nodded and

picked a stray goobie off her husband's shirt.

'You know, I think I am.' It was all Colin could hope for as he pulled a fluff ball from Vivian's hair and flicked it in the water.

CHAPTER 5

'Happy birthday, darling.' Vivian planted a kiss on her husband's forehead and then reached over and handed him his present which she had hidden under the bed. Colin sat up and played the game of shaking the parcel then trying to guess.

'An angle grinder?'

'No.'

'A remote-control organiser?'

Vivian shook her head.

'Just open it' He obeyed and ripped off the paper. Vivian looked for some sign off recognition that she'd got it right.

'Colin,' Colin held the brass clock and barometer set and smiled.

'Beaut Viv, just beaut.' The instruments were made to look like real port holes with screw down glass.

'Connie on the catamaran helped me. Rowdy said they would last years.'

Colin checked out the time.

'Perfect.'

After a leisurely breakfast Vivian made everything ready for the day .They had discussed what to do for Colin's birthday on the Easter long weekend and a family outing on Moonlighting seemed the obvious choice. What better way to spend the weekend than mucking about in boats.

'What time is everyone getting to the boat?'

'Around 10:30, I think' Vivian answered as she packed the esky.

A knock at the door interrupted the pair and Gloria from next door, popped her head into the kitchen

'Happy Birthday Colin,' she said, proffering a gift.

'Thanks Gloria. I didn't expect anything.' Gloria smiled. She was one of those infuriating people that never forgot a birthday, anniversary or date of any kind and always had something on hand. The Tripps on the other hand subscribed to the view that unless it was written on the fridge it didn't get a mention.

Colin unwrapped the present and held it up for all to see. The hand knitted jumper in navy blue had an anchor emblazoned on the front in gold thread and could have passed as kitsch if it wasn't so gaudy.

'Nice.'

'I didn't know your size so I had the idea you were the same size as Ted.' Colin held up the jumper against his chest and the bottom band hung around his thighs.

'Nice.' he said again.

Satisfied her largess was appreciated, Gloria launched into 20 questions.

By the time Vivian had finished packing Gloria knew where they were going, what they were eating, who was coming, how they were getting there and why they decided to go in the first place.

She hung about in the kitchen like a dead fly on the windowsill and Vivian shot Colin a look as if to say - you utter one word about an invite and you won't see another birthday. Colin bit his lip. He fiddled with the toaster, he re-clipped the esky and shuffled the tea towels, but when Gloria asked what it would be like on the boat the invitation just popped out,

'Why don't you and Ted come along?'

Vivian almost dropped the flask of milk and turned to glare at Colin who had decided it wasn't wise to wait for the definitive answer from Gloria and shot outside quicker than a scalded cat.

'We don't like that full cream milk in our tea,' Gloria pointed to Vivian's supplies.

'Is that so?'

Gloria nodded and then said she was just popping home to let Ted know.

'You do that Gloria, and let him know we are leaving in 15 minutes.'

'Right. Toodle loo. See you there.'

'Right. Toodle loo,' Viv mimicked through gritted teeth. She watched as all 4 foot 9 inches of her pesky neighbour hot footed it across the side grass to the gate.

'Colin McCalum Tripp,' she shouted into the yard, but the only reply was the mocking of the early morning crows in the gum tree.

It was only 10 minutes and Gloria rang and explained that Ted, as much as he'd like to come along and help Colin with the sailing and technical side of things, had far too much to do at home. Vivian hung up and thought Ted's reticence wasn't a busy schedule, but something more to do with sea sickness. She beckoned Colin inside and wrapped her arms around his neck,

'The Gunns can't make it.' She smiled and planted a large kiss on her husband's cheek and Colin breathed easy. Things were looking good. When each of the children cried off at 20-minute intervals Colin thought things were looking even better.

Moonlighting waited, bobbing gently at the dock as Vivian and Colin ferried their picnic on board and went through their checklist.

'Sun cream?'

'Check.'

'Bottle opener?'

'Check.'

'EPIRB?'

'Check.' Colin felt proud that he now was the owner of his own EPIRB. With everything ready they started the engine and slipped, without incident, from the berth and into the channel and out into the bay.

The day was perfect for boating with a decent breeze to fill the sail and not much in the way of cloud. There were others on the water and as the Tripps sailed they felt relaxed and happy.

'Shall we head for Horseshoe Bay straight away Col?'

'Let's just Jill about for a bit, you know, get the feel of the girl. I read that the discerning owner should know their boat, you know, really know their boat.' He smiled at Vivian and added, 'You could sunbake, if you like?'

Viv took off her shirt and sat back in the cockpit

soaking up the sun.

'Why don't you take 'em off?'

'What?'

'You know, take 'em off. No-one will see.'

'Do you think?' Colin nodded and raised an eyebrow.

'You could lie back there,' he pointed to a spare space at the stern. Viv gathered a few cushions and threw caution to the wind and took off her bra and lay down.

'Nice Viv,' Colin said.

'Oh Col, you've seen them a hundred times.'

'Can't help it, I still like 'em.'

Vivian smiled and closed her eyes as the boat skipped along the sea in an easy rhythm.

Colin sat back and began to read the wind, the sails and every now and again tweak the helm to keep the boat on course. He found he could lounge right back in the cockpit and just take the wheel between his toes to keep her steady. It was a masterful feeling knowing how to keep the boat gliding along with minimum effort. Nothing could go wrong, Colin thought and smiled to himself when there was a crackling below and the VHF radio sparked into life and a helicopter suddenly chopperd overhead.

'White hulled yacht. White hulled yacht on heading 230 degrees.' The radio squawked. Colin looked at the compass in the hope the Coastguard helicopter wasn't talking to him. He squinted at the authorities and waved.

'Nice puppies,' the radio operator said and then the copter flew off in the direction of Magnetic Island.

'What was that?' Viv sat up and put her hat on. 'I must have dropped off for a minute there.'

'Oh, nothing dear.' Colin answered taking another look at the puppies.

The trip around Orchid Rocks, past Radical Bay and into Horseshoe Bay on Magnetic Island is a well-worn track for the locals. In a South Easterly the anchorage is safe and calm and best of all, the pub is right on the foreshore, just a short dinghy ride away.

The Tripps approached the bay and brought down the sails and cranked the motor up. Moonlighting swung into calm waters and joined about two dozen other yachts, motor cruisers and powerboats, all with the same idea.

'Where are we going to park?' Viv looked at the crowded water.

'Anchor Viv. Where are we going to anchor?' Colin corrected his wife. They scanned the water for a spot.

'Over there Colin, near that blue one and the white one.' Vivian pointed to a gap that looked promising. Colin squinted.

'Nope.'

'Well what about there, next to the green one and the yellow buoy.' Colin sized up the area.

'Nup.'

'Oh look,' Viv pointed to a spot near a white cabin cruiser. 'That looks big enough.' Colin blew out a considered breath.

'Well...' he said. 'Maybe.' He eased off the throttle and Moonlighting glided in the general direction.

'Just check the depth honey,' Colin asked. Vivian scooted downstairs and yelled,

'Fifteen metres.'

'Right.' Colin said trying to drum up some courage for their first anchoring experience. Viv came into the cockpit waiting for instructions.

'You take the wheel Viv and I will let the chain out.' Viv nodded and took up her position.

'Throttle right back when I say.'

'Ok,' she replied. Colin went to the bow and reacquainted himself with the beast. The windlass was a monster that looked like it could pull a diesel locomotive from a standing start. The chain was bleeding rust, but Colin gave it a kick and it still had a bit of movement in it so he let go the break.

'Throttle,' he yelled adding hand signals that didn't mean anything to Vivian, but looked like he knew what he was doing. She slowed the engine and watched as Colin played out the chain when there was a ruckus on the port side.

'Eh. Eh. You. You're too close. Get outta here.' The Cabin Cruiser Captain stood on his back deck and waved wildly at Moonlighting. Vivian smiled and waved back.

'P#** O#%' he yelled. Vivian couldn't mistake the next hand signal and called to Colin.

'Col, that man says we should move.' Colin looked up to see his near neighbour gesticulating with just one finger in the air. He hit the break and the chain jagged to a halt.

'Turn her around Viv,' Col yelled and slowly Moonlighting did an arc and headed out to sea.

'Where now?' Vivian asked as they looked behind them.

'Bloody anchor hog.' Colin fumed at their dismissal. 'Over there Viv,' he pointed to a spot near a trawler. 'Fishermen must know a good spot when they see it.' Vivian swung the yacht around and they tried again.

'What's that noise Colin?' Colin concentrated and then remembered he had about 8 metres of chain out and they were dragging it and the anchor through the water.

'Hang on. Just go-slow Viv, we still have the chain out.' He scurried to the bow and along the bowsprit then looked over the side. The chain was carving a nice rusty mark down the side of Moonlighting as it was carried along.

'Oh hell. Stop Viv stop.' Colin yelled. Viv obeyed and cut the throttle. With no forward motion there was no steerage and they began to drift straight towards the trawler.

'Colin?' Viv could see what might happen if they didn't do something.

'What?' Colin replied with an exasperated tone as he looked at the damage.

'It's just that we seem to be drifting.' Colin looked up to see three fishermen staring at him as Moonlighting inched closer.

'In gear Viv, NOW!' Colin raced back to the cockpit and rammed the lever into reverse and gave the engine a come along by pushing the throttle to the max. Everything remained the same for what seemed like ages then with a great churning of water Moonlighting gradually began to back away.

'What did they say?' Vivian asked her husband. 'Was it amateurs?'

'I couldn't say.' Colin would rather not repeat

what he heard. They were gathering speed in reverse and heading for the rocks.

'Col...'

'What now.' Colin snapped.

'Well, it's just that I think we should go forward a little.' Vivian turned to look at the rocks about 300 metres away. Colin looked around.

'Oh hell.' He put the boat into neutral, cut back the revs and then had the idea that they could just jolly well anchor where they were and their reverse motion would set the plough anchor.

'We are anchoring here,' he said. 'No questions, no - it's just that... We are staying here and that's final.' Vivian pinched her lips and bit her tongue. Colin stomped down to the bow and let go the windlass break. The chain rattled down the long bowsprit and disappeared into the sea. He watched as it just kept coming out of the chain locker, throwing off its rust flakes all over the deck. After a full five minutes Colin put the break on and Moonlighting stopped moving. He looked over the side at the chain, then satisfied, walked back to the cockpit.

'See, nothing to it.' He smiled. 'Now we just take our bearings so we know if we have moved, then I fancy a drink at the pub.' He looked to the shore. They were anchored quite a way from the dress circle of boats that ringed the beach.

'Big yachts never get too close Viv.' Colin looked at the distance they needed to cover to get a beer. 'No worries about the tide out here eh?' Vivian frowned.

'I read that you should stay on the boat for a bit after anchoring, just to make sure.'

'Viv, I put out heaps of chain. Don't worry.' Colin said. 'Now, how about a beer?'

Once the dinghy was lowered and Vivian installed at the bow, Colin started the engine by the swearing method.

'Just a bit of fiddling to get it going.' He pulled.

'Probably needs a few pumps on the primer bulb.' He yanked.

'Two strokes are dead reliable, really they are.' He pulled again.

'You give me any trouble and you are going straight to Davy Jones.' He strangled it.

'Right that's it you Chinese mongrel. If you don't start now. He stood up and yanked like machine gun fire just as Viv leaned forward and she copped an elbow in the chest.

'Oww.' Viv clutched her chest.

'Will you just let me do this?' Colin barked at his wife. He gathered all his strength and pulled the starter cord so hard it ripped right out. The engine gave a cough, cleared its throat and burst into life.

'Easy eh?' Vivian kept silent as she let go the painter rope and they began the painfully slow ride to the beach in silence.

The dinghy came up to the beach and Colin directed Vivian to hop out to hold it steady. The beach at Horseshoe Bay is deceptive as it has a sharpish drop off and Vivian scrambled over the side and went up to her waist in water.

'Keep her steady Viv.' Colin tried to lift the outboard to stop it dragging in the sand, but lost his footing and landed in a heap on the dinghy floor.

It was rapidly turning into a matinee show for the back packers, loafers and holiday makers.

'Hang on,' Viv took the rope and skull dragged the wayward boat up the beach and Colin plopped out like a beached whale. There was a small round of applause as the Tripps made their way up the sands to the grass.

'Stronger than she looks eh?' A tourist said, eyeing up Vivian's wet slacks.

'I need a tap,' Vivian looked at Colin and smiled. 'I think we need to practice that particular manoeuvre, don't you?' Colin took a look at his trousers covered in sand and began to giggle.

'How about a wash up and a nice beer?' They found a tap and after a rinse off headed for the pub. Once a soggy ten-dollar note was handed over and they had sat down Vivian mused,

'Col, how do you think we can start the engine to get back?' Colin supped his beer and pondered the question. Without a pull start rope it would be a bit tricky.

'I think there is a small poofteenth of an inch hanging out. We just need to tie some more on and bingo, back in business.'

'Oh.' Viv wasn't so sure. She offered up a silent prayer to the God of small things and crossed her fingers. After a second beer and an order for a bowl of chips and gravy the logistical problems melted away and once more boating was 'just wonderful'.

'Er, hello.' A briny looking fellow came up to the Tripps.

'Hello,' Viv replied.

'Saw you come in. Mick's the name.' He

74

introduced himself and sat down at their table. 'Where's your vessel.' Colin liked the thought of calling Moonlighting a vessel and stored the word away to impress someone at a later date.

'She's over there,' Colin pointed out into the bay.

'Where?' Mick asked, squinting to the horizon.

'There. Out there,' Colin waved his hand in the direction of New Zealand.

'Bit of a hike eh? Why you out so far? What's ya draft?'

'We are 1.4metres.' Vivian chimed in.

'Ya could have come in a bit.' Colin didn't want to sound like a novice and so piped up with,

'Well, we know the fishing is really good out there, and my wife wanted to catch a fish and so I said, well if you want to catch a fish we will have to anchor here and so that's about it.' Vivian widen her eyes and took a sip of beer to stop herself from saying something.

'That so.'

'Yup.' Colin and Mick looked at Vivian and she shrugged her shoulders and smiled.

'I just *love* fishing,' she said.

'So how is the holding?' Mick asked rapidly turning the chance meeting into twenty questions.

'Not bad'

'What you using?'

'The usual.' Colin said, not quite understanding the shorthand questions.

'A C.Q.R then?'

'Yup.'

'How much chain?'

'Oh, you know.' Colin sipped his beer.

'Right.' The men nodded and then the bowl

of chips arrived. Mick helped himself as Vivian went for another round of drinks. By the time she had returned to the table Mick and Colin were best mates and Mick was just launching into an anchoring story.

'So, the bloke was laying out his chain while in reverse and all he did was make a big turning circle when the tide changed. He swung around on a 30-metre circle and collected two yachts along the way.' Mick was laughing and Colin felt he needed to get back to the boat.

'So,' Colin began, just to get the whole idea straight. 'all he did was lay the chain straight out and then sort of...just...pivot.'

'Yeah. Crazy eh?'

'Crazy.' Colin said thinking on his own technique. Once the chips were eaten Mick said he had to go and Colin felt he needed to get back to the boat.

'Are you ready Viv?'

'I guess.' They were just rising from their seats when a couple came over and introduced themselves.

'Darren, and this is Jill.' The man held out his hand. 'We saw you come in,' he pointed to their dinghy.

'Colin and Vivian,' Colin said and shook Darren's hand.

'We are from the 55-footer. Capricious.' Jill said with a wave of her hand in the direction of the bay. Vivian nodded and smiled.

'Ours is called Moonlighting. It's out there.' Vivian pointed to the horizon.

'Where luv?' Jill asked putting on her sunglasses

to get a better look.

'Over there.' Viv pointed.

'New to this are you?' Darren asked. Colin shot Viv a look and then 'fessed up.

'Pretty much.'

'Thought so.' Darren looked to his wife, 'Didn't I say Jill. Those people are new to this, didn't I say that?'

'Yep, that's what you said alright darl.'

'So, what you got?'

'It's a 38-foot sloop, ferro.'

'Oh,' Darren said nodding knowingly. 'A ferro.'

'Mmm.' Colin nodded.

'Cee-ment.' Jill said like it was a dirty word.

'Well, nice to meet you. We better get going. Isn't that right Jill?'

'Sure is honey. Got to get going. By-ee.' Jill waved and they strode away almost breaking into a trot.

'What's up with them?' Viv asked Colin.

'Well, Arnold said something about it.'

'What?'

'Well...it seems there is a bit of...snobbishness about boating and ferro...cee-ment,' Colin mimicked Jill's disgust, 'is not exactly fibreglass or traditional wood.' Then Colin regurgitated Arnold's pontifications on the subject of boat building materials ending with the pronouncement that 'some' ferro boats are home made with chicken wire.

'Is ours chicken wire?' Viv asked.

'Pedro didn't think so.'

'Oh.'

They looked out to the bay and ruminated on the thought of chicken wire when Colin perked up and said it was time to go.

As they walked the beach it became apparent that the tide had receded and the Tripps had to drag the inflatable to the shoreline. It didn't look heavy, but it was akin to lugging a stubborn beluga whale who didn't want to get wet to the water's edge, a good 50 metres away. They heaved, slogged and pulled the dinghy until it was floating. Getting in it while it was still close enough to shore to push off was another matter and once again Vivian was waist deep in water. Colin hoiked her in like landing a prize catch and she landed on the folding anchor and chain catching the shackle in the knee.

Once onboard there was still the matter of the pull start and Vivian suggested the string keeping Colin's shorts together. It was an ad hoc arrangement, but seemed to work. They pushed off and drifted into deeper water and Colin gave the engine a stern talking to, then pulled. His technique included a hip twist which under normal circumstances wasn't a problem, but with nothing keeping his shorts up except prayer the inevitable happened.

'First time, how is that?'

'Colin,' Viv grabbed his shorts at half-mast and pulled them up.

'Oh.' Col grabbed his clothing and sat down.

'Wonderful Col.' Vivian sat up the front away from Colin's elbow. The dinghy putted into the bay and everything seemed to be going smoothly when the engine stopped.

'What is it?'

'Dunno?'

'Petrol?'

'Nup.' Colin tried the pull start. Nothing.

He took the cover off and fiddled with the spark plug, then pulled. Nothing.

'I just don't understand it.' He scratched his head.

'Well I guess we better row.' Vivian pulled out the paddles.

The makers of inflatable boats have a sadistic streak when it comes to rowing. They skate, they scoot, they skid, but they do not row. Vivian put the paddles in the oarlocks and tried to get some movement. The boat went around in a circle.

'Here, let me have a go.' Viv shuffled to the bow and Colin took up the rowing position. He gave it his all. He huffed. He pulled. He pushed and the boat went around in a larger circle.

'Whoever made these things knows nothing about boats.' Colin said, 'It rows like a shampoo bottle.'

'Perhaps we should sort of just do it like a canoe,' Viv suggested. Colin took out the middle seat and they knelt down and took a paddle each.

'Together now.' Slowly but surely they made progress towards Moonlighting.

'I didn't think it was this far,' Vivian said as she dipped her paddle in and out.

'Nearly there,' Colin kept his eye on the prize. It was only when they had grasped the ladder to Moonlighting that Vivian saw the petrol hose had been pinched by the folding anchor and starved the engine of fuel. She declined to mention it to Colin, as some things are best kept in the dark if boating was to be a fun thing to do.

'Right, let's have a look at our position.' Colin took his bearings. The boat had swung in an arc and if it continued they would hit the rocks in an hour or so.

'Are we ok?' Viv asked.

'Well, I reckon we should just reset the anchor, now we have time on our hands.'

'How do we do that?'

'Well...' Colin scratched his head. 'We bring up some chain and then let it drop down, more or less, in the one place, rather than play it out.'

'Right.'

The exercise was completed without incident and after an hour on deck to see that everything was ok Colin finally relaxed.

'What's for tea?' Col asked. He sat easy watching the sun go down and anticipating their first night on Moonlighting.

'Isn't this fun?'

Viv declined to answer as she looked at the blueish bruise on her chest, the blister developing on her hands and her new slacks, which were slowly leeching their colour onto her legs and had a small tear on the knee.

'I know, let's have a BBQ.' Colin said, adding, 'This is the life.'

Viv had to think about that one as she imagined a smorgasbord on a cruise liner and no dishes to do afterwards.

CHAPTER 6

After their first excursion the Tripps were fired up on boating. Bruises, cuts, sore fingers and sunburnt noses were conveniently forgotten as they waxed lyrical about their magical weekend.

'And then we pulled up the anchor, and went right around Magnetic Island without a hitch.' Colin leaned on the dividing fence and smiled at his neighbour.

Ted nodded,

'Didn't I tell you it would be fair weather?'

'Something like that Ted.' Colin felt he had a bit of one upmanship and wanted to give his neighbour one more twist of the knife.

'And turns out Ted,' Colin smiled and raised his eyebrows in exclamation, 'Vivian and I just don't get sea sick.' Ted saw he was losing the upper hand and waved to his back door.

'Coming dear. She wants me. Must go.' And with that convenient excuse he hot footed it to his house. Colin did a little jig on his lawn as he walked back to his shed. It wasn't often he could get one over Ted.

Col was tinkering with his roadster when Vivian

appeared in the doorway.

'I contacted the electrician, Mr Sleck. He said he could come on Monday arvo. I said could he make it around 4.30 because you could get off early and he said that was fine.' Colin nodded at the information.

'Rowdy said he was the best with 12 volt. I don't suppose it will be a big job to get the mast lights working properly. Probably just a bulb or something.' Vivian waited in the doorway.

'What is it?' Colin new that look.

'Well it's just that we usually shop around and we don't really know how much he charges and all that sort of stuff.'

'Can't be too much. A call out fee and a light bulb.' In Colin's mind the job was a five-minute thing and he would have change from a $50 dollar note.

'Oh well, we will see tomorrow.' Viv folded her arms and frowned,

'Colin? Do you think we might go on a night sail?'

'Quite possible, why?'

'Well it's just that there is a meteor shower coming up in about three weeks and wouldn't it be lovely to see it at sea where there wouldn't be a loom of lights.'

'Sounds like a good idea Viv' Colin took his wife by the waist and pulled her in close, 'We could get all romantic.'

'Colin Tripp.' Viv said and kissed her husband. This boating could work out to be fun after all, she mused.

Colin drove single mindedly through the traffic. He didn't want to be late and miss Mr Sleck. Walking down the dock to the boat he felt a sense of pride and belonging as he casually waved to his near neighbours and new friends. Arnold and Connie were sitting on their back deck when Colin came up to Moonlighting.

'Nice afternoon,' Colin nodded at Arnold.

'Yes.'

'Come down for a look.'

'Well, yes.' Colin looked at his watch. 4:26. He didn't want to start a lengthy conversation with the Burkitts just as the electrician arrived.

'Always something isn't it.'

'Mmm.' Colin looked at his watch again.

'Waiting for someone?' Arnold and Connie sipped their drinks and smiled.

'Actually, the electrician will be here any minute.' Arnold looked at his wife and they shook their collective heads.

'Sleck?'

'Yes.' Colin didn't like the way he said Sleck. He bit his lip and shuffled his feet, put his hands in his pockets and then brought them out again and finally asked,

'He's reliable, isn't he?'

'Well if you ask me...' Connie began when Arnold shot her a look to say keep your mouth shut. Connie took a long drink.

'He's just a bit...different.'

'Different?' Colin said.

'Sort of...different.' Arnold huffed and grinned

'Oh.' Colin looked at his watch. 4:32.

'Why don't you ring him and see if he's caught

in traffic or something.' Connie stood up and motioned to Arnold that they should go inside. No-one wants to see a grown man cry.

The advice sounded good and so Colin pulled out Sleck's card and gave the number a ring. The conversation went something like this.

'Mr Sleck?'

'Yep.'

'Colin Tripp here.'

'OK.'

'Colin Tripp who owns Moonlighting.'

'Right.'

'Colin Tripp who owns Moonlighting and has a mast light that's not working.'

'Oh.'

'So...'Colin started hoping to jog Mr Sleck's memory.

'What?'

'Well...it's just that...I just thought that we had an arrangement.'

'Did we?'

'Yes.'

'Oh.'

'Well Mr Sleck, I'm here now and it is 4:40.'

'Right.'

'So...are you free.'

'I can't say just now.' Mr Sleck coughed and cleared his throat. 'Do you want me to....?'

'Yes,' Colin interrupted.'

'Right. Now when would a time suit you?'

'Now?'

'NOW?'

'Yes.' Colin could sense Sleck was losing the plot.

'My wife arranged for you to come now.' Colin pleaded.

'Look, give me your number and I'll give you a call.' Mr Sleck fell back on the old chestnut that has been getting tradesmen out of trouble ever since Mr Bell invented the telephone. Colin dictated his phone number and rang off. He looked at the mast. Perhaps, he thought, he could do it himself. Heights weren't his specialty, but the mast didn't look that high. After all, he mused, it probably only needs a new bulb. He walked up the dock to the chandlery and consulted Rowdy on the logistics of getting up the mast. After a lengthy discussion at 98.6 decibels Colin came away with a bosun's chair, a length of Spectra rope and all on the account.

'So, what did the electrician say?' Vivian handed Col a beer when he came home.

'Well...' Colin began. He didn't want to be seen as a complete idiot or just a weakling in front of his wife so he toyed with the idea of lying.

'He said he had an emergency and we had to reschedule.'

'What sort of emergency?'

'Didn't elaborate. Probably life or death.'

'So...' Vivian began to get suspicious. 'So, when *is* he coming Colin.'

'I couldn't say. So, that's why I bought you this.' He offered the Bosun's chair as his get out of jail card. 'It's a bosun's chair. For going up the mast.' Vivian looked at the contraption which was all straps, buckles and clips. 'Rowdy says we can do things like this ourselves. Everyone does it Viv.'

'Everyone?'

'Well, Rowdy said...' and here Colin launched into 'what Rowdy said' ending with 'Easy.' Viv wasn't too sure.

'Well I have some news too.' Viv said, then sipped her beer at the patio table.

'What?'

'I rang the shipwright, Mr McKee. He said he would be free on Wednesday to look at the rust marks. He said he knew Moonlighting and doubted that it would be chicken wire bleeding through.'

'Well, that's good news.' Colin smiled at his wife. She really was getting into this boating thing. 'Wednesday eh?'

'Yeah. I said I could meet him there at 10.'

'You?'

'Well why not. It's our boat and I think I can handle one tradesman.'

'But, I...I just thought that...' Colin pushed his glasses up his nose and peered at his wife.

'Colin?' Viv had seen that hang dog look before. 'Remember I said I wanted some input. Mr McKee sounded nice on the phone, and all he is really going to do is tell us if we need to fix the little bits of rust.' Colin mulled over the idea of being usurped, but it was a fait accompli and so he just nodded and pulled another beer from the bar fridge.

It was a cloudy and humid day as Vivian walked down the dock to the boat. She smiled and nodded to the other people going about their day and waved to the coastguard fellows washing their boat. They grinned at her and took more than a passing interest as she walked by. Viv dismissed their interest as just being polite and made her way to the boat.

'Morning,' Connie popped her head through a hatch and smiled. 'Doing some work?'

'I'm waiting for the shipwright,' Viv spoke to the bodyless head.

'Simpson or McKee?'

'McKee.'

'Oh.' Connie said with just a little of an ominous tone in her voice. 'McKee.'

'He's ok isn't he?' Viv asked.

'Yes. Yes. You'll be fine. Must go.' Connie pulled her head in and Vivian was left with the feeling she had just lost a winning lottery ticket. She climbed on board and opened up when there was a knock on the hull.

'Hello,' she held out her hand.

'I'm here.'

'Yes.

'So, what is it?'

'Well you see, we have just purchased the boat... yacht,' she smiled 'and we were sailing the other weekend, over to Horseshoe bay,' Vivian pointed in the direction of Magnetic Island, 'and when we were in the dinghy,' she pointed to the dinghy, 'well we sort of around the boat and we noticed these little marks. Really small marks, sort of pin pricks really, just about as big as a dressmaking needle, and well we thought that they might be something important.' She sighed and smiled.

'Hmmmmm.'

'And we thought they might be nothing really, but we just wanted to make sure.'

'Hmmmm.' Vivian wondered if this man was going to be the silent type when her phone rang.

'Is he there?' Colin asked.

'Yes, just talking to him now.'

'Put him on Viv.

'My husband just wants a word.' Vivian, much to her chagrin, handed over the phone.

Colin went over the same ground adding that they had a beer at the pub and Rowdy suggested they call him, just to make sure.'

'Hmmmm.' Mckee handed back the phone.

'So, can you take a look?' Viv hovered.

'Spots you say.'

'Yes spots.'

'On the hull you say.'

'Yes, on the hull.' Viv could see this conversation could go on for days.

'I better take a look then.' McKee took a ball point pen and bent down to take a look. He came in close and then with his pen began to dig. A sizable hunk of boat was levered out with his biro and plopped into the sea.

'Well, that's never happened before.' McKee stood up and scratched the crown jewels. Vivian bent down and looked at the hole.

'Can it be fixed?'

'Yes, yes, no worries. Just call Nino, he does this type of thing.'

'Nino?'

'Hmmmm. Nino Labotte. We call him El Nino.'

'Umm, are the tiny little holes anything to worry about Mr McKee?'

'Well that depends my dear.'

'On what?'

88

'Well it all depends.'

'Yes?'

'You should get that,' and here Mr McKee pointed an accusing finger at the hole he created, 'fixed pronto. Don't want the air getting in.'

'And the others.'

'Hard to say.'

'Well can you give it a shot Mr McKee?' Viv was getting peeved at his dodging every question.

'Look, it's like this little lady...' Mr McKee started when his phone rang. He retreated up the dock taking the call and Vivian stared at the hole. What would Colin say, she thought. She was bending over when someone politely coughed.

'Oh, hello.' Viv stood up to see a tall lanky fellow watching her.

'Sleck.' The man said and frowned.

'Sleck?'

'Yep.'

'Oh, you're the electrician. I thought you were going to ring first Mr Sleck?'

'Yep.'

'Well, I guess now you are here.' And Vivian explained that when they turned on the toilet the mast head light came on and off and when they wanted a fan they needed to operate the compass light at the same time.

'Right.' Sleck said looking into the distance.

'So...' Vivian tried to coax a definitive answer from the sparkie.

'Yeah.' Sleck raised his eyebrows.

'Can you take a look?' Vivian jumped on board and Sleck followed. She glanced up the dock to see Mr McKee striding off, probably to a life and death emergency, she thought and turned to tell Sleck to mind his head. Too late as a loud crack reverberated through the cabin.

He came inside and put his tool box down on the polished table. Vivian brought out a mat of non-slip to save the woodwork and offered it to Sleck, but he ignored her offer.

'That's a big tool box.' Viv tried to make conversation.

'It's my lunch box.'

'Oh.' Viv looked at the box and wondered what was inside. Sleck bent down and looked like a stick that had broken in two and pronounced,

'Oh. One of those.' Sleck looked at the circuit breaker board and rubbed his head.

'Is it bad?' This open-ended question is like manna from heaven to a tradesman. It can mean a week's work with call out fees and spare parts, 'that are virtually impossible to find these days and cost a fortune'. Fortunately, Sleck was too lazy for such shenanigans and if he could fiddle about and fix a problem with a bit of creative electrical wiring in twenty minutes it was 'all good'. He pulled a small screwdriver from his pocket and went to work dismantling the circuit board. Vivian watched as he teased out a bird's nest of wire in varying colours. She hovered expectantly.

'So,' Mr Sleck began, 'here is the problem.' He was about to start when his phone rang. There was a garbled conversation about relay switches and power grabs and he rang off. Once again he bent to the task and grabbed a white wire and yanked it from the innards of the board. There was a sort of wrenching noise, then a squeak and a thud and the wire flicked out with half a fuse in tow.

'Oh. Wrong one.' Sleck looked at the wire hanging like a criminal and tried to stuff it back in.

'Won't we be needing that one?' Viv asked.

'Leave it to me.' Sleck said. Vivian wasn't so sure. She watched as he produced a coat hanger and began to fish about up the wall. His phone rang again and he left the coat hanger - hanging, and went into detail about power consumption, solenoids and potted circuits and hung up.

'Um, excuse me Mr Sleck, but we had a bit of a look and it just seemed to me that.' Sleck held up his hand.

'Look here. Do you want me to fix it or not?'

'Well, yes, but you see, we thought that...' Sleck looked over to Vivian and tsked.

'You have a multi double switch integrated duel functioning 40watt overarching connecting system here. There is a ...' and Mr Sleck went on with unintelligible jargon. Vivian nodded a few times, but was lost after multi.

'So...do we need a new something or other Mr Sleck?'

'That's about the size of it.' Sleck stood up and his phone went off again. He assured the caller he had an inline fuse and a momentary switch and hung up, then turned to Vivian, 'I can get you one, but with your requirements I wonder if you don't just rip it out and start again.'

'You mean...'

'Yep.' Sleck put his hands in his pockets and raised his eyebrows.

'Oh.'

'You have my number give me a call.' Vivian

watched as he sloped off the boat and headed up the dock. She took another look at the hole in the hull and then through the window at the wires hanging out of the panel and bit her lip. How was she going to explain all this to Colin? Then she remembered Mr McKee's words. El Nino was her man. She fairly ran up to the chandlery and scooted inside to see Rowdy reading the paper behind the counter.

'Mr Rawlinson,' Vivian began.

'What cha young lady.' Rowdy boomed.

'Do you know of El Nino?'

'Weather patterns or odd jobs?' Rowdy yelled.

'Odd jobs.' Rowdy lent over the counter and pointed to the pin-up notice board around knee height on the front of the counter. Vivian had never noticed it before and wondered why anyone would put a notice board where it couldn't be noticed. She bent down and scanned the cards. Nino had a crude hand-written note extolling his virtues as an all-rounder.

#Fibberglassings, #hal repears, #boat mantenence # Underwatering Molto bella work.

'Saw him a half hour ago. On G finger.' Rowdy waved his hand in the direction of G finger and then as the hand was already in the air he put it to use picking his ear.

'Right.' Vivian shot out the door and trotted to the next dock down from Moonlighting. She let herself in the gate and walked down the dock looking left and right in the hope of spotting the Italian handyman. She had gone to the end and back again with no luck and so stopped and asked a fellow who was watching the water.

'I'm looking for El Nino. Have you seen him?'

The man pointed to the water,

'There.' Vivian looked at the dirty water and tried again.

'Sorry, I mean I'm looking for Nino the handyman.' Once again the man pointed to the water and frowned. They looked over the side of the dock and then Vivian noticed an air hose draped over the dock and bubbles coming up.

Oh, there,' she said and pointed. 'What's he doing?'

'Scraping my bottom.' The man frowned and fidgeted.

'Is there a problem?' Vivian couldn't help notice how agitated the owner looked.

'It's $100 an hour and he's been down there for 20 minutes already.' Now Viv had a frown as she thought on how much her hole and rat's nest of wires might cost.

'Will he be much longer do you think?'

'I bloody well hope not.' The man wrung his hands and began to pace.

'I'll wait.' Vivian stood on the dock and watched the bubbles as they worked their way along the hull of the motor boat. Presently she saw a black head appear and Nino popped up and hoiked himself onto the dock like a sea lion out for a sunbake.

'She's a good to go,' he smiled at the owner who was looking at his watch.

'Er. Mr Nino,' Vivian butted in, 'Can you come over to Moonlighting,' she pointed to the next finger, 'when you are finished. Just a small job.' She threw in the last bit in the hope of a small bill.

'Okey dokey.' Nino began to pull off his wetsuit. Vivian watched as a bronzed, pumped, young torso appeared and her mind wandered to the striking resemblance of the statue of David or the fireman calendar she had in the kitchen at home.

'Hhumm,' she cleared her thoughts. 'I'll just go and wait, shall I?'

'Nino flashed a perfect smile with perfectly straight, white teeth. 'Not a problemo.'

Once back on the dock next to Moonlighting Vivian was hailed by Connie.

'Oh Darl, have a look at this.' Connie flapped a magazine at Vivian.

'What do you think lovvie, the green or the blue?' Connie pointed to a picture of a cutlery set with little anchors printed on the handles in a catalogue.

'Well, I guess it depends.' Viv said, thinking she sounded like the shipwright and his shifty answers. 'What is that book?'

'The bible darl, the bible. Here you can have this one, I have another inside.' Connie handed over the boating catalogue and Vivian flipped through the pages. There were things in the book she had never seen, never knew existed and they made her open her eyes wide and she felt her bank account wasn't far behind.

'Thanks Connie.' Vivian clutched the bible to her chest and was interrupted by Nino.

'Hello.' he flashed his perfect smile.

'Oh, hello.' Vivian blushed. She turned to her neighbour and mimed she was busy. 'Later,' she said and turned to the bare-chested Adonis standing next to her.

'It's just that we have a little problem Nino. With this hole.' Viv pointed to the damage left by

McKee. Nino bent down, his muscles in his thighs bulging in his shorts and took a look. Vivian took a good look as well.

'Can you fix it?'

'No problemo.' Nino jumped up and smiled.

'Will it be a big job?'

'No problemo.' Vivian had a sneaking suspicion that to Nino everything was 'no problemo'. She tried her few words of broken Italian.

'Quanta costa?' and rubbed her fingers together to signal money. Nino rubbed his chest and frowned. He mimed small with his fingers and smiled.

'Now?' Viv pointed to her watch.

'Si, now.'

'And if you could just pop inside Nino.' She mimed for him to follow. He put his hands around her waist as she hoiked herself on the boat and Vivian didn't resist. Once on board she showed him the rats nest of wires Mr Sleck had left behind.

'Fix this.' Vivian pointed.

'No problemo.' Nino once again did a squat and looked at the mess while Vivian stood back and watched.

'I have tools.' Nino said.

'Right.' Vivian said, thinking she had it all under control. By the time Colin would come down after work everything would be as it should. Nino sprang out of the boat and fairly trotted up the dock and was back in a jiffy with a bag of tools. He worked quietly and diligently. Vivian sat in the cockpit and flipped through the catalogue.

There was a whole world of things that seems essentials for boating. Dinner sets made of melamine with sea faring motives, cup holders, fruit nets, fruit baskets, and all manner of handy things for the galley. Striped cushions, back rests, outdoor cushions and tablecloths were put under absolutely necessary. Then there was a whole section on teak accessories. Magazine racks, cup racks, toilet roll holders, binocular holders, fancy fiddles for shelving and the list just went on and on. Vivian looked downstairs and it wasn't long before she could envisage all the necessities of boating in place. She was just getting to clothing when Nino popped his head up and said,

'She's a good to go.'

'Really,'

'Si. Come.' Nino took Viv's hand and helped her down the companionway stairs in a gallant gesture and then pointed to the electrical power board. He flicked the toilet switch and gave an O.K signal. Then he did the same with the mast light and a little red light came on.

'No problemo.' Vivian smiled and watched a small bead of sweat run down his muscled chest.

'Would you like a drink Nino?'

'Si.' Viv fished about in the fridge and produced a can of lemonade and handed it over. Nino drank it and then gave her back the can startling her out of her daze.

'Oh. thanks.' she giggled and took the can.

'Outside eh?'

'Yes.' She watched him jump up the stairs and start work outside.

'I do all yes?'

'Ok.' Vivian would have let him excavate Pompeii and patch it up again as long as he kept his shirt off. He was working at the hole while she perused the clothing section. Hats, gloves, jumpers and shoes all seemed to be a must as Vivian looked at the pictures. Next came first aid kits, torches, antique brass hanging lanterns, survival packs, waterproof bags for just about every electrical appliance and by the time Nino had finished Viv needed the gross national product of Belgium to pay for her wish list.

'She's a good to go.' Nino smiled. 'She's a wet.' Vivian nodded.

'Quanta costa?' She asked.

'Tomorrow. Domani.' the Adonis said and Vivian smiled and nodded again. Nino flashed a grin and picked up his tools and trotted off. Vivian watched him until he reached the gate and thought she had found a gem, one worth hanging on to.

When Colin came down at the end of the day Vivian had a cold beer waiting and ushered him into the cockpit.

'So, what did they say?' Colin asked.

'Well that depends.'

'Depends on what?'

'Well, that's what I said and the shipwright said it depends.' Colin frowned and sipped his beer.

'Oh, and Mr Sleck came.'

'And what did he say?'

'He said we have a multi something or other with an over something and a 40 watt something else. He fiddled about a bit and then said we needed to replace everything.'

'What, everything?'

'That's about the size of it.' Vivian shrugged

97

her shoulders and grinned.

'Buuuuut...' she began.

'What, there's more.'

'Hmm.' Vivian smiled and gave Colin another beer. 'I found a man and he fixed the wiring and he fixed the patch on the hull.'

'What patch?' Colin began to feel uneasy about what had been happening in his absence.

'Well a bit of the boat fell off,' Vivian was interrupted.

'Fell off?'

'Yes. When Mr McKee did a bit of prodding and Nino fixed it.' Colin stood up and they jumped off so Vivian could point out the patch. It was a fine job and only need a lick of paint to be virtually invisible.

'And he said he could do the rest if we wanted. I said yes.' Colin looked at his wife and felt a swelling of pride. She really was taking to the boating lifestyle.

'And Connie lent me a catalogue.' Vivian brought out the bible and put it on the cockpit table. She opened the book and introduced Colin to the world of shopping for a boat. He started at aerials and it was getting dark by the time he reached fenders.

'I guess we better head home?' Vivian finished her Gin and Tonic as the sun dipped below the horizon.

'I guess.' Colin took a deep relaxing breath.

'Colin?' Viv began.

'Yes.'

'Do you think we need some cushions out here? Comfy ones?'

98

'Yeah.'

'And a few drink holders would be nice.'

'Yeah.'

'And maybe a lantern?'

'Yeah.'

Vivian sighed. Things were working out just fine.

CHAPTER 7

Vivian set the morning tea out on the patio, waved to Gloria who was at the side fence and called Colin. She had an idea and wanted to run it by the Captain. Colin clumped up the three steps to the decking and sat down.

'I don't know what makes those weeds grow so quick.' He looked at the back yard and sighed. It was no surprise to Vivian. They had been spending every waking moment down on the dock. She pushed Colin's coffee a little closer and began with her idea.

'Colin, I was just thinking.' Colin raised his eye brow. He was always wary of Vivian thinking - it could lead to all manner of 'ideas' that usually involved drilling a hole, tying something up or pulling something down.

'Yeeeerrrrrs.' he said cautiously.

'Well it's seems to me that we have been spending a lot of to and fro lately and not really getting on top of things.'

'What things?' Colin narrowed his eyes.

'Boat things.' Viv explained. 'And I was thinking that perhaps, maybe we should just go
100

and live on the boat for a week or so, just to get a real push on the things that need doing. That way we could be ready for the meteor shower in two weeks. An overnight sail and then three days just mooching about on the water.' Vivian sat back and let the idea sink in.

'What? You mean live on the dock?'

'That's right. Sort of move on board for a week or two and then we can save a lot of time.' Vivian smiled at Colin and took a sip of her coffee.

'But what about...' Colin began. Vivian held up her hand.

'Gloria said she would look after things and the sprinklers are on a timer so really it's not a problem. Anyway, we can come back if we need to.' Colin sipped his coffee and frowned. He huffed a bit and then twiddled with his tea spoon. For once Vivian had come up with a bright idea.

'You know we *could* do without the commute.'

'Yes, that's what I thought. I rang the marina and they said it's not much more for live aboard rates. Vivian took a piece of cake.

'And we could be up early every day and tackle something so that we can be ready for a big trip. Colin nodded and Vivian wondered how she would bring up the subject of installing the teak drink holder, the magazine rack and the toothbrush holder she had ordered without it sounding like a set up.

The morning was bright and warm as the Tripps packed for their adventure. Vivian had booked in for two weeks and they had made a 'To Do' list over the preceding week, so as 'not to waste the time'. Colin had taken two weeks leave. They were ready.

'All set?' Vivian asked as she closed the boot.

'Yep,' Colin replied putting the last of his tools in the back seat.

Once at the Marina they purloined a rickety old cart and loaded up for the walk down the dock. It felt like coming home. They said morning to the regular live aboards. Connie and Arnold spied the load. Arnold asked,

'Moving on board?'

'Just for a bit. To get some things done.' Colin said. The Burkitts nodded, knowing a thing or two about 'getting things done'. It took most of the morning to get the boat sorted with stores and after only two trips to the supermarket, three trips to the hardware store and a longish shouting match with Rowdy to buy an extension lead they settled in and put the kettle on.

'So,' Vivian looked at their extensive list. 'We should check out that light,' she pointed to the mast. Colin looked up as he sat in the cockpit drinking his tea. Heights weren't his favourite occupation.

'Do you want me to go up?' Vivian offered. 'Or...' Colin smiled at his wife.

'If you *really* want to.' He played his get out of jail card. They went over the logistics and then Arnold came over.

'If you need a hand or anything?' He had escaped Connie's crocheting, patchworking and scrapbooking looking for an excuse.

'Well we were just wondering how to get up there.' Vivian pointed to the top of the mast. 'We have a bosun's chair.' she offered.

'Bloody piece of cake.' Arnold said and explained the rope situation, the winch manipulation

102

and the safety lines.

'You want to do it now?' Mr Burkitt asked. Viv looked at the time.

'I guess so.' She shrugged her shoulders at her husband and went downstairs to get the bosun's chair.

'Now we are looking for cracked lenses on the light, loose wiring, anything like that.' Colin prepped his wife and she nodded.

There was a moment when her feet left the deck and then she began the climb up the steps of the mast with the chair acting like an over-full nappy hanging from her backside. Arnold and Colin watched and winched as she made her way past the spreaders to the top.

'Alright Luv?' Colin shouted.

'Fine.' Vivian checked her ropes, gave the thumbs up and kept going.

Once at the top she tied herself off and looked at the view. Spread out before her was the coast and Magnetic Island all bathed in bright sunlight looking just perfect.

'Everything ok?' Colin yelled as he belayed the line.

Yep, fine.' She wrapped her arms around the mast and took a look. Straight away Viv could see the problem. There was a bird's nest in amongst the pulleys and wheels and they had pecked the electrical cord to the bare wires.

'I'm just going to chuck some stuff down.' Vivian began to pull out the nest and saw it had two eggs in it. It was a toss-up whether to leave them in peace or get rid of them. She pocketed the eggs and then went to work on the light. Its screws were a mishmash of sizes and it took quite a bit of cajoling to get them loose. Eventually she pulled the light free and put it in her swinging bucket with her tools. Everything else looked in good order and so she gave the order to descend. Colin and Arnold were nowhere to be seen.

'Er, Colin.' Vivian shouted from the top. She looked around, but there was no-one about.

'Colin,' she tried again.

'Hello.' Nino appeared down below.

'Hello,' Viv said hoping she wasn't blushing. 'I need to get down.'

'She's ok.' Nino took charge. He lowered Vivian at a gentle pace and when she reached the deck he took her by the waist and held on until she stepped out of her harness with her arms around his neck.

'Oh, thanks,' she said over Nino's shoulder. Viv saw Arnold and Colin appear from below decks.

'Colin, this is Nino.' Vivian extricated herself from the young man and made the introductions. Colin set his jaw and looked Nino over.

'Bit young isn't he.'

'Oh, I don't know.' Vivian twirled her hair in her fingers. She hadn't seen Colin jealous for quite some time.

'I have the bill.' Nino produced a piece of paper and handed it to Viv. Everyone was watching Nino as he took off his shirt. Colin momentarily tried to 'suck it in soldier', but his six pack these days was in the fridge.

'She's a hot.' Nino said.

'Yes.' Vivian giggled and then she remembered the eggs. She gently picked them from her pocket and explained the birds nest.

'I take them.' Nino cradled the eggs in his hands. Colin wondered why he hadn't thought of that as Vivian gushed at the kind, sweet young man.

'And the light?' Vivian handed over her bucket and the boys disappeared down the hatchway to ponder the light.

'Well, thanks I'll pay this tomorrow ok?'

'She a okey dokey.' Nino flashed a smile and left Vivian feeling all aflutter.

'Cute isn't he?' Connie called over.

'Hmmmm.' Viv answered.

'My Arnold over there?' Connie pointed to Moonlighting.

'Downstairs.' Viv replied.

'Well come over here luv and have a drink.' Vivian scrambled across the ropes and boarded the Burkitt's boat called 'The Love Nest'. It had a very lived in look.

'Come in,' Connie held the door open. Pot plants hung from the bimini and other pots gathered on the back deck with a gaggle of folding chairs and tables and old milk crates and a huge esky. Vivian's hair caught in a rather elaborate wind chime made of copper wire and beads which were fashioned and bent to look like a star fish.

'I think I'm stuck,' she pulled at a tentacle.

'Here let me help you with that.' Connie untangled her hanging dangle and the women went inside.

'Cuppa or a coldie?' Connie asked.

'Cold one if it's not too much trouble.' Connie pointed to a small settee covered with patchwork throws and lace doilies over the arms and back.

'Sit.' Vivian went to sit down and Chester, the

105

small yappy dog shot out and flew past her ankles and disappeared down to the galley. She sat down on the spot left warm by the dog and marvelled at the room. There was hardly a spare space to be seen. A cross stitch 'Home sweet Home' adorned the top of the windows which were heavily veiled with lace and sun catchers of dolphins, turtles and whales in various poses. There were love heart cushions scattered around like confetti and brass anchors as book ends which vied for room with a Spanish flamenco dancer doll propped up on the VHF radio. But the centrepiece, which had pride of place on the table, was a gaudy water fountain of King Neptune with spritely water nymphs playing with a revolving ball under an arc of dolphins jumping over a rainbow.

'Here you are,' Connie offered a glass of soft drink and sat at the kitchenette table.

'Thanks.' Vivian tried to drink slowly so as not to comment on the room.

'What do you think?' Connie smiled at her masterpiece.

'Well...' Vivian smiled.

'We only got it yesterday. And how much do you think it was? Go on... guess?'

'Well...I really...'

'Just 200 dollars, that's all.'

'Really.'

'Yup.' Connie looked at Neptune and then said, 'Watch.' She leaned down and flicked a switch and the whole thing lit up.

'Gosh.' Viv said. She knew that if she stayed, there would be that awkward moment when she would be asked if she liked it. 'My word, look at the time. We really have a lot to do and so thanks for the drink Connie, but I better get back. Colin likes an early tea and we want to get going early tomorrow. Thanks again.' Vivian stood up and shot out the cabin door, vaulted over the back railing and hurdled onto Moonlighting and took the companionway stairs two at a time.

Colin and Arnold looked up from their beers,

'Arnold has invited us over to his boat for sundowners Viv.' Vivian deflated like a made in china hypolon dinghy.

'Nice,' she said as graciously as possible.

As Vivian put on a clean blouse Colin mentioned that they should rustle up a plate of something to take.

'What? Now you tell me. I don't have anything Col.'

'Oh, just some of those things you do. The nice things with the other stuff on the top. You know. My favourite stuff. I think it's sort of red and green.' Vivian looked at her husband.

'Well we don't want to be too long you know. We have a busy day tomorrow and we don't seem to have ticked off much of our list.' Vivian began to assemble a pick and mix for their first invitation to sundowners. 'And I should just warn you that the Burkitts have...varied cultural tastes.'

'What?' Colin was picking the olives as fast as Viv spooned them out.

'You'll see. Just try to keep your mouth full so you don't put your foot in it.'

'Right.' Colin said getting a head start with the cheese and sun-dried tomatoes.

'Hello.' Viv knocked on the hull and the Tripps were ushered on board.

'We thought we'd sit on the deck, it's such a lovely evening.' Everyone took a seat around a coffee table which had a top made out of beer bottle caps.

'Beer?' Arnold took two stubbies and said 'Watch this.' He put one of the bottles under his armpit, flexed his muscle and the lid popped off, then he handed the bottle to Colin.

'Er, I have my own, thanks all the same.' Colin produced a can and supped.

'Oh, Arnold, stop showing off.' Connie thumped her husband on the arm and everyone laughed politely.

'You got a bit to do?' Arnold asked. The Tripps nodded.

'We did all this ourselves, didn't we luv?' Connie said. She looked puppy-like at her husband.

'Just about Munchkins. I installed that.' Arnold pointed to a bait board on the back of the deck. It was fixed with rusting screws that pointed up through the nylon board and a piece of wood kept the whole thing from throwing itself into the sea to end its miserable life.

Everyone looked at the board and Colin stuffed his face with crackers and cheese and smiled.

'Oh, I know. Do you like music?' Connie gushed. The Tripps nodded still munching. Connie went inside and then they heard the music from the outdoor speakers which Arnold had installed with a blunt bread and butter knife on a dark night. They were lopsided and hung from their holes in the walls with sticky velcro tabs.

108

Connie came out,

'We just love country music, don't we Arnold?'

It was late in the evening when the snacks had run out that the Tripps finally left to the strains of someone's dog dying on the road and the girl they left behind. Once down below and with their dinner cooking Vivian said,

'Well they are really nice people...really.'

'Really friendly.' Colin added.

'And Arnold does know a bit about boats. He was telling me we need to take a look at our chain locker. They are an overlooked area that can cause trouble.'

'Put it on the list.' Vivian said, 'and then I want to go out and buy one of those water fountains.'

'Anything for you munchkins,' Colin mocked as he tucked into his dinner.

Vivian thought it would be a good time, with Colin in a fine mood, to bring up her recent purchases and tomorrow they could make real progress with the instillation.

CHAPTER 8

Colin and Vivian lay in bed listening to the morning sounds on the water. The birds were squawking, engines were buzzing and the halyards were slapping against the mast. Vivian looked up through the open hatch above their bed,

'Bright blue sky,' she said. They lazed about for an hour talking on the day ahead and then had a revitalising breakfast of bacon and eggs to get the day started. By the time they had walked to the showers, done the dishes, and read the paper it was 9:30ish.

'Shall we get some morning tea at the shops first, then we won't have to stop later?' Colin asked.

'Sounds good.'

Once back from the shops it was decided that they might as well have morning tea before they got stuck in and so the kettle was put on and they mulled over the jobs to do. It was 11 o'clock by the time Colin decided to have a look at the chain locker.

Moonlighting had a massive locker. At a pinch it could fit about 6 refugees or at least 150kg of cocaine. Viv peered into the depths then they made a plan. What they needed was those cable ties that everyone seemed to have on their chain to count the depth. That entailed laying the chain out on the dock.

With a quick trip to the hardware store for cable ties of different colours and a set of riggers gloves for Viv, when they got back to the boat it was lunch.

After lunch it was decided that they could tackle the job and so the boat was moved closer to the walkway and Colin marked out their 20 metres on the dock. The idea was to lower the anchor and then lay out the chain right to the bitter end and this would have been the next step, except Colin got to talking to Max on Max-a-million.

'So, if you just use this app then you can see where you are,' Max thrust his iphone at Colin and said, 'See, you are here.'

'Yeah, I know.'

'Now if you swipe your finger over here you can see the view.'

'Really.' Colin said.

'Mate, you should get one of these. I could download the app for you. You do have an ipad, and an iphone that hook up to your laptop, don't you?'

'Er...my wife takes care of all that.' Colin said not letting on that he had trouble even using a remote control on the television.

'Well, if she wants to come over sometime.' Max offered. 'Colin nodded and smiled.

'You doing your chain?'

'Yep.'

'Well, you know you can get an electric counter for that. It's an easy unit to install and you can have a read out on your consol. Then if you want, you can patch it to your ipad and see it on your gps reading.

'Fancy.' Colin scratched his head.

'Yeah, and then you can co-ordinate that with your depth sounder and that can be patched to your

Iphone so you know how much chain to let out.'

'Amazing.' Colin said looking for Vivian to rescue him.

'You want to see mine?'

'Well...'

'Only take a minute.' Max dragged Colin by the arm and led him to the opposite walkway and they stepped onto Max-a-million, a 50 ft flybridge powerboat.

Vivian came out with sun hat, riggers gloves and an expectation of getting started. When she saw Colin disappear into the cabin of the powerboat she took off her gloves and went below to take a good look at her purchases and where they should go and just how many magazine racks and egg cup holders did she really need.

It was afternoon tea time by the time Colin came back and Vivian presented him with 'his very own drinks holder, magazine rack and toilet roll holder'.

'I just knew you'd like them Col.' Colin frowned and looked at the teak fixtures.

'Do we really need all this?'

'Well, I just thought...' Vivian started. Colin smiled. He couldn't resist his wife when she had so much enthusiasm about the boat and they spent the afternoon, or what was left of it, deciding where to drill, screw and plug. It was 5 o'clock when they sat back in the cockpit and cracked a beer.

'Well, we seemed to be getting on,' Colin looked at the drinks holder.

'A good day's work.' Vivian said using her own drink holder. She had to perch the beer on the top as it didn't seem to fit in the thing.

The evening was mild so after their tea the Tripps decided to take a stroll down the dock. Boats with their interior lights on can show the casual observer the insides. Vivian peeked into a few boats looking at their wood work, their soft furnishings and general layout. Colin, on the other hand, came up short and grabbed Vivian's arm.

'Look.' he whispered and pointed to the reflection in a forward hatch. There, for all to see, was a snatch in the hatch. The reflections acted like a mirror above the V berth and the occupant was none the wiser.

'Don't look.' Vivian dragged her husband away.

'Did you see that?' Colin was astounded at the clarity of the picture. It only took about a minute for the Tripps to think on their own situation. They hurried back to moonlighting which was bow in to the dock with the V berth hatch wide open and the light on. Vivian and Colin could see their bed, the book Viv had been reading open on the coverlett and if they had been lying down...well it didn't leave much to the imagination.

'You don't think...?' Viv said.

'Nah. We had the light off, didn't we?' Col answered.

'I guess so.' Viv tried to think. They quickly convinced themselves that there were no indiscretions on Moonlighting and went on board for a cup of tea and to close the hatch.

Lying in bed that night Vivian conceded that they hadn't done much on their 'to do' list.

'Well, we have a good head start on the chain tomorrow. I don't think we need anything from the hardware store.' Colin remained hopeful.

'Shouldn't take too long do you think?' Viv snuggled up to Colin.

'Nah, not long at all.' he said as he drifted off to sleep, remaining the eternal optimist.

CHAPTER 9

The Tripps jumped out of bed early and made an effort to get going. All the morning chores were home and hosed by 8:30 and Vivian was just putting on her rigging gloves when there was a,

'Yoooohoooo,' from the dock. She popped her head up like a prairie dog and spied Connie.

'Honey,' Connie began, 'We are having a girl's lunch today and I thought you might like to come.'

'That's very kind of you Connie, but we need to get some work done here.' Vivian showed Connie her gloves ready for action.

'If you change your mind dearie, we are at the pub across the road.' Connie said. Vivian smiled and waved and ducked back inside.

'Why don't you go luv?' Colin had heard the conversation. Vivian picked up the 'to do' list and waved it in front of her husband.

'OK, ok. I just thought it might be an opportunity to get to know some of the people, that's all.'

'Well, if we get some of these done,' Vivian had another look at their list, 'I might pop over for a drink. Shall we get this chain locker thing happening?'

They trooped up on deck and surveyed the job. Colin had an idea on how to go about it and Vivian had a different idea on the logistics. There was a tense moment when neither was going to budge when Max, Arnold and Mr Ashcroft from Wanderlust came over to have a good look at the job.

'You need to get that over here first,' Mr Ashcroft said.

'You really should put the anchor in the water,' Arnold advised.

'I reckon you'd be better to pull the whole thing forward a bit.' Max suggested. Colin and Viv nodded at all the advice and then said they had it sorted, but thanks all the same.

The experts departed and Colin stood on the dock ready to take the anchor. It didn't look that big or heavy, but 60lbs of pointy metal can be a handful when it drops in your lap.

'Right let it go.' Colin said. Vivian played out the chain. The theory was fine, but Colin didn't count on the boat moving back on its mooring ropes. As he held onto the anchor to lower it to the dock the whole thing began to get away from him.

It often happens that somehow the brain has a blockage and the last thing on a person's mind is to let go. Colin hung on and slowly lost his precarious footing and ended up dangling from the anchor as the boat shifted with the tide. Vivian, being on the deck, and way behind the enormous bow sprit, couldn't see the dilemma and was awaiting further instructions.

'Do you want some more chain Col?' She shouted. Colin kept quiet and waited knowing the boat would swing back any moment...and so it did...

116

eventually. Once again standing on the dock, Colin wrapped the chain around a cleat and then shouted to Viv to let go the brake. Being the dutiful wife Viv 'let go the brake'. The chain rattled out over the bow sprit and onto the dock as Colin began to stretch it out. The first line is always the trickiest, but with a bit of back work and perspiration the chain begins to follow a course and get laid out in rows. Colin walked the 20 metre lengths when Viv shouted to stop.

'What's up?'

'I think we have a big problem. It's stuck. It looks like there is a big blob in the locker.'

'A blob?' Colin asked.

'Sort of a knot or something.' Vivian peered into the depths and knelt down to give the chain a jangle.

'Hang on, I'll have a look.' Colin clambered up to the bow and then lowered himself inside the locker. The chain had been sitting in water and was rusted together in one big lump. He jumped on it. He thumped it with a hammer, but it refused to oblige. He prodded it with the boat hook.

'Angle grinder Viv.' Vivian trotted downstairs and came back with the angle grinder.

'Won't we need all that chain Col?'

'I don't think so. We have 65 metres on the dock as it is.' Colin turned on the grinder and began to cut the chain at the point just before it went up the hawser pipe while Vivian watched on.

As the last link was cut the tension on the chain pulled the cut end through the pipe and it clattered down the bow sprit and fell into the water. Vivian raced to the bow to see the neat corn rows of chain get pulled down into the water like dominos.

'Colin quick.' Colin climbed out of the chain locker and was just in time to see the last of the chain disappear in the water then the dock cleat that was holding the anchor gave up on its rusty coach screws in rotten wood and the whole kit and caboodle took a flying leap and plummeted to the bottom of the murky depths.

'Oh.'

It was around morning tea time when Rowdy, after telling them that the chain and ground tackle would be virtually impossible to find in the thick viscous mud, assured the Tripps he had a special deal for chain and anchor and could get it to them in three days.

'Shall I put it on ya tab?' Rowdy yelled. Viv and Colin nodded.

'Just look at it this way,' Rowdy began, leaning in close, 'it's like bloody insurance. Something you can trust. New chain, new anchor equals good night's sleep.' He rummaged about in his vest for a bit and then had a scratch. 'In-sure-ants' he shouted.

The walk back to the boat was a sombre march as the Tripps contemplated their bad luck.

'Well I guess we would have had to buy new stuff at some point.' Vivian said.

'Yeah.' Colin muttered. They climbed on board and looked at the lump still in the chain locker.

'It's a pretty big lump.' Vivian prodded it with her foot.

'Well it's got to come out I guess. Do you feel like tackling it now?' Vivian looked at her dejected husband. Their to-do list wasn't getting any smaller and she smiled at Col and gave him a kiss to try to alleviate his pain.

'So, what's next on the list that we can totally cock up?' he asked.

'Hmm. We need to get the gas bottle out and tested.' Vivian thought that this would be a small, quick job and likely to have a good 'I'm achieving *something*' feel about it.

The designer of Moonlighting, like other boat designers, all have an unhealthy obsession of trying to fill every space, every void with something. Moonlighting's gas locker and the 9 kg bottle were made for each other.

Colin lifted the lazarette hatch at the back of the steering station and took a good look at the bottle. It was wedged into a corner of the hull that was about as big as a 4kg gas bottle. He grabbed the collar and tipped the bottle on its side, but it was too big to roll. He turned it around and tried to pull the bottom out first, but it couldn't tilt. Vivian sat on the back rail and made a suggestion.

Colin huffed, 'I just tried that,' he said through gritted teeth.

'Alright Colin. I' m just trying to help.' Colin tipped the bottle on its side as far as it would go and then rolled it forward, but it jammed at the hatch lip.

'Bloody hell.'

Arnold heard the cry for help and came over to investigate.

'Why don't you pull it forward and then lift the back?' Colin stepped aside to let Arnold find out for himself that that particular manoeuvre didn't work. Max came into the mix and suggested they pull

119

the bottom out first. Arnold stepped aside and Max had a go. Connie came over and thought that they needed to grease the sides, but this was dismissed as ridiculous. Mr Ashcroft came over and said they should just cut it out and patch it up after. Colin wasn't so sure about that idea. All the while Vivian sat on the rail and pondered the problem.

'I think,' she hopped down from her perch and began to get everyone's attention, 'I think, that if you put the mouth of the gas collar to the left and over the hinges, then roll the bottom up so it's 90 degrees then just pull forward it should work.' The assembled crowd looked at the problem, then at Viv and then back to the problem.

'Viv,' Colin began. He put his hands on his hips, rolled his eyes, and pushed his glasses up his nose. 'I think it's a bit more complicated than that.' He looked over to the men and gave a little shrug of his shoulders and a 'phhhhfffff'.

'Excuse me.' Viv knelt down at the locker. She positioned, rolled, pulled and the bottle came out without touching the sides.

'I was going to suggest that.' Arnold said.

'It's obvious really.' Max started walking to the side of the boat to jump off.

'They often come out that way.' Mr Ashcroft followed Max and they hurried down the dock.

Connie began to laugh. 'Trust a woman to get it right.' She patted Viv on the back and retreated back to The Love Nest chuckling to herself with Arnold not far behind.

'Rowdy said we can leave it with him and he will send it away to be tested.' Vivian looked at the embossed lettering and numbers on the collar. 'I'll take it up, shall I?' Colin gritted his teeth and nodded.

While Vivian was gone Colin thought he might take a look at the list and get something finished all on his own. Seeing the magazine rack, he felt he could tackle that without too much trouble. Viv had said she wanted it somewhere, but he couldn't quite remember where, so he thought he'd just surprise her and get it done. There was a spare space near the toilet and this seemed ideal to Colin. Every man knows he does his best reading on the throne. It was a tight fit but the rack slotted in and it didn't take a jiffy with a goodish dab of glue, the drilling of some holes and a few screws to get the thing in place. It was only when he stood back to admire his handiwork that he realised he had put the rack over the access hole to the piping. It didn't seem a big thing and so he figured it would be alright.

'I mean,' he said to himself, 'how often would I need to get to those toilet pipes.' He shut the door on his misgivings just as Viv came down the companionway stairs.

'Rowdy says he won't be sending anything off for a bit and so suggested I take it over myself. He gave me directions so I thought I'd just go and do it.'

'Yep.'

'So, I'll go, shall I?'

'Yep.'

'You're not sulking are you Col?'

'Nope.' And with that unequivocal answer Vivian left to go to the camping store which just happened to be a mega chandlery as well.

Gas, Gear & Boating Goods was out of town,

121

but when Vivian walked in she could see right away she had found the Mecca of the boating world. There was so much stuff she just knew she needed, and all of it, the shop assistant assured her, was essential if she was to have a trouble-free boating experience. Her boating experience could take several hours and so she rang Colin and said she'd be a while and did he prefer stainless steel coffee mugs or melamine?

It was after a big fry up lunch and a quick five-minute lie down, which turned into three hours, that Colin woke up and was putting the kettle on when there was a knock on the hull.

'Hellllloooo there.'

Colin popped up and saw a large bearded man beaming at him.

'McGregor.' He held out his hand.

'Tripp,' Colin offered.

'New are you?'

'Yes.'

'Well we are having a few drinks later, down there,' McGregor pointed down the dock. 'Everyone's invited.'

'Thanks, that would be great.' Colin smiled.

'I knew the owner of this boat. Did you know the history?' McGregor leaned on the gunwale.

'Not really.'

McGregor sat down on the set of steps used to get on board and seemed to be settling in for the conceivable future. Colin offered a cold one and that was the end of the list.

Vivian found the two men hard at it when she

came back to the boat and frowned.

'Darling, this is McGregor. He knew the owner of Moonlighting,' Col was talking fast to get out of trouble, 'and he was just telling me about the history.'

Viv nodded and put her shopping bags on the deck.

'And did you know that Moonlighting actually won a race and that it was designed by a naval architect.' Colin smiled, 'Drink?' He popped downstairs and came back with a beer for his wife.

Arnold heard the 'phhssssh' of a beer can and joined the group.

'Ol' Simpson loved this boat,' Arnold said. The Tripps listened as their boat was given some history and kudos. Max soon came over with a drink and added to the story then gradually as people passed the growing crowd, they were drawn in and by the time the sun had set, it was a party.

Vivian had a gaggle of women pouring over her purchases from the 3Gs as the mega chandlery was known, and the women could see a complete makeover, with their experience on offer, for Viv and Moonlighting. Colin hung off every word of the old salts as they plied him with drink and advice about shaft alignments and pump schematics. Food appeared, more drinks came in eskies, someone produced a ukulele and as with all dock parties, there were lies, tall stories, bragging rights and booze. Bodies draped themselves over Moonlighting and The love nest, people brought folding chairs, stools and steps and then Lionel off Gunna-go produced some chilli peanuts from Thailand.

'I like shillii,' Colin slurred.

'Col?' Viv giggled, 'He does you know,' she nodded. The crowd hushed as Lionel passed the bowl to Col. There was silence as Colin grabbed a handful and threw them in his mouth. He smiled and chewed. Everyone waited.

'He really likes chilli.' Viv said to the silence. Colin chewed and swallowed. A minute passed and then - nothing.

'Maaaaaaate.' Lionel patted Colin on the back and the party cheered. Colin was so drunk he didn't know what he'd done to deserve the accolades, but he felt right at home and at that moment counted about twenty-four of his best friends in the whole wide world.

It was only the next day as he was on his hands and knees pulling the magazine rack to pieces and trying to unblock the toilet pipe of paper while nursing a splitting headache and a burning clacker ring, that he began to curse his best friends, while at the same time wishing he had never been born.

CHAPTER 10

Vivian sat in the cockpit and sipped her cup of coffee. She surveyed the scene of last night's party. Wine bottles were stacked three deep on the dock, there was the odd folding chair, abandoned by their owners, a rubbish bin had been dragged from somewhere and was spilling its guts onto the dock and a couple of lonely shoes sat forlorn, waiting to be adopted or claimed. Arnold appeared on his back deck and rubbed his eyes.

'Morning,' Viv trilled.

'Ug,' Arnold said then took a good look at the dock, the mess and cast his eyes over the side of his boat which seemed to be carrying its fair share of empties. He fished about for a cold drink in his fridge and then, with a swig to restore his vocal cords and get his brain working, he smiled at Viv.

'You pull up alright?'

'Yes, sort of,' Viv said. Arnold digested the information and then spied something on his rod holder. He came in close to get a better look. The thing was wirey, hairy and a reddish colour. He tentatively picked at it and then held his prize up in his fingers like it was a left-over sock from the

125

rugby dressing room floor.

'What is it?' Viv looked at the thing.

'Beats me.' Arnold let it fall into the sea then sloped off inside out of the light. It was, Vivian decided, a wild night.

Colin appeared with a coffee and spanner in hand.

'Finished?' Viv asked. He nodded and then regretted the sudden movement.

'Did we say we would go sailing on the weekend with McGregor?'

'I can't remember.' Viv shrugged. 'Did you know that Susan and Douglas have been around the world?' Col slowly shook his head. As feeling began to return to their jangled nerves there was the after party review with quite a few of 'did you know, have you ever seen, she said, he said and more gossip than Mr Bell ever dreamed of with the invention of the telephone.

Colin went downstairs to brew some fresh coffee and Vivian was hailed from the finger.

'Hey there. Wild night eh?' A troll like yachty came up to the boat and shook hands.

'Bongo,' he said.

'Viv.'

'We met last night.'

'I guess,' Vivian wasn't quite sure if she did or not. She looked at Bongo and suddenly in one of those rare lucid, lightening strike moments knew just what Arnold had deposited in the sea. Bongo had a large patch of beard missing from his chin.

'Well, thanks for a great night.'

'My pleasure.' Vivian watched as he walked away thinking some things are best left unsaid.

'Who was that?' Colin reappeared.

126

'Bongo, apparently we met last night,' Viv giggled.

'What?'

'I'll explain later.' She snickered.

With a second cup of coffee under his belt Colin brightened up and they once again looked at their 'to do' list.

'Well, we have been up the mast,' he ticked the box.

'And we installed the drinks holders.' Vivian looked at her accessories.

'Half-finished the chain locker.' Colin said.

'Then just really got rid of the old stuff, but there is still a bit to do.' Vivian said and pointed to the paper.

'And...well...that's about it.' Colin looked at the A4 sheet. 'What do you fancy doing today?' Viv looked at the list.

'I guess...there is the magazine rack,' she leant over and gave Col a peck on the cheek.

'Yes, the magazine rack.' Colin didn't quite know to explain that he had to demolish the said rack to get to the toilet pipes. 'I don't know where that rack is. I hunted high and low for it, but you know it just seems to have walked off the boat somehow.' He gave a little nervous giggle and absently fiddled with the compass cover then began to polish his glasses.

'Oh.' Vivian frowned.

'Nowhere to be found.' Colin put his glasses back on and thanked his lucky stars he had so successfully wrecked the rack that the biggest piece could probably hide itself in the toothpick holder and no one would be the wiser. 'Oh well, I guess it will turn up. What else on the list?'

'Hmmm. I was thinking since it's going to be a sunny day I'd give that mattress a good wash. I'm not keen on sleeping on other people's gunge.'

'Right.'

There is a belief that what went in must come out. It seems an obvious thought, but on a boat nothing is that simple. The Tripps had inherited a thick, stiff, foam mattress that had the dimensions of a Mac truck with all the nobbly bits sticking out. It was in three pieces all joined together somehow and looked like it would just fold in half and go through the door. Vivian pulled and the thing sprung back like a sciatic nerve. Colin tried to roll and it flipped over taking him with it as a contender for World Championship wrestling. They employed some rope and tried to put the two ends together and ended up wrapped in it like a kebab.

'I think we need to be a bit canny here.' Viv thought on the problem. 'What if we take it out of its cover, then we will have three separate bits. She found the zip and gently gave it a tug. The zip was welded shut with rust.

'Who puts a bloody metal zip on a boat, ridiculous!' Colin was ready to rip the thing into shreds as his frustration level grew.

'What about if I...' Vivian began. Colin held up his hand. 'Right, I'm taking charge.' He grabbed the unwieldy mattress and wrestled it into a nonagon and then via brute force pushed it through the doorway to the saloon. It jagged, caught and snagged on the table, the engine box, the latches and knocked a light off the bulkhead. He heaved the monster past the table and threw himself at the companionway stairs. The mattress sprung out and much like trying to put a cat in a bucket of water it wasn't going outside come hell or high water.

It was a close call who won the first round as Colin pushed and shoved and the monster sprang, flipped and bounced and finally was squeezed through the companionway hatch and into the cockpit. It hung on to the last, catching on the rigging and the ropes before it was unceremoniously dumped on the dock.

'We're getting hammocks.' Colin said as he wiped the sweat from his face.

Vivian prised open the zip with a pair of pliers and began to pull the cover off. What she found was almost gag material. Long tendrils of hair had worked their way into the foam and now it looked like a client waiting for a full body wax. There were bits of tissue, stains, and balls of what Viv later called, goobies, when they went to Eddy's Mattresses to order a new one cut in more manageable bits, with a delicate floral designed cover and piping at no extra cost.

The blow-up mattress that was borrowed from the Burkitts was inflated and installed without a word from Viv about the expense as she was already imagining the new sheets and quilt covers she would need to buy and had seen a nice set at 3Gs with an edging of nautical flags.

It was after lunch when Colin went to the chandlery to find another magazine rack, with no success, and was walking back from an ear bashing from Rowdy about rules and regulations and the need for stickers to denote where the life vests are stowed or a $200 fine, that Colin was waylaid by the stinky mob.

The stinky mob in boating talk are those without mast or sails, (stick and rag), but have a diesel or iron jib. They usually congregate on the back of a boat and talk dirty. Ian, Malcolm, Trevor and Rob were sitting on Gofasta and beckoned Colin over.

'Listen, we have a problem mate and were wondering if you could help?'

'Me?' Colin suddenly felt like an old salt and wished he'd had the forethought to wear his peaked cap. He adjusted his glasses, puffed out his chest and smiled.

'Yeah. Hop onboard,' Trevor said and he opened the transom gate. Colin jumped onboard the 44ft powerboat and took the offer of a beer.

'I don't know if I can be of much help.' Colin offered. He felt he was beginning to get a handle on things, but nevertheless to be asked his advice on boating matters was a big morale boost.

'Nah, she'll be right.' Malcolm said. He picked up a boat scrubbing brush and Ian picked up another one.

'So, which is softer?' Ian asked. All the men looked at Colin expectantly. Col felt the bristles, he rubbed his hand over the brushes, he looked at the colours and fingered the feathered ends.

'Er...this one, I think,' he said pointing to the yellow one Malcolm was holding.

'See, I told ya.' Malcolm put his brush down and Ian shook his head.

'I've seen the new double shanked, triple

130

bristle with a twist and they say you can wash with confidence knowing they won't scratch, bend or break.' Trevor waded into the debate.

'Yeah, but I still reckon my brush has, with its nylon bristles, more staying power.' Ian said.

'Well it all depends on your choice of shampoo.' Rob came into the conversation. 'Without a wax treatment you're just wasting your time with brushes.'

'Er...' Colin began, 'Are you talking about washing the boat?' The four men stared at Colin as if he has just asked if they wanted to wash their boats in truck wash with a cheap synthetic chamois, God forbid.

'Mate...of course.' Trevor answered.

What Colin failed to realise was that boat washing is almost an Olympic sport with stink boat owners. The talk moved onto buffing and here things began to get technical. Colin listened in while drinking beer and began to learn a whole new vocabulary. He left the boys talking on the merits of non-kink hoses and squirters and staggered back to Moonlighting which would have needed a whole flock of sheep's wool buffers to get a shine.

'Where did you get to?' Vivian looked at her husband who seems a little worse for wear.

'Just chatting with the lads.' Colin slopped down the stairs and kissed his wife. He threw himself on the blow-up bed and closed his eyes,

'Just five minutes Viv,' and he began to snore.

As the days slipped by the list took second place to networking, climbing a steep learning curve (as Colin described his drinking habits) and gossip. Vivian found her nautical friends a mine of information on whose wife has left whom, what mistakes had been made with soft furnishings and the merits of pressure cookers versus hot cobs with a variety of quilted covers. A whole week had passed and all they had managed to do was spend money and find their limit when it came to drinking.

'Hellooooo,' there was a knock on the boat. Viv and Colin popped up in the companionway hatch like prairie dogs.

'Hello,' Viv replied.

'Just wondering if you could give a hand?' the man asked. Colin climbed outside and shrugged to his wife.

'Just going to give a hand.' He smiled and jumped onto the dock and followed the fellow to the berth across the way.

'Windward is coming in,' the stranger explained. Colin nodded and introduced himself.

'Colin,' he held out his hand.

'Steve.'

'This Windward, a big boat is she?' Colin thought he better prepare if he was going to catch lines.

'Nah, not too big. It's just that Peg and Tom are old and well you know...'

'Right.'

Windward, a big wooden trawler type came into view and slowly made its way to the waiting berth. The noise from the engine was deafening, the black billowing smoke leaving a trail in the air. Its glory days were past and as Colin watched he could see two wizened old people on the deck getting lines ready. Peg and Tom resembled two brown sultanas

132

which had been left out in the sun way too long. They were thin, weathered and looked like they knew what they were doing. Colin watched their expert handling of the boat as it slid effortlessly into the dock and Peg threw him a line and shouted,

'Springer.'

Steve grabbed the other line and Tom yelled,

'Stern.' When the boat was safely tied to the dock Peg climbed down and helped Tom down and they surveyed the mooring.

'Thanks,' Peg shouted.

'Not a problem,' Colin answered.

'We've just come back.' Tom yelled, then turned to his wife, 'I just told him we've just come back.'

'Yeah, just come back,' Peg shouted to her husband. It soon became obvious that Peg and Tom yelled all the time because of their noisy engine. Colin related the story to Viv when he came back to Moonlighting.

'What do you say?' he shouted and they giggled. There were more characters on the dock than at a midnight screening of the Rocky Horror Picture Show.

It seemed to Vivian as they drank their sundowners at the end of the second week that working on their list was a lost cause. She looked at her drinks holder and idly wondered where the magazine rack had gone when Colin interrupted her musings.

'I saw there is going to be a garage sale this weekend. It's on the lawn in front of the toilet block. S'posed to be good.' Vivian knew from long experience garage sales were a bad thing where Colin Tripp was concerned. He could never resist a bargain whether he needed it or not.

'Just junk I suppose?' She tried to ameliorate his excitement.

'No. All good stuff. The blokes said it's a big thing.' The jury was out on that one, Vivian decided.

Saturday dawned as a bright and sunny day, just right for a garage sale. Colin was up early after another uncomfortable night on the blow-up mattress which squeaked as he rolled, slid as he turned and generally made itself as unaccommodating as possible like it hadn't read its job description. He knew from experience you had to be early to catch the worm when it came to bargains. He nudged Vivian awake and reminded her of the opportunities that were waiting.

'Come on Viv, we don't want to miss anything.' Vivian stirred and looked at Colin.

'You go, I'll catch up later.' She had decided she would try to do at least one job on the list and the oven was it.

'Well don't blame me if you miss out.' Colin jumped out of bed and made coffee and toast. He gulped down his breakfast and then was gone.

The bargain hunter strode up the dock in expectation and arrived at the designated spot just as the other hunter gatherers arrived.

Boat sales are a breed apart from garage sales. In the latter there will always be the useful odd bits and pieces, that piece of guttering, the missing wheel for a trolley and an old lawnmower. At a boat sale most of the things on offer are well used, way past their sell by date, fittings that don't fit anything and, in Viv's words, junk. Colin started at the end trestle and looked over the items.

'Does this work?' he asked of an extension cord that had so much sun damage it could have done with a complete skin peel.

'Couldn't say,' came the reply. Colin continued looking and picked up a book on splices and knots.

'How much?' The man looked at Colin and read sucker on his customer's forehead.

'$15.00.' It seemed an opportunity too good to miss and Colin parted with his money. Moving on to the next table he found a bag of misshapen cleats with their holes flogged out. A good rummage brought up one that didn't look too bad. It was added to his treasure hoard. As he moved along he couldn't believe some people would actually not want their stuff. There were bits of rope, wire and anchors in various states of retirement. He spied a huge Hereshoff anchor that weighed in at 95lb. Men were trying to lift it and it was a great talking point. A crowd was gathering as Colin watched. He felt he could really do with an anchor like that. It would be excellent for a cyclone season. He could deploy it in the mangroves if it came to survival and as it came in three bits it would be a doddle to store. He was eyeing up the competition when Vivian slid up next to him.

'I thought you were sleeping in?' Colin bit his lip and tried to take his eye off the anchor.

'Well, I just thought that you would like me to come.' Viv would rather shop than clean the oven.

'Oh,' Colin held his treasure trove close to

his chest.

'Oh no. No Colin.' Vivian caught him looking at the anchor which wouldn't have been out of place on a container ship.

'No of course not Viv, what are you thinking?' Col moved on to the next table. The seller was getting rid of hoses, hose clamps, old tools and the like. Colin picked over the hose clamps when a pushy customer fronted the table and grabbed some hose. He measured the length and then to all assembled he put the hose to his mouth and gave a blow as if in rehearsal for a didgeridoo recital. It was a crowd stopper, but for all the wrong reasons as the seller quietly said that the hose was sanitary hose that had come off his boat toilet. There was a collective, 'Eewwwww' as the crowd thought on the implications. The fool put the hose down and strode away without a backward glance.

'I wouldn't want to be his wife when he gets home.' Colin said and there was a small titter through the crowd.

They moved on and Vivian found a boat hook.

'We need one of these Col.' She picked up her find and twisted the telescopic neck. Colin examined the hook and found it in good order and handed over his money.

'Nice one Viv.'

When they had come to the end the Tripps were full of useful junk and happily made their way back to the boat talking on the merits of square fry pans, a broken spice rack that just needed a little work, a good solid plank of Oregon, a flat fender plus the book, the boat hook and a wonky cleat. They laid out their stuff on the dock when Arnold spied the haul.

136

'You didn't buy that did you?' he pointed

'Well yes.' Viv said defensively. Arnold shook his head and frowned.

'Well, takes all sorts.'

'I'm sure it does Mr Burkitt.' Viv gathered all their goods and made a point of going inside.

'The cheek.'

'Well I think we did really well Viv. All this will come in handy.' The Tripps were yet to find out that things that will come in handy on a Saturday soon become a waste of space on a Tuesday.

With just one remaining day to knock off their list, it wasn't looking good and so they made a plan to do just one more thing before they returned home, but as much as Vivian hunted, the magazine rack had just disappeared and Colin couldn't imagine where.

CHAPTER 11

Colin poured over the cruising guides on the kitchen table while Vivian made tea.

'It says here in *Alan Lucas's Cruising the Coral Coast* Viv, that this part of the coast is the most idyllic in the whole region.'

'Great.'

'And Alan says that at this time of year the winds are light and from the South East. That means we should have a fairly easy run to Orpheus Island.'

'Good.'

'And that if we wanted to- mind you, only if we wanted to- we could stop overnight at Great Palm Island.'

'Nice.'

'Are you listening to me Viv?'

'Yes of course Col, but I'm trying to get tea and I trust you with all the navigation stuff. I' sure you will have it all worked out. We have a whole week before we need to go.'

'Mmm.' Colin pondered his 'whole week'. They didn't seem to achieve much when they spend 2 weeks on the dock, however much they had planned.

138

'I think I will ask Ted to help me with the chain when it arrives tomorrow. You'll be victualling I suppose.'

'Vic-ta what?'

'Victualling Viv. It's in Percy Landers Nautical terms. It means provisioning.'

'Oh, you mean shopping.' Viv said. Colin studied his wife as she served up the curry and rice.

'You must learn to use the nautical terms Viv otherwise no-one will know what you mean.' Vivian sat down at the table,

'Aye-Aye Captain.'

'That's the way.' Colin tucked into his evening meal and idly wondered if Captain Cook ever had beef curry and pappadums on his voyage around Australia.

It was one of those mornings when the BOM (Bureau of Meteorology) forecast a dull day of 22 degrees. Of course, it was bright and sunny and the temperature was climbing by 9am to a sweaty 29 degrees. Some doubted the BOM had any idea at all and used a roll of the dice or a stab in the dark with a knitting needle to produce the forecast.

Ted bounded over to the Tripps yard through the side gate and knocked on the back door, then spying Colin through the kitchen window, waved and let himself in.

'Coffee Ted?' Colin asked.

'Is it decaf, cause Gloria only has decaf and I'm not supposed to have the full bottle. She says it's bad for me.'

'This is just the ordinary stuff,' Colin looked at the label, 'Coffee,' he read.

'Well...alright. But don't let on.' Ted acquiesced.

With coffee and cake well underway Colin began to outlined the order of the day.

Ted butted in, 'We're not going out on the boat, are we?'

'No Ted, just the chain.' Colin continued the run down. There was the picking up of the chain, getting it from the chandlery to the boat down on the dock, the purchase of tested shackles, fixing the bitter end inside the chain locker and finally stowing it away after measuring it and putting cable ties on at 10 metre intervals. Colin held up the coloured cable ties that had already been purchased and didn't want to go into details about where the old chain had gone.

'Don't you worry about that,' Ted said and helped himself to the last of the cake just before Vivian came into the kitchen and spied the empty plate and realized the boys had eaten the cake she'd made for their sail and was going to freeze.

Colin found a parking spot not far from the Chandlery and had the bright idea of loading the chain into the boot of the car and driving it the short distance to the dock then borrowing a trolley for the last leg to the boat. Ted, on the other hand, snaffled a shopping trolley that had made a run for it from the supermarket and was now press ganged into service to carry 100 metres of 10mm short link galvanised chain.

'This is just the ticket,' said Ted wheeling the
140

trolley up to the chandlery loading dock, Colin looked at the trolley and scratched his chin.

'Do you think it will take the weight Ted?'

'Don't you worry about that,' Ted waved away the question optimistically and they walked around the front of the store to ask Rowdy to open up.

'There it is,' Rowdy pointed to a great big lump on a wooden pallet. 'I moved it near the door for ya.' The men looked at the shopping trolley and back to the lump.

'It looks do-able.' Colin said with a nervous giggle and pushed his glasses up his nose.

They found the end which was tied with a bit of red string and began to hand over hand the chain into the cart, when it soon became obvious that they needed to lay it with a little more precision. So, they pulled it all out and started again, this time curling around the wire basket. A good half an hour later the 100 metres was in the trolley which was taking the strain. A 100 metres of chain is a bit heavier that 2 cubes of Pepsi and a week's worth of groceries. The men tried to get a bit of momentum. Colin and Ted pulled, huffed and puffed, but a mere 3mm step out of the loading dock was an obstacle too large to overcome. They pushed, but the trolley wheels were stuck.

'How about we tow it with the car?' Ted suggested. It sounded, once again, do-able, so Colin hitched the load up with a bit of rope.

'Right-ho.' Ted gave a wave as Colin put the car into gear and the trolley began to move. It jagged and then slowly plinked over the step and onto the driveway. Now to the naked eye there doesn't seem to be a discernible slope on the delivery dock driveway, but with the inertia of over 200kg of chain the trolley began to move. Ted hung on and tried to wave at the same time that things were getting out of hand. It was a dismal effort and as the trolley gathered speed he began to yell,

'Hey, Hey, HEY.'

Colin put on the brakes and Ted and the trolley careered into the back of the station wagon with a sickening crunch.

'Lost my footing,' Ted said rubbing his shins. Colin inspected the deep crack in the plastic bumper bar.

'Oh well,' he resigned himself to the fact, 'We better walk it.'

The two men pushed and pulled the dead weight to the dock entrance and took a good long look at the walkway.

'It would be low tide.' Col scratched his chin.

'Don't you worry about that,' Ted spat on his hands, took a deep breath and a firm grip.

'I'm not sure we can 'just hold on',' Colin said. 'It's mighty steep. I think I'll just get a rope, you know, just in case.' He went to fetch a rope from the car. Colin was walking back to the gate when he heard a scream and ran to see Ted being dragged down the steep walkway to the dock, his sneakers having a hard time trying to grip the wood and his knuckles white, much like the whites of his eyes. Colin raced down - threw a line around the trolley - threaded it around the gate post and tied it off for a world speed bow line record and went to Ted's aid. He gently prised off Ted's fingers one at a time from the handle and sat him down.

'Alright mate?' All Ted could do was nod as his mouth was as dry as an out of season sheep dip and he seemed to have bitten his tongue in the excitement. Colin in times of stress often got the giggles and this was no exception. It started with a little titter, just a mere squeak, then it gathered pace and he let out a guffaw or two. After that it turned into a laugh proper and by then it was all over red rover. He tried to stifle it, but every time he saw Ted's face full of fear he was off again.

'Sorry mate,' Colin giggled.

Ted glared.

'Phaaah, really it's a miracle,' Colin blurted and laughed.

Ted glowered.

'Geez, that was close,' Colin bahhahahahed. It was only when he looked the other way and took a deep breath that he could regain any composure and he blew out a load of air, screwed up his face and clenched his teeth to control himself.

'Right,' he said not looking at Ted who had set his jaw and narrowed his eyes at his neighbour.

'Lucky eh?' Colin said checking the rope and letting off a small titter. 'OK. Let's get this show on the road.'

The logistics were quickly reappraised and with the aid of the rope the trolley was gently lowered to the dock and the lads pushed it carefully down to Moonlighting and tied it off to the dock cleats. Now it seemed just a matter of laying the chain on the dock for the coloured cable ties and the putting it on board.

'I marked out 10 metres so we should just be able to put it in rows,' Colin pointed to his electrical

143

tape on the dock denoting the measurements. They went to work laying the chain down with Colin making sure it wasn't too close to the edge and in the sun things began to get hot after just 20 metres.

'Wanna stop for a drink?' Colin offered. Ted looked like he could slay a coldie and the men went onboard and cracked a tinnie. It was after their third that Colin began to tell Ted about their planned trip to Orpheus Island for the meteorite shower and their first night sail.

'You'll be wanting crew then?' Ted asked. Colin tittered, swallowed hard and took a gulp of beer. He pinched himself on the leg and wished he could cut his tongue out with a razor blade. Vivian would kill him if he somehow, without knowing quite how, invited Ted and Gloria along for the trip.

'Well, we kinda, sorta, really...'

'I'd love to Col, but well... I sorta, kinda...' It was an easy men's truce as Colin side stepped the question and Ted didn't want to repeat the sea sick experience he had had on Moonlighting previously.'

'Oh well...' Colin said and they cracked another beer.

It was well past lunch when they had solved the world's political problems, made poverty history and had given those good for nothing people at motor vehicles registration a piece of their collective minds, that there was a knock on the hull.

'Er, just wondering if you're nearly done on the dock, only it's just that I've got a shopping trolley coming with people and well it's...' Mr Ashcroft shrugged his shoulders letting his participle dangle.

'Don't you worry about that.' Ted stood up and swayed, like he was holding on in a force 10 gale.

144

'Right on it,' Colin said and the men staggered outside. Ted and Colin looked at their slovenly effort and it wasn't long before they had sweated out their alcohol content and had 10 neat rows of chain laid out on the dock.

If you don't follow the lay of the chain it can be a bit confusing when it comes to measuring. Ted began at one end and Colin the other and by the time they had finished the chain looked like a Christmas decoration with coloured cable ties all over it. Putting the tinsel in the chain locker was the next step. When Colin opened up the locker there was the rusted piece of glob at the bottom.

'We really should get rid of that,' Col pointed to the glob that used to be the 3/8th short link chain. Ted took the nearby boat hook and tentatively prodded the conglomeration of rust. Anything that looked like hard work was to be avoided at all costs. Ted though he'd done enough for the day and suddenly clutched his back,

'Ouch,' he made a sour lemon face. 'Sorry mate, me back's gone on me.' Colin eyed his neighbour suspiciously.

'Bit sudden?'

'It's like that sometimes. Just comes on all of a sudden.' Ted winced and contorted his face into something resembling a bit of roadkill.

'I think I'll call it a day Col. Sorry.'

'Right,' Colin gave Ted an uncomfortably long stare, polished his glasses furiously and then shut the chain locker,

'I guess we can finish tomorrow,' he said trying to bait his neighbour.

'Well, I'd love to Col, but...' Ted sucked his

145

teeth and clutched at his back and went all out for an Oscar.

'Oh, I see.' Colin said through gritted teeth. 'Well, that's it then.'

'Yup.' Ted gingerly made his way to the edge of the boat and eased himself onto the dock. Colin followed and made sure Ted kept up the act all the way to the car. It was a silent drive home and a cursory goodbye that was directed at Ted and then Colin parked the car.

'Back early?' Vivian said as she finished the washing up.

'Ted 'hurt',' Colin used his fingers to display the quotations, 'his back.'

'Oh.'

'Hmm.'

'So how far did you get?' Viv could picture herself heaving and shoving on the morrow. After Colin had started at the beginning and acted out the trolley, the rope the cable ties and the glob of rust, Vivian made a mental note to wear her old jeans and hunt out the deep heat liniment.

It was around 8pm when the phone rang and Vivian answered.

'Yes,' she said.

'Well I'm sure it would be,' she answered as the caller went on and on.

'Of course, I can see that,' she tried to placate the other person.

'What? Now?' she nodded.

'Oh,' she looked over to Colin who had fallen asleep on the settee.

'It can't possibly wait I suppose?' she asked.

146

'I see. Alright then.' she hung up. Vivian gently nudged her husband and he shot up mumbling,

'I've got it, I've got it,' and grabbed at the air.

'Col, darling,' Viv cooed.

'Huh?'

'Col, that was the marina on the phone.'

'Phone?' Colin began to enter the real world.

'Apparently someone's complained you left the chain on the dock and although it's late there has been a bit of a kerfuffle and someone's lost a trolley of shopping or something.' Suddenly all became clear to Colin and he remembered the conversation with Mr Ashcroft.

'Geez,' he rubbed his eyes and ran his fingers through his hair.

'They said we have to move it - tonight.'

'What, now?' Colin frowned. Vivian nodded.

'Something about a breach of the agreement or something.'

'Are you sure?'

'That's what the man said.'

'Who?'

'Well I didn't quite catch his name.'

'Right.' Colin marched to the telephone and pressed return call. It was after a good 10 minutes of ear bashing he finally hung up and blew out a sigh of relief as Vivian looked on.

'Mr Swink, the Marina Manager,' he said. 'About the chain,' he added as if the news was new to him.

The Tripps looked at the clock on the wall and thought on the task ahead. It wasn't as if they could just ignore the summons as a prank call and have their rental agreement torn up. Moonlighting wasn't a trailer sailor to be parked in the back yard.

'Well, I guess...' Viv began. Colin nodded in agreement.

Once on the dock they whispered as they walked down to the boat.

'It's awfully quiet,' Viv held her husband's hand.

'I've had an idea Viv. Why don't we just put it in the shopping trolley and it'll keep 'till the morning.' Vivian rubbed Colin's arm,

'Ok,' she whispered.

The chain had been pushed to one side and when Colin looked about, the trolley had gone, probably to emergency for a bit of chiropractic care.

'Damn,' Colin said in a lowered tone. 'We'll have to put it onboard.' He jumped on to Moonlighting and opened the chain locker to once again see the old chain leering up at him.

'Damn.'

'What is it?' Viv asked.

'Look Viv, just hand it up to me and I'll get it going on the windlass.'

'Ok.' Viv mouthed and nodded. She took one end and passed it to Colin who stood on the bow sprit and once in possession he then threaded it back to the gypsy and down the hawser to the locker. There was no way he could get the old stuff out and so he snaked the chain in on top and flicked the switch.

'Right,' he gave the thumbs up to Viv and she stood ready to stomp on any run-away chain should it try to throw itself in the drink and join its predecessor. Colin stepped on the foot switch and there was an almighty wrenching, a grinding and a dreadful racket as the chain began to come onboard. Lights flicked on as people popped up to see what all the noise was about. The old windlass sounded like it was about to explode while chewing nuts and bolts as it did its duty.

The chain gradually began to make its way down the hole, when about 15.5 metres in according to the cable ties, the gypsy - that vital little wheel that locks the chain links in place, shuddered, the chain slipped and the machine stalled.

'Darling?' Vivian called.

'Hey, do you know what time it is?' a voice shouted across the water.

'Sorry,' Collin yelled back.

'Colin?' Viv whispered.

'Jammed. Hang on.' Colin pulled and fiddled and realigned the chain on the gypsy. Once again the antique took a deep breath and began to haul. At 27.3 metres by the look of Ted's handiwork, the chain jumped off again. this time sounding like a freight train off the rails.

'Knock it off,' a voice rang out in the night.

'For the love of....' an irate liveaboard shouted.

'For .... sake another disembodied voice began and was thankfully drowned out by the old workhorse as it once again grabbed the chain.

'I don't know why it's jumping off,' Colin leaned over to tell his wife.

'Why don't you jump off?' Someone shouted as the neighbourly love melted into something a bit more like hate. 100 metres of chain on a disgruntled windlass can take a long time. Vivian and Colin laboured into the night to get the job done, the chain slipping at every 20 metres or so and at 90 metres the old windlass gave a grunt, a loud bang, several expensive sounding crunches and it was all over red rover.

'Damn.' Colin tried the foot switch, but nothing happened.

'Col?' Vivian looked at the last 10 metres on the dock.

'That's it Viv. It's broken. We'll have to do it by hand.' Vivian pulled the chain to the boat and Colin heaved it the last few metres to the hawser and finally, with some satisfaction, he watched the last link disappear down the little hole into the locker.

'Right, all done.'

'What about the anchor Col?' Vivian looked at the offending object on the dock.

'Oh, we'll do it tomorrow.'

'You won't live that long if you don't shut it.' a gruff voice threw the threat over the dark waters.

'Come on,' Vivian beckoned her husband off the boat. 'Tomorrow,' she said knowing all could be fixed in the daylight.

Colin woke up to aching arms and as he climbed out of bed he found sore leg muscles he never knew he had. He struggled to the kitchen and took a welcome cup of coffee from his wife.

'Hells bells, I feel about 100 years old.' Colin eased himself into a chair with much face pulling and grunting, trying to elicit some sympathy. Viv smiled at her husband,

'We still have to do the anchor and now we

need to get the thingame bob looked at.'

'What?'

'The thingame that makes the chain go up and down.' She mimed the chain moving and stopping and then the action of the foot switch.

'Windlass Viv. How can I possibly know what you're on about if you refuse to use the nautical terms?'

'Alright, alright,' Vivian said, 'I'll try.'

As the Tripps walked down F finger there was none of the camaraderie evident from the dock party. No 'hey there' greeted them, no 'hi' or 'howdy' propelled them to Moonlighting. Vivian looked at Colin and shrugged,

'P'r'aps it's the weather or something,' she offered a feeble explanation, although by the time the Burkitts had snubbed them they knew; The Tripps were on the nose because of their extracurricular activities. Arnold Burkitt washed his boat and glared at Colin.

'Just following orders,' Colin giggled and adjusted his glasses.

'Didn't help Hitler,' Arnold muttered and continued spraying water.

'So what we need to do,' Colin began explaining to his wife, 'Is just thread the chain back up the hawser,' and here he pointed to the pipe protruding from the deck, 'and take it to the bowsprit,' he pointed again, 'and thread it into the rollers,' he touched them with his foot, 'and then hook it on with the tested shackle I bought,' Colin fished in his pants pocket and held the shackle aloft. 'Ok?'

'Right,' Vivian said. 'Hawser, bowsprit, rollers, shackle.' Colin nodded and opened the chain locker. He lay down on the deck, put his head down into the depths and considered the problem.

'I'm ready Col.' Viv said from the dock.

'Hang on a minute will you.' Col said. Vivian waited. Colin didn't want to look a dill, but on a closer inspection the chain didn't seem to have an end. He tentatively moved a bit and it cascaded a little. He lifted a strand that looked promising, but it wasn't going anywhere. The coloured ties were so confusing that they didn't offer any solution.

'Colin?' Vivian enquired.

'What?' Colin snapped back.

'I'm ready.'

'Alright, alright.' Colin huffed with growing irritation. He grabbed some links and pulled. A steady tumble of chain fell over itself. He yanked a bit more and a purple cable tie briefly came into view then was covered by an avalanche. It was a fine line whether he was making it better or worse.

'What's the matter?' Viv asked. From the depths of the chain locker there were a few choice words then Colin admitted defeat. He was sane enough to know when he was beaten. He grinned, popped his head up and gave a little guffaw.

'I seem to have lost the end,' he giggled, his stress level around 60%.

'I don't understand?' Viv came on board and knelt down next to Colin to look inside the dark hole.

'Oh,' she said as she gave the pile of chain a poke and it shifted to make itself comfortable like someone settling into a comfy chair with a good book.

152

'It just keeps moving around, like it's alive or something.' Colin knelt beside his wife and if they had had a small prayer mat it wouldn't have looked out of place, as an offering up to the Gods was the only thing between the Tripps and lugging the chain out to repeat their night time exercise.

'If you think about it logically,' Viv began, 'It should be under that little hole.'

'Hole?'

'This thingo,' Viv pointed to the pipe through the deck.

'Hawser.' Colin threw the word at Viv.

'Well it's not my fault. I did say about the anchor last night.'

'Well it's not last night now it.' The Tripps were having their first boat argument. Viv fleetingly remembered the article Col had shown her. Her lifetime boating companion was quickly turning into something she could do without.

'Everyone's a blood expert aren't they?'

'I wouldn't know.' Viv retorted.

'Well you think you're so clever.'

'I never said that.' And so it went on and the chain just sat and watched. There was that tense moment when each combatant can't think of anything more to say and the Tripps looked at the chain as if it was the culprit all along.

'Oh well...' Vivian picked up some links and hauled the length onto the deck. Colin sulked for about 10 metres then gave a hand to his wife as they laid the chain on the deck.

'Thanks,' he said as she handed him some more length.' Vivian conceded the thanks and gave a smile. It took a good 40 metres then Vivian pulled and the end flicked off the pile and came away in her hands.

'Oh look,' she held the end up.

'Well done Viv,' Colin took the end and threaded it through the hawser and Viv caught it and continued down the bowsprit to the rollers and then Colin finished the job by attaching it to the anchor. They gave each other a high five and laughed.

After shoving all the chain back in its locker Colin shut the hatch and looked at his wife.

'Sorry.'

'Me too,' she said adding, 'How about a cuppa?'

They went downstairs and Viv was confronted with empty beer cans and several raided packets of breadsticks.

'Colin?' she looked at the mess.

'We only stopped for a minute or two. It was hot.' he gathered up the empties and fussed about in the kitchen making tea. Over cream biscuits and tea they congratulated themselves on a job well done when Vivian asked,

'Do you think we can get the...the...windlass fixed in a week?'

'I'll ask Rowdy.'

'Well let's go now,' Viv began to clear away.

Rowdy was in an expansive mood. He eyed his customers coming through the door and smiled.

'Heard you had a bit-o-trouble last night,' he yelled. Vivian smiled.

'I remember a bloke,' Rowdy began at mosh pit volume, 'he had some chain, 100 metres or so...' and Rowdy went on for a good 20 minutes telling the story, backtracking to get his facts right, introducing the relationship between the chain fellow and his neighbour and what his wife did for a living before he petered out, ending with 'and he never knew.' He scratched his underarm and picked his ear then leaned in on the counter and asked,

'Trouble?'

'A bit,' the Tripps said. There was a pause when Colin piped up,

'It's just that we need our windlass looked at.' He rested on the counter and fiddled with the tide tables.

'Windlass?' Rowdy bellowed. The Tripps nodded.

'See Darryl Downer.' Rowdy leant right over the counter and pointed to the notice board at knee height. The Tripps bobbed down and hunted for the card.

'Not there?' Rowdy shouted. He got up and walked around to the front of the counter and bent down in front of Viv. There are some sights that qualify for the Guinness Book of records and Rowdy's plumber's crack was right up there. Viv copped the lot as he hunted for the business card. She took a deep breath and staggered back and knocked in to a stand of hats and thongs, thanking her lucky stars Rowdy wasn't wearing the lycra variety of the latter.

'Here yar.' Rowdy straightened up and hitched his pants at the same time. 'He's ya man.' He wistfully looked at the card and began, 'I remember a bloke once...'The Tripps settled in, too polite to steal away. Half an hour into the story the phone rang and Vivian seized the opportunity to grab her husband's arm.

The Tripps smiled politely and Colin said,
'Amazing eh?'

Rowdy fell into a musing for a bit with the phone to his ear, then pulled himself together. 'Right you all sorted then?'

Darryl Downer was a tradesman of the old school. He knew just about everything about machines and had all the carcasses since the invention of the first Ford (around 1903), left over in varying degrees of undress in his workshop, to prove it. The Tripps found their way to the pokey office at the back of the tin shed and called,

'Cooee.'

From a large grease spot stacked with tractor parts a short stout man appeared and ambled towards the pair. He seemed genuinely surprised that there were other people on the planet and that they had made their way to his shop. He stopped, looked the Tripps up and down, gave a grunt and shuffled into the office.

Colin and Vivian followed and watched as Mr Downer sat down, fiddled with some papers, blew his nose, adjusted his overalls and then looked up, once again surprised that there was someone else in the room.

'Er, Mr Downer,' Colin started with a little giggle. Mr Downer looked vacant.

'We have a problem with our windlass,' Vivian smiled and tried to look engaging. Mr Downer studied the pair.

156

'Windlass,' Colin spoke up thinking the man a little hard of hearing. Mr Downer frowned, stood up, thought some more, and took the two steps to the counter at about the same pace as a 3 toed sloth. It often happens that when you meet someone for the first time you form an impression and have the individual pegged neatly in your mind. The Tripps waited for a reply from the mechanic, but didn't expect the quiet, low pitched voice that said,

'Is it here?'

'Pardon?' Colin tittered.

'Is it here?' Mr Downer almost whispered.

'Well no, it's actually still on the boat.'

'Oh.' Mr Downer said and went to sit down. Colin could see if he didn't act fast then they might need to start all over again.

'Can you come and look at it?' Darryl Downer turned and looked as if Colin has asked him to come to pole dancing practice on Tuesday and could he bring an extra set of leotards.

'Out.' Downer said. The Tripps looked at one another then Vivian pulled her husband towards the door thinking they were banished.

'In or out?' Mr Downer whispered stopping them in their tracks.

'Oh, you mean in or out,' Colin giggled. 'It's in the water actually.' There was a very long pregnant pause, enough for the gestation of an elephant and then Mr Downer shoved a notebook and pencil at Colin.

'I think he wants our details,' Viv elbowed her husband. Colin wrote the details and Downer took the paper and walked past them to his beloved workshop and the Tripps followed not sure if the transaction was at an end, but when Mr Downer disappeared into the gloom and seemed to blend in they headed for the door.

'Do you think he will come?' Viv asked.

'Beats me,' Colin answered pushing his glasses up his nose.

It was two days before the Tripps could get back to the boat and only five days before their sailing adventure to catch the meteorite shower. They hadn't heard from Mr Downer and didn't expect any progress, so were pleasantly surprised to see a small luggage label attached to the windless, fluttering in the breeze.

'I think he's been,' Vivian climbed onboard and examined the tag. 'Colin look,' Viv held out the tag. It had a grubby greasy thumb print on it and the imprint of what was once a rubber stamp.

'Well he might be a little strange, but he's prompt.' Vivian said. 'Shall we try it?'

'How do you mean?'

'You know, do the switchy thing and let the anchor down. A practice on the dock couldn't hurt could it?'

'Switchy thingy?' Colin rolled his eyes skyward. 'Alright.' Colin went inside to the fuse box and flicked the switch and the green light came on. He popped his head up and told Viv to let it go. She unwound the brake and put her foot down. The anchor didn't budge, but the chain started to pile up. It was a small matter to run forward and give the anchor a push. It lunged forward and then the bunched chain followed and for some reason the windlass began to do its own thing letting the chain go at a terrific pace. It clattered out as Vivian watched, disappearing into the water.

'Take your foot off now,' Colin yelled from inside as he saw the green and red lights come on together.

'But I haven't got my foot on it.' Vivian yelled back. Putting 100 metres onboard may take all night, but letting it out again is just a matter of minutes. Colin raced upstairs just in time to see the last metre come out of the hawse-pipe, rattle down the bow sprit and disappear over the side including the bitter end which he had neglected to attach the night before.

'Oh.' The Tripps studied the water. Mr Burkitt looked up from his bottle of beer,

'Oh, Colin. Downer was here. Said he was taking a bit away to realign or whatever. Clutch plate or some such.'

Colin and Viv looked at the windlass and then back at the water. Even an 'oh' couldn't escape their stunned silence.

'Nino said he could do it tomorrow Col.' Viv hung up the phone.

'How much?' Colin could see dollar signs in front of his eyes.

'Didn't say exactly, But it will be worth it if we can get rid of the old stuff and he can retrieve the new stuff and then all the stuff will work.'

'Stuff?'

'Oh, you know what I mean Colin.'

After work Colin went around to Mr Downers to check on the progress of his windlass. The door was open, but any sign of life was sadly lacking. Colin coughed and waited. He yelled,

'Hellllooooooo.' Nothing.

'Mr Downer,' Col hollered into the gloom. From way down the back he heard a clanking and watched as Mr Downer plodded into the afternoon light.

'Colin Tripp,' Colin held out his hand. Mr Downer looked at it and then at Col and frowned.

'You have our windlass parts.' Colin looked for some recognition. 'Off Moonlighting,' he added. Mr Downer looked like a door mouse that had just woken up.

'Just wondering if it will be fixed soon?' Mr Downer pulled out a greasy rag and wiped his hands then beckoned Colin to follow.

'Look at this,' Downer pointed to an ice-cream container full of bits.

'Is that it?'

Downer picked up a doughnut shaped metal bit and wiped it on his overalls then handed it to Colin.

'That bad eh?' Colin felt he had to say something.

'Not too bad. Friday alright?'

'Yes, Friday's fine.' Colin smiled and as his eyes became accustomed to the dark he saw the shed was full of wonderful old machinery with embossed plates, some saying 1926 Emerson and the like.

'My word, you have a lot of old machines.' It was all Darryl Downer needed to get going. It was like cranking over a one-cylinder engine, but when it was away it just went on forever. Darryl loved his machines and began to tell Colin the history of each in great detail. It was well past 7:30 in the evening when he finally ended with the lathe that

160

came out from Liverpool, England in '32 and was used in the Railways for a good many years until his father acquired it and it ended up on the shop floor. Colin sat on a wooden crate fascinated by the depth of knowledge. He looked around the workshop and felt a deep and abiding bond with Darryl Downer.

Right through tea Colin regurgitated to Viv what he'd learnt from Downer trying to instill some sense of the man to his wife.

'So when will it be ready?' Viv had her eye on the practical side of things.

'Friday, Darryl said.' Colin felt he was on first name terms with Downer.

'Good.'

The plan was coming together.

FIG. 133.—Matthew Walker (complete).

CHAPTER 12

'I'm going victualing,' Vivian told Colin on the phone.

'What?'

'You know - vic-tua-ling.' Colin dug around in his brain and came up with supplies for the trip.

'Right, shopping,' he qualified.

'Yes, if you must call it that. I'm taking Connie Burkitt too.'

'Well just remember it's only four days Viv. Townsville to Great Palm to Orpheus then back again.'

'I know,' Vivian said trying to keep the exasperation from her voice.

Samuel Pepys said a navy travels on its stomach and the same can be said of cruising. Food is a vital ingredient to having a good time. Vivian remembered all too well their camping trip when the portable fridge/freezer failed and they had to eat everything in three days, then survive on packet noodles and salami on crackers.

'Nothing,' she said to herself, 'was going to stop her this time as the boat had a good size fridge and the portable fridge would act as a freezer.

Connie directed Viv to the wholesalers out of town. Mrs Burkitt had a 'card', that magic thing that allowed one to buy coffee by the kilo and toilet paper by the pallet. The car park was full as Vivian cruised around looking for a spot.

'Market day,' Connie explained, 'bargain prices.' Vivian parked on the grass and the women entered what can only be described as shopper's paradise. Everything is big. The trolleys could accommodate a family of four if they were all sitting down. The aisles were wide and three stories high and the produce was mainly in something akin to 44-gallon drums.

'Let's start at dry foods.' Connie led Viv to pulses, flours and noodles.

'Just think of the money you'll save love,' Connie cooed at Viv as she put 48 packets of noodles in the trolley.

'Er, not noodles Connie.' Viv knew she had seen enough noodles to last her well into the afterlife.

The women walked down the aisles, Connie sharing her vast sea going experience with Vivian on how to cook spam in a multitude of ways.

'I'm not sure Colin likes spam.' Viv said as they stopped in front of meats and corned beef in tins that were as big as a rolled sleeping bag.

'Nonsense,' Connie said. 'Just take two.' She heaved the tins that would fit a pickled baby into the trolley. They mooched along and stopped at flour.

'I don't think I'll be making bread, Connie.' Vivian eyed the 10kg bag of bread mix.

'Listen, you say that now, but when you're out

163

there and you want something to do, kneading bread is a great stress reliever. Quietly Vivian wondered if Connie needed quite a bit of stress relieving, where as she had already decided what the Tripps would be doing in their 'spare time', and it didn't include bread making.

'Just take one.' Connie humped the sack into the trolley. The confectionery aisle was an eye opener. Family packs of chocolates that were big enough for a whole refugee camp run by UNESCO, jubes in multi packs that could last a lifetime, and coloured popcorn by the ton.

'Treats are very important.' Connie looked at the variety. 'What-cha-like?'

'Col likes snakes.' Vivian looked at the catering pack of snakes.

'Take three and chocolate too.' Connie loaded up the trolley. Three hundred dollars later the women were in the car park stacking the boot.

'It looks quite a lot,' Vivian wondered how they would ever get through 5kg of black olives and 1.5kg of peanut paste.

'You'll soon see. Sailing gives my Arnold such an appetite,' Connie said as they drove back to the marina.

Once all the stores were onboard Vivian had the task of storing it away. Nothing fitted and so she had to put things all over the place. Pickles in with the life jackets, spam in the chart table and it was late in the day by the time everything was hidden away. She just had to remember where it all was.

'Did you get everything? Colin asked when he came home from work.

'Just about - only some fresh veg and fruit to go.'

'How much?' Colin asked.

'Are you excited darling?'

'Yep, it's going to be great.' Colin said. Viv looked at her husband and side stepped the shopping bill.

'Nino gave me the bill today. He did a wonderful job. The old chain is gone, the new installed and apparently he worked really hard.'

'How much?'

'He even cleaned the mud off the deck.'

'How much?'

'Arnold said he worked like a slave.'

'Viv, how much?' Vivian handed over the bill.

'What!' Colin looked at the paper and flipped. '$870! What did he do, lick the deck clean?'

'Well he's good, not cheap, but good. And it's done now so we don't have to worry about it.' Vivian tried to put things in perspective.

'Jeez.' Colin sat back in his chair.

'How much was the shopping?' Vivian bit her bottom lip. She could lie about it, but it was best to have it all out so as not to spoil their holiday.

'Well...they *do* everything so it's not as if I have to buy anything else...much.'

'Viv?'

'And it's cheaper than the supermarket...in the long run.'

'Viv?'

'$300,' she blurted.

'Over $1,000 for four days.'

'Don't forget Mr Downer Col?'

'Bloody hell.' Colin put his head in his hands and lent his elbows on the table.

'Anything else?'

'Well...'

'What?'

'Well Rowdy said our tab is due.'

'Well I'm confident there. We haven't spent much at the chandlery.' Col looked at Viv, 'Have we?'

'Um. It sort of adds up darling.'

'How much?'

'I really don't know how we could have spent so much. I don't remember half of these things.'

'How much?'

'$700.'

'What!?' Col jumped out of his chair and grabbed the bill from Viv.

'I told you we didn't need that thing for your thingo.'

'What?' Viv frowned.

'Oh, never mind.'

'When Rowdy gave me the bill he said, do you know what boat stands for?' Viv shouted mimicking Rowdy. Colin looked at his wife and shrugged. 'Bring on another thousand. I thought he was joking.'

'Not bloody likely.' Colin said.

CHAPTER 13

'Are you sure he said this morning?' Vivian asked as she packed away the last of the shopping.

'First thing.' Colin watched his wife try to fit a jumbo pack of pretzels into a plastic container.

'It's just that high tide is at 8.42 and...' Viv began. Colin held up his hand,

'I know Viv. Don't get all thingy. Everything will be fine. Downer said he'd deliver the part first thing and I believe him. We are like that now.' Colin crossed his fingers to demonstrate his friendship with Darryl Downer. As if he knew he was being talked about Darryl tapped on the side of the boat and climbed aboard. Colin shot up and ushered the mechanic to the windlass then watched as Downer worked in silence putting the machine back together. Colin hovered expectantly in case Darryl needed anything, but the man looked like he could do it in his sleep, such was his expertise. With a quiet grunt Downer tightened the last bolt and stood up.

'Done?' Colin asked. Downer nodded.

'Shall I pay now or...?' Downer took out a small notebook and wrote a figure on a scrap of paper.

'Oh, ok. I'll get it to you next week alright?'

Downer picked up his bag, wiped his hands on his overalls and padded in his sock feet to the side of Moonlighting.

'Right,' said Colin and followed. He watched Darryl slip on his boots, which were waiting on the dock like a dog waiting for their owner outside a shop, and walk away. Vivian came outside,

'What did he say?'

'Absolutely nothing,' Colin replied.

With everything stowed and anything that looked like it might move strapped down with bungy cords the Tripps decided they were ready. Or to be more precise, Vivian decided they were ready; for it is widely known that the Captain might have command of the ship, but the Admiral has the last word. If the Admiral is happy, everyone's happy!

Colin fired up the engine and Viv slowly backed out of the dock, did a turn and headed for an idyllic four-day holiday on some of the most beautiful coast of Queensland, Australia, or so Alan Lucas and his cruising guide suggested. They had boned up on their course and decided that a short cut across Cleveland Bay would be a good plan rather than go around Magnetic Island. Moonlighting came out of the marina and turned left. The morning was clear and the Tripps could see The Palm group of island in the distance and their expectations grew.

'See Viv, there they are.' Colin pointed. 'Not far at all.' Viv fiddled with the GPS and saw their route mapped out in red dots in a very neat direct line.

168

'It says 37 nautical miles.'

'An easy day,' said Colin. 'Right, let's get sailing.'

The Tripps looked at the wind direction and considered which side to set the sails. The little wind indicator swung about like a drunk on a light pole.

'It doesn't seem to be from anywhere.' Vivian concentrated on the arrow. 'Shall we just motor for a bit?' It sounded like good advice to Colin and so he sat back and let his wife helm. Moonlighting rolled from side to side in the swell as it couldn't make up its mind which side was more comfortable.

Cleveland Bay looks inviting, interesting and fun. The locals call it a washing machine. Shallow water, a reef, the confluence of the tide and wind all conspire to mix up the sea so it doesn't know what it wants to do. Vivian tried to keep to her little red line of dots, but Moonlighting had other ideas. The boat rolled, bucked, slew and floundered along in an erratic way for over half an hour.

'Here, let me have a go.' Colin climbed behind the wheel after Viv had lost feeling in her fingers trying to hold the course. Col's effort wasn't much better except for the odd swear word and they didn't seem to be getting anywhere fast.

'Shall we try the sail?' Viv offered. 'The one at the front.'

'You mean the Genoa?'

'That's it,' Viv said and pointed. She arranged all the winches and ropes and then waited for Colin to give the word. He considered the wind, looked at the GPS, studied the compass while Viv watched.

'Now.'

Viv let go the furling rope and the sail filled

169

with wind. She tightened the sheet rope and all looked good - for about 20 seconds when the wind died and the sail began flapping.

'It's not working,' Vivian said and winched the sail tight. 'Perhaps we should go over there.' She pointed at 90 degrees from their position. 'The wind would fill it from there.' Colin turned Moonlighting and although they were heading straight for Maggie Island it was enough to fill the sail and pick up the boat to a decent pace. It took the best part of an hour to reach the other side of the bay and their trail on the GPS was like the zig zag stitching on a canvas bag, but the Tripps had tacking down to a fine art.

Once past the influence of the Island the wind picked up and again Vivian tried to follow her red line. It was all going swell so they decided to put up the main.

'Now remember, Viv, you have to go straight into the wind until it's up.' Viv nodded. 'And then when it's up swing back on course and we can do the adjusting. OK?'

'OK.' Viv looked at the wind and watched Colin make everything ready at the mast. There was a bit of trial and error as Colin became confused with the winches and clutches, then he signalled to Viv to come up into the wind. She turned the boat and the Genoa began to complain, flapping and carrying on as Colin slowly pulled the main up the mast. The rope screamed, the winch pulled and they kept going into the wind heading for New Zealand. As Colin hauled the last metre to the top he was sweating and out of breath. He waved his arms around for Viv to turn and sat down to try to breathe. Moonlighting turned, caught the wind and both sails filled making the boat heel over. This precipitated a loud crash and bang from below. Trapped as she was at the wheel, Vivian tried to look downstairs for the trouble, but couldn't see.

'Colin,' she yelled.

'Just- a- minute,' Colin took a few deep breaths.

'Colin, we have a big problem.'

'What?' Colin returned to the cockpit.

'Something is going on downstairs. Can you steer and I'll look?' Vivian had a sneaking suspicion her spam was making a bid for freedom. She left her husband at the wheel and scooted below. The spam wasn't the problem. Viv could see straight away what all the noise was about. The cutlery drawer had flung itself to the floor as the boat leaned and rolled and now the steak knives were embedded into the floor and looked like a circus act.

'All good,' Colin shouted.

'Nothing serious.' Viv replaced the drawer and employed yet another bungy strap to keep it shut. She grabbed two beers and reappeared in the cockpit.

'For my Captain,' she handed over the can.

'This is what it's all about.' Colin grinned.

Everything was just perfect until they reached Rattlesnake Island and their VHF radio crackled into life

'Vessel on Co-ordinates 19°02'639 South, 146°33,993 East requested to vacate the area immediately.' Viv and Col sipped their beer and looked around for the naughty boat.

'Vessel on Co-ordinates 19°02'639 South, 146°33,993 East requested to vacate the area immediately.' Vivian fetched the binoculars,

'I don't see them.' She scanned the horizon.

'Sailing Vessel Moonlighting you are...' The Tripps looked at one another, then it dawned on them that they were in the live firing range of the air force. Colin threw his beer overboard and panicked. He turned to port, changed his mind and swung to starboard, then the sails went in a slow death of flapping and he turned again.

'Heading 17° NNE,' the radio barked. Colin looked at the compass and made the turn. Moonlighting's sails took some of the wind and filled. She picked up her skirts and on a broad reach gained speed.

'Phew,' Colin said. Viv grabbed the radio.

'Er, um, we didn't know. Sorry.'

'OUT.' came the terse reply.

We should have checked the paper,' Colin giggled.

At that particular heading the wind was perfect, but it wasn't the direction they needed to go and their next stop might have been Fiji. Col kept the heading revelling in the feel of sailing, the wind, the water, the exhilaration.

'This is the life isn't it Viv?' Viv nodded.

'We still have a way to go, don't we? And isn't that Palm Island over there?' She pointed to the port side as they headed out for the shipping channel. Colin took a look, then adjusted his glasses and peered at the GPS.

'Hmm.' He studied the map as Moonlighting skipped along.

'Col?'

'Well, we do need to go there, but this is one

172

hell of a ride.'

'So, you think we should turn soon?'

Soon.' Colin sat back as the boat cruised along. Vivian watched as they slowly started to edge away from their destination.

'Col, do you think we should turn now?' Colin looked at the GPS again.

'These things are relative Viv. We may look like we are heading in the wrong direction, but it's only a degree or two. We can adjust our course in small steps and you watch - we will be there in no time.' The Admiral wasn't so sure.

Half an hour passed as the Tripps sailed their course - and then for some inexplicable reason the wind changed direction. The sails began to flap and it was action stations as the boat began to roll with the swell, lines went slack and things began to fall about in the cabin. Colin looked up at the wind indicator and then at Palm Island and his projected course. It wasn't working.

'I think the wind is from the North Col.' Viv suggested.

'Impossible. The weather said South East 10 to 15.' Col took another look at the compass. 'Get Alan Lucas's cruising guide Viv.' Viv shot downstairs and retrieved the bible, that indispensable book about the Coral Coast.

'Alan says here,' Viv began to read, 'That on *very rare* occasions there can be a northerly wind, even in the persistent South East trade winds.' She looked at the wind indicator. 'It's a northerly.'

Col swung Moonlighting to get some wind and they, once again, were heading out to sea. Beating into a head wind is as much fun as filling in a tax return, although for Colin, as an accountant, tax time was the highlight of the year. Moonlighting bucked and rolled and the only recourse was to tack or motor. He put the options to his wife.

'Well, we want to get there in daylight, don't we?' She asked.

'I guess.'

'We should just motor in a straight line.' It bothered Vivian that they hadn't kept to her plotted course and it seemed sensible to go from A to B regardless of what the weather wanted to do.

'It could be mightily uncomfortable.' Colin looked at the increasing swell as they sailed east and didn't relish a bout of sea sickness.

'But we'd have to go ages before we could come back.' Viv frowned. Colin shuddered,

'Yep.'

The wind increased and the boat began to cut through the swell.

'Viv look,' Col pointed to the water on the port side, 'Dolphins.' Vivian squealed as she watched the dolphins ride the bow wave. It was the omen they needed to keep sailing.

'We could go out to the shipping lane, then come back in again.' Colin looked at the map. 'It's all an adventure anyway,' he giggled.

They sailed most of the day going back and forth and eventually as the sun was setting rounded the corner of Great Palm Island and pulled the sails down and started the engine.

'Alan says to anchor here,' Col held the book up to Viv so she could get her bearings. The little

174

picture showed an anchor just tucked in behind the headland near the township. Viv steered the boat to the spot and Col made ready the windlass and his new chain. When everything was ready he signalled Viv to slow and then dropped anchor. The chain clattered over the side, jumping now and again off the gypsy and Colin counted the metres, which Nino had marked with bright coloured chain counters. He repositioned the chain on the windlass a few times then stopped at 30 metres and gave the thumbs up to Viv.

'We made it.' Viv plotted their course on the GPS.

'Only 67 miles,' she said.

Palm Island has a sheltered bay and anchoring there is a welcome rest from the motion of the sea. Moonlighting gently bobbed in Casement Bay and as the Tripps sipped their sundowners they felt a sense of triumph watching the last rays of sun dip over the horizon.

'Now, take a position Viv. Look for visual markers so we can check where we are.' They looked around and collected a mental picture.

Friday night on Palm is disco night, or so it seemed to the Tripps. The bright lights flashed, the music thumped over the water and they could see bonfires on the beach.

Vivian had planned a special meal for their first proper night away and so once they were settled she busied herself in the galley preparing dinner. The little stove did its best and the Tripps sat down to a sumptuous feast of beef chow mien, fried rice and prawn crackers. It didn't take more than half an hour after the dishes were done for a day in the sun to catch up with them. Colin fell asleep on one side of the table and Viv dozed on the other. Sometime well after the disco had gone home Viv woke up and rubbed her neck.

'Col,' she nudged her husband awake.

'Huh, what time is it?'

'Late,' said Viv. She stood up and looked out of the windows. It was dark. No town lights to be seen. She studied the shore line, but the town was dark.

'Shall we go to bed?' Colin made a move to the blow-up mattress.

'Well, it's just that...' Viv peered outside.

'What?'

'Well, I think we have a big problem.'

'What now Viv?'

'Well... I'm not sure, but I think we've moved.'

Colin stood next to his wife and peered into the night.

'We were near the town - and now...' The Tripps went up on deck and slowly, by following the shore line as it disappeared into the darkness, they could just see some lights in the distance.

Collin grabbed Viv's arm, 'I think we've dragged.' They looked at one another, then at another island which was looming large on their stern.

'What'll we do?' Viv tried to get her bearings.

'Get the hell out of here.'

There was a flurry of frantic activity as the engine was started, and Colin pressed the windlass into action. The chain refused to stay in the gypsy

176

and Colin lost quite a bit of skin on his knuckles trying to keep it on the little wheel.

'What's wrong?' Viv asked.

'It keeps jumping off and I don't know why.' Colin said.

'Praps you should,' Viv started.

'Look, you just concentrate on your job and I'll do mine. Alright.'

'No need to get shirty.' Viv huffed.

Eventually the 'useless bloody anchor,' as Colin described it, was pulled up and it took a good 25 minutes for Moonlighting to motor back to their original spot.

'I can't believe it. I can't believe it,' Colin kept muttering as they found their GPS co-ordinates.

Colin dumped a heap more chain as he dropped the anchor and it was a restless sleep had by all for the remainder of the night.

It was only in the daylight that the Tripps realized their luck as they had drifted past a wreck, the lead lights for the ferry, two fishing boats and about a dozen crab pots marked by floating cordial bottles.

'I can't believe it,' Colin said, but this time for an altogether different reason.

The north wind was still prevalent, but the mood on Moonlighting was high as Casement Bay saw a bright day with light winds. The wind was so light in fact that it was virtually non-existent.

'Not much point in putting the sails up,' Colin stood on the foredeck and looked at the glassy water.

'Shall we just motor darling?'

It was decided to chug out of Casement Bay

177

and see what the sea was like. Vivian took the helm and the anchor was pulled up amid much cursing, flapping of arms and a few threats. It was given a stern talking to by Colin and then they were on their way.

Passing near to Islands is quite a thrill and the Tripps came in close and puttered around Fantome, which used to have a leper colony, and made a course for Orpheus. The sea calmed to an oily slick and Moonlighting chugged along.

Sailing has often been described as 90% boredom and 10% terror and now the Tripps were in the 90% zone. They ate. They drank. They boiled the kettle and took photographs. When there is nothing to do the mind can invent things and takes off on tangents. Colin's mind decided to take off his clothes. Viv went down to get some snacks and when she returned there were more than peanuts on offer.

'Colin,' she giggled.

'Well, it's comfortable.' He sat in the sun and enjoyed the freedom of being on the sea can bring when your closest neighbour is miles away.

'Go on Viv,' Colin nudged his wife, 'It's so liberating.'

'Well...' Vivian took the plunge and striped off and they ate their pick and mix a la naturale.

Orpheus Island isn't too far from Great Palm and by lunch time the Tripps had come to their next anchorage. Little Pioneer Bay is just around the corner from the exclusive resort on Orpheus and as they passed the holiday destination for people who don't have to ask the price, Viv began to get dressed.

'I don't want Mick Jagger or some gazillionair

to see me do I?' she said to Col.

'What about me?'

'Colin Tripp. You know the answer to that.' Vivian laughed.

The boat rounded the small headland and Colin pointed out their destination. A small sheltered bay with a tiny bit of beach fringed by a coral reef.

'Looks idyllic, doesn't it?' Colin pointed the boat in the right direction.

'Just perfect.' Viv answered.

'Now. We are going to pick up a mooring Viv.' Colin handed her the boat hook, their bargain from the garage sale. 'Just as I ease the boat up to the buoy, you pull the small rope up and feed it through the fairleads,' Colin pointed with the boat hook at the opening in the gunwales, 'and then put the big rope on the bits. OK?'

'OK.'

The boat slowed and gradually made its way to the blue, Great Barrier Reef Marine Park Authority buoy. This particular buoy was actually missing the smaller rope, which gets pulled up first, so Vivian had no option. She made a few hand signals to Colin, left, right, left a bit, and leaned over the bowsprit. The boat hook was only just long enough and Vivian swung wide and snagged the large hawser as thick as a world record French stick and tried to bring it up.

Some things aren't meant to happen. Viv's boat hook took one look at the job and did its back in, bending in half. Viv could see it all going to hell in a hand basket and lunged at the rope just catching it in time, while a stray bit of wire caught her shirt and

179

gave it a decent size rip. Slime, weed, barnacles and other nasty stuff flung themselves at Viv covering her shirt, shorts and face, and her sunglasses slipped off and headed for the bottom.

'Everything OK?' Col yelled.

'Fine,' Viv said though gritted teeth lest she get the catch of the day between her teeth. There wasn't much she could do except haul the rope in and loop it over the bits, those knobs sticking up at the bow of the boat.

Colin shut the engine off and went to inspect the job. He looked at his wife, sans sunglasses, covered in smelly slime, the bent boat hook, the ripped shirt and the hawser now resting over the bits.

'Piece of cake.'

With the whole of the anchorage to themselves it didn't take Colin a minute to figure out that Viv could do with a swim, 'to get cleaned up a bit, cause you stink'. The Tripps stripped off and were about to jump overboard in an act of gay abandon, when Vivian remembered that movie she had seen where the occupants of a yacht perished because they couldn't climb back onboard.

'We need the ladder down Col.' Colin threw the rope ladder over the side and they bombed into the crystal-clear blue sea, like a couple of kids on school holidays. There was much splashing and squealing and larking about, so much in fact that the arrival of another boat wasn't noticed until it was close enough to see the tattoo on the skipper's chest.

'Hellooooo there,' the tattooed man called. Vivian scampered behind Colin and tried to hide.

180

'I hope he isn't wearing polaroids,' Viv whispered to Colin.

'Er, hello there.' Colin waved.

'Where is it you are headed?'

'Well...we actually are just on a bit of a break. My wife here,' Colin pointed behind his back while treading water, 'and I are just...' Vivian gave Col a dig in the back to get on with it as she could see Colin getting up steam and forgetting they were both naked, in the water, and the ladder was in full view of the neighbour. Col giggled.

'Eh?'

'We could come over later if you like.' Colin smiled and the Tripps swam backwards towards Moonlighting.

'You get up Col and then toss me my bathers.'

'Why me?'

'Well, it was your idea.'

'No, it wasn't.'

'Yes, it was.'

'Wasn't. Anyway, we could just wait 'till the boat swings around the other way and then we won't be in view.'

'And we could just wait for the sun to go down.' Viv snapped back and swam into the shade.

' Oh, alright.' Colin rolled his eyes and paddled over to the ladder. A ladder is a very useful thing in the right circumstances. This rope ladder had all the makings of a useful thing, except the last rung was about half a metre from the surface of the water. It may not look like a lot, but when you have to put your foot on it and haul yourself up, it can be a mighty obstacle. Colin tried to get a grip with his foot by putting his toes around the rope and pulling. With one leg up around his ear and the other flapping about in the water there wasn't much left to the imagination. It reminded Viv of a rhyme she had learnt about the angle of the dangle. He flopped back in the water and tried a different tack. Lunging at the rope he gained a hand hold further up and then managed to get his knee on the last rung. The ladder swung wildly to the side as Colin hung on, bent double, all thoughts of modesty lost to the prevailing wind. His toe struck a hold in the exhaust outlet and he splayed himself out on the hull and gradually inched his way up and rolled over the gunwale onto the hot deck. His beche de mer sizzled on a sun-baked stainless-steel fitting, and Colin shot up howling in pain. For a crazy split second, he had the idea of jumping in the sea, then sanity prevailed and he rushed downstairs and grabbed a cold beer can and put it on his burnt offering. It was only when he had finished the beer and thought about a second one that he remembered his wife. Whipping on a pair of shorts he rushed up on deck and peered over the side.

'Viv?' He looked around.

'Viv?' He went to the other side of the boat.

'Vivian?'

'Here,' came a terse reply. 'Under the front of the boat.'

'Bow darling.' Colin couldn't help himself and regretted he had corrected her the minute he said it.

'Just a minute honey.' He rushed downstairs and grabbed Viv's sarong. 'Coming.' He lent over the bowsprit and lowered the cloth to Viv. With it secured Vivian swam to the ladder.

'Wait, I need to lower it.' Colin let out some

slack and the rungs hit the water. Vivian climbed aboard and huffed downstairs to change.

'I didn't forget you Viv. I had an accident.' Colin began to take his shorts off. 'Look.'

There was the beginnings of a blister in the unmistakable shape of a D shackle on his sea cucumber. Viv came in for a good look and began to titter.

'It hurts.'

Viv giggled.

'It's really sore.'

'Viv cackled and pointed. There, on the burn was the reference number RF 151.

It is amazing what rubbing a soothing salve into a wound can do for morale. The first aid was administered, lunch was had, beer was drunk and the Tripps were out for the count having a nanna nap when there was a loud bang on the hull. Colin shot up and in a panic rushed out on deck. Everything looked normal. They hadn't drifted and then he remembered they were on a mooring.

'What was that?' Viv appeared.

'I don't know. A fish maybe?' They listened and then it happened again. A huge thump reverberated through the boat.

'Are we sinking?'

'Of course not.' Colin frowned. He followed the noise and ended up at the bow of the boat. The blue mooring buoy was bashing itself on the hull in the growing northerly swell. The Tripps looked down as it had an irresistible attraction to the boat and was trying to rub every vestige of paint from the topsides.

'Why is it doing that?'

'It looks to be too short or something.' Colin studied the problem.

'Perhaps we should do what that other boat has done.' Viv pointed to their neighbour who had threaded another rope through the hawser and given himself a longer lead.

The Tripps gathered some rope and then pulled the boat forward and lengthened their lead. The buoy floated away to a safe distance and Colin gave Viv a high five.

'Job well done.' They retired to the bed once more when there was a loud banging again.

'What now?' Colin climbed off the bed and went to investigate. The companionway doors were banging in the swell. First the starboard and then the port. He thought on the problem and the easiest solution was to close them.

'What was it?' Viv asked as Colin jumped on the bed.

'The doors. Fixed.'

Viv gave her husband a high five. 'Job well done.'

It was Vivian's big night and she had planned everything to the last minute so as not to miss the meteor shower. Nibbles and drinks, early tea, camera set up, then sit back and watch the show. She outlined the evening to Colin as she prepared the nibbles.

'And they said it should go on for a good hour or so.' Colin didn't mind one meteor, maybe even three or four, but an hour was stretching it. He screwed up his face.

'What?' Viv said.

'Why do there have to be so many?'

'What do you mean?'

'So many meteors. I mean, do we have to watch them *all*?' Viv frowned and pursed her lips and was just going to get into an argument when there was a knock on the hull.

'For Pete's sake,' Colin thumped up the stairs to take a look at the buoy again and came up short when he saw a face bobbing next to the gunwale.

'Er, hellooooo.' The neighbour held onto Moonlighting and tossed a rope. He was tied off and proceeded to climb aboard.

' I am Jerk,' he held out his hand.

'Colin.'

'I was thinking you would like a drink.' Jerk held up two bottles of Vodka and raised his eyebrows.

'Um...' Colin looked at the bottles, took a second to think about all those meteors and invited his guest downstairs.

'Viv, this is Jerk.'

'Hello.' Viv smiled. Jerk looked like an old salt from the sea. He had tanned, leathery skin, periwinkly blue eyes and the biggest walrus moustache Viv had ever seen. Where are you from?' Viv asked.

'Sweden. Have you been to Sweden?'

'No, we haven't.' Viv fished out some nibbles and put them on the table between the two men. They dived on the pick and mix and poured the Vodka.

'Sweden eh?'

'Ja.' We drink to Sweden and Oztralia.' Jerk and Colin tipped glasses and downed their drinks.

'You don't drink?' Jerk asked Viv. 'You must

drink. It is special night. Night of stars.' Jerk threw his hands about mimicking shooting stars.

'Yes, the meteor shower.'

'Ja.' We drink to shower.' Three more drinks were poured and downed followed by a beer or two. Jerk then brought out his pipe.

'You are not minding if I smoke.' Colin liked the fellow and the beer mellowed his sensibilities. He pushed his glasses up his nose and patted Jerk on the back with a

'No. Not in the least.'

The pipe and tobacco took a good few minutes to connect. There was the tapping, the twiddling, the filling, more tapping, and finally he struck a match. Viv watched as he puffed up a good stack and screwed up her nose.

'You like it ya?'

'Well...' Viv started when three more drinks were poured and they toasted Jerks pipe, his tobacco, his sister and if she had one, her pipe too. The party was getting quite jolly and tipsy. Jerk kept the Tripps entertained with stories about sailing. Stories about women and sailing and stories about sex, women and sailing. The evening slipped away as the Vodka, beer and gin disappeared. Around nine Vivian suddenly remembered the reason they were at sea and the party rushed up to the deck to see the last meteor cross the sky. Viv pointed and tried to take a picture. Colin and Jerk, it turned out, missed it completely as they pissed over the side to the tune of jingle bells, the only song that they both knew. Two bottles of Vodka, twelve beers and five decent size gins later the party broke up, as all yachting parties do, with the promise to never

186

lose touch with one another and the swapping of addresses. Jerk fell into his dinghy and rowed back to his boat and the Tripps collapsed on their blow-up bed and wished every day could be as good and everyone as nice as the Swedes.

Dawn broke with an increasing wind from the north and a more direct blast from Colin as the Vodka made its way south.

Boating brings on a selective memory. What seemed horrendous at the time soon becomes a yarn or an anecdote of survival. The Tripps slipped into the latter as they lay in bed and by the time they were thinking about coffee they needed a reality check like a dose of Epsom salts to a case of indigestion. The journey so far wasn't a trial at all, everything was going according to plan, the sunburn didn't really hurt and spam could be made to taste wonderful. It was a classic case and the Tripps had it bad.

'I just wish we could do this forever - don't you Colin?'

'Yeah.'

'People do you know. They sell up everything - a sea change.'

'Yep.'

'And just travel.' Viv lay back on the blow-up bed and looked at the clouds appearing and disappearing as the boat rolled with the swell.

'We could do it you know.'

'Mmm.'

'Col, we could become cruisers.' Colin propped himself up on his elbow and looked at Viv.

'I think they are called grotty yachties.' He

plopped back down and closed his eyes taking a deep breath and hoped like hell he didn't have a hangover and sea sickness at the same time.

'Grotty yachtie. I like it.' Viv said. Colin hung onto the side of the bed to stop the motion of rolling. It wasn't working. He blew out a few stagnant breaths and then staggered to the toilet and sat down. It was just the motion of the loofa, swinging back and forth, back and forth that set Colin off and he just had time to do a reverse twist, before the inevitable happened. Vivian appeared in the doorway and looked like she'd had a stroke as she tried to keep her stomach contents on the inside. Colin's retching was the call of the wild to her stomach and she lurched up the stairs and let rip. Moonlighting rolled from side to side and all Viv could do was hang on when she heard someone hailing her.

Jerk was standing on his deck, buff naked doing calisthenics with his pipe in his mouth. She waved and shot back inside. It took a good hour before Colin could speak and stop his eyes from rolling into the back of his head.

'I think I've got two tongues.' He poked his tongue out for Viv to take a look.

'No, just one. You want coffee?' Viv asked. Colin nodded and regretted it. He sat at the table and closed his eyes as Viv gingerly moved about the rolling boat.

'I wonder if we should go back today Col?'

'What do you mean?'

'Well, we're not 100%, and well...' Vivian sat down with their coffee and they thought on the idea of extending their holiday. 'I just don't feel up to sailing back.'

'I guess I could ring work.' Colin sipped his drink.

Viv smiled. 'We could take an extra three days maybe?'

'Sounds good.' Colin sat back and studied the empty bottles left on the table. 'Is Jerk still around?' he asked. Viv nodded and related her vision of him doing his daily dozen.

'What a sailor. What a man.' Colin said as he looked at all the burnt spots on the table from the tobacco and then somewhere in the dark recesses of his mind he remembered it was supposed to be Viv's special night.

'Did you get any shots of the stars or anything?' Viv grabbed her camera and flicked through the shots. There were three of her feet, one of the winch, several of the sea and one fuzzy one of the moon.

'Not your best effort.' Colin tried to be pragmatic. 'Never mind, there is always another meteor.'

'Not really. The next one will be when I'm 120 years old.' She giggled. Colin tittered and they were soon laughing at the situation.

All the prep for a picture of a winch and her feet. After a second coffee and toast Colin rang work and, without going into details, said he needed three more days. He gave the thumbs up to his wife and put his mobile phone down.

'So where shall we go?'

'Hinchinbrook Channel.' Viv pointed to the page from the guide, 'Alan says, one of the most spectacular waterways on the Queensland coast and a fisherman's paradise,' she read. 'This is going to be fun.'

Colin smiled, 'Do you think I should get a pipe?'

CHAPTER 14

Vivian stood at the helm while Colin unhooked the mooring line and when he gave the all clear she swung the boat out to sea and their next leg of the journey. Hinchinbrook channel is entered at the south by following the 6km long Lucinda Sugar jetty. Vivian pointed to the jetty which was visible in the distance.

'Not far.' she said to Colin as he came to sit in the cockpit. The swell was building as they left the relative calming effect of Orpheus Island and by the time they came into the sea there was a fair chop and increasing winds.

'Er, Viv.'

'Yes?'

'Don't look behind you.' Colin studied the rising waves. Saying 'don't look behind you' is an invitation that no-one can resist. Viv swivelled around and her eyes widened in alarm. The waves were building and rushing to their stern at around 2.5 metres. As Moonlighting dipped into the troughs they looked a lot bigger.

'Col, do you think we will be alright?'

'No worries Viv. She can take it. Just stick to

this course.' Colin unfurled the headsail and it whipped tight taking the wind. Moonlighting took up the challenge and the Tripps felt this was what sailing was all about. The motor was cut and all they could hear was the whoosh of the water on the hull, and the companionway doors banging at every roll and dip.

'I don't know why they bang like that.' Colin looked at the doors and there didn't seem to be any logical reason.

'Just stuff something behind them.' Viv said. Colin followed the advice and the doors kept quiet.

'Fixed.' He smiled and looked at their projected course. It didn't look far in a straight line. It was a pity they had to tack because of the contrary north winds and the straight line turned into a zig zag. Eventually the jetty took form and Vivian made the turn to run parallel to the monster sugar terminal jetty. Now the wind was in the right direction for a grand sail and the boat skipped along when Colin noticed the depth sounder. He tapped the glass and frowned, then had a look at the charts. Then to confirm his growing suspicions he looked up the tide tables for Lucinda.

'Er Viv,' he came into the cockpit with a frown.

'What?' Viv smiled. She was enjoying the feeling of sailing on a broad reach.

'I think we have made a miscalculation.'

'What do you mean?'

'Well, it looks like we are coming into the channel on a falling tide and it gets pretty low. We either have to really hurry or hang about until the tide turns.'

'How low?

192

'Bottom low.' And then just to prove the point there was a judder as the boat scraped the sandy bottom. 'That low.' Colin added.

'How...' but Vivian didn't finish as Colin jumped downstairs and started the engine. Moonlighting was given a rev up and the Tripps left a trail of mud and sand and they ploughed their way into the channel at speed. Colin spotted the red and green markers to show the way and they hurried to deep water. Moonlighting began to shudder at the strain as Vivian tried to keep her on course. They made the dog leg to get to the Island side of the channel and deeper water. Colin watched the depth gauge slowly creep up in numbers.

'Col?' Viv said.

'What?'

'I think we have a big problem. Just look at that rock.'

'What rock?'

'The one we don't seem to be passing.' Colin studied the rock on the Island. Moonlighting was revving hard, the sail was doing its duty, but they were standing still.

'What the heck?' He grabbed the cruising guide and read on. *There can be a 3-knot tidal flow at either end of the channel.*

'Oh hell.'

'We need more power.' He looked at the rev counter on the old engine. She was giving her all. 'We will have to put up the main and tack.' He rushed to the mast and hoisted the mainsail. The wind grabbed it and Viv turned the boat to zig zag across the narrow channel that had the deep water. Gradually Moonlighting made slow progress albeit as fast as the New Zealand, Fox Glacier and as the tidal race slowed their tactics paid off.

'We are heading for Haycock Island.' Colin pointed to the map. 'Just up around the bend.' Viv nodded and steered the course watching for the markers and admiring the scenery. The hills looked like something out of Jurassic Park and untouched by human hands. Dark gullies erupted with bird life and huge tree ferns crowded the hillsides. The wind dropped, the tide slackened and they inched their way along. Colin could see the sails weren't adding anything with the engine doing its bit and so pulled them in.

'Pretty spectacular eh?' Colin said. Viv nodded, lost for words. 'This is the life eh?' Viv nodded some more.

Haycock Island is a small pimple of an island in the middle of the channel from south to north. It is a favoured spot for anchoring in calm idyllic waters. Moonlighting slid around the Island and Viv took a look at the book and parked Moonlighting right on a little anchor sign.

'Ok Col. Anchors away.'

Colin let go the break on the windlass and the chain rattled over the side. He held up his thumb and Viv reversed to set the anchor. Anyone watching might have thought they had been doing it for years, so practiced was the procedure.

'All good.' Colin came back to the helm and kissed his wife. 'Magic.'

They surveyed their surroundings. Tucked between towering Hinchinbrook Island and

Haycock they were sheltered, out of the main tidal flow and very comfortable. The sand-flies saw them as fresh meat and the mosquitoes were thinking of dining out that night. Colin began to scratch and itch as Vivian started to swat and wave her arms about.

'We need repellent.' Colin scratched his face. His growing stubble was no barrier for sand-flies. Viv went downstairs and came back with her herbal remedy.

'Not this stuff Viv. The real stuff.' Colin went downstairs and fossicked about. All he could find was the fly spray. When a man is in need necessity takes precedence and he liberally applied the spray while Vivian dabbed on her herbal oil. They settled in and enjoyed the feeling of not moving, rolling or bucking around.

'I think I've found my favourite spot.' Viv said as she made lunch.

'Me too.' Colin came up behind his wife and gave her a kiss. Their reality meter was red lining at selective memory.

After a late lunch, a snooze and some R and R, Colin came up with an idea.

'Viv, I need a haircut.' Viv looked up from her book.

'Well when we get back I'll make an appointment.'

'Can't you do it now?'

'Well, I don't have the right scissors or anything.'

'I do.' Colin produced a pair of $2.00 scissors he had found in the cutlery drawer. 'Just a trim.'

'Oh alright.'

Colin started to take off his clothes. 'Just do it in

the cockpit, that way we won't get hair everywhere, including our clothes.'

Vivian smirked. 'And I suppose you want me to take my gear off too?'

'Well, just sayin'.'

Viv began to undress. Colin sat down and Viv went to work trimming and shaping, concentrating on the job and enjoying the sunshine when she looked up from her labours and there about 60 metres away was a tourist crocodile boat getting a bonus on their cruise.

'Aahhh.' she ducked down in the cockpit and hissed, 'boat,' and pointed. Colin turned around and joined his wife on the cockpit floor.

'Hells bells.' Colin looked around for something to use to cover up. The Croc tour moved in closer and they could hear excited voices.

'Make a run for it.' Colin pushed Viv to the companionway stairs.

'You make a run for it.' Viv hunched over. Colin grabbed a fender and eased himself along the seat to the stairs. He took them two at a time and found a tea towel, then threw a couple of cushions at Viv. She did the best she could with what she had and dashed downstairs. Col began to giggle, and Viv took up the joke and they began to laugh.

'That's the second time we have come undone without clothes Colin.'

'Want to make it three?' He grabbed Viv and led her into the bedroom.

The Tripps reappeared as the sun was just dipping below the horizon and were startled to find they had visitors. Three foreign boats were anchored around them. One from Canada, another from England and a Swede, for Jerk had made the trip up the channel as well. Colin grabbed the binoculars and started to spy.

'Can you see anyone?' Viv asked. Col shook his head. They stared at the boats when the VHF radio crackled into life.

'Sailing vessel Moonlighting go one up.' Viv looked at Colin and shrugged her shoulders.

'What does that mean?'

'Dunno.'

'Sailing Vessel Moonlighting, go to channel 17.' The penny dropped and Viv took the call. She fiddled with the buttons and then replied.'

'Er hello. This is Vivian from Moonlighting, over.'

'Hello Vivian. Norma here from Sassafras. We are having drinks and a pot luck tonight. Would you like to come? Over.' Viv looked at Colin and smiled. He nodded.

'Yes, that would be lovely. What time? Over.'

'5:30, Over and out.' Viv put the microphone down. 'It's just like talking on the phone really isn't it.'

'And if there is one person who knows how to talk on the phone it's you honey.' Col felt a growing sense of pride at the way Viv was taking to this boating lifestyle. 'What's pot luck?' he asked.

'Sort of bring something for tea and we all just, dig in.' Colin liked the idea of what seemed to him to be free food. 'What do you fancy?' Col thought on the question. He had a great list of favourites.

Viv was a good cook and he wasn't a fussy eater so anything she put in front of him soon became a favourite.

'How about those things with the stuff that is mixed up in it and then you dip them in that other stuff.

'You mean Vietnamese spring rolls and dipping sauce?'

'That's the one.'

Vivian went to work and Col spied on the neighbours. He scoped the boats. What they had, didn't have, what he would like that they did have, and ruminated on what he would do if he had what they had. In boating circles it's a pastime that has whiled away many an hour from the coracle to the Queen Mary. By the time they had freshened up, packed their meal, drinks and made the dinghy ready it was just on 5:30. Vivian took a look at the other boats. There didn't seem to be any movement.

'We don't want to be first.'

'Why not?'

'Well, we don't want to be seen to be too keen.'

'Why not?

'Colin. Trust me on this.'

Colin's stomach began to growl as he waited. Five minutes went by.

'Oh, heck. Let's just go. We'll get a good dinghy park.' Viv pursed her lips.

'Look, there goes someone now.' They watched an inflatable take off from the English boat and make its way to the Canadians.

'Now we can go.' The Tripps bundled into their dinghy and Colin tried the pull start as Viv held onto the side of the boat. He pulled and the engine politely coughed. He flexed his muscles and pulled again. The engine spluttered. He rolled up his sleeve and gave an Almighty pull. His elbow connected with the plastic container Viv was cradling and she lost her grip. The Vietnamese spring rolls did a back flip and landed in the bottom of the dinghy. It wasn't the best of outcomes as they now looked like chop suey. The engine gave a splutter and started and Colin giggled.

'Just get going Col, we don't want to be late.'

'What? You say don't go, then you don't want to be late. Sheeesh.' Colin sat down and they made their way to Sassafras. Viv threw the rope as they came along side and Jerk caught it and hauled them in. As Viv stood up she saw a fender step and with a quick step was on the deck, thinking that step was the first thing she would get when they were back home. Very handy. Colin passed up the Tupperware and then climbed aboard and Jerk escorted them to the cockpit of 60 feet of pure luxury. Viv smiled at the assembled crowd and introductions were made. Norma and Bob were from Ontario, Barb and John from Surry and Jerk, well they had already seen quite a bit of him in more ways than one.

'Would you like a tour?' Norma took Viv by the hand and led her downstairs as Colin settled in for men's business. Vivian followed down the companionway stairs and entered a different slant on boating. Sassafras had everything. Norma thought nothing of having a dishwasher, washing machine, dryer, ice maker, household fridge/freezer, office... and the list went on. Viv thought they were doing well on Moonlighting when she brought her coffee plunger along.

'My word, you seem to be well set up, she said looking around and making a mental list as long as your arm.

'Oh well. It's home.' Norma went to the ice maker and proceeded to make her drink. She plopped some cubes of ice the size of a lamington in her whisky beaker and then went to the drinks cabinet that swung out on a revolving hinge and chose her poison.

'I like a bourbon and bergs.' She smiled.

'Bergs?' Viv frowned.

'Icebergs. That's what we call them back home honey.' Viv thought on the 6 cans of light beer they had brought over to the party.

'Nice,' was all she could say. They re-joined the group in the cockpit and the Tripps sat silent as the pot luck club talked of trips they had done, mistakes they had made and sailing adventures they had had. Colin lapped it up and Vivian's mental list grew. Now she knew her life wouldn't be complete until they had been somewhere and done something. It all seemed so possible. As the darkness fell the group retired inside the boat to serve up their dinner. There was curry, pasta, stew and rice and then Colin looked around on the table for the spring rolls.

'Viv, where...' It was as far as he got as Viv shot him a look.

'Oh,' she feigned disappointment. 'I asked Col if he had the spring rolls and he must have forgotten them. Sorry.' Everyone looked to Colin and he giggled. There was no way Vivian could serve up her chop suey rolls to the pot luck club. She'd be mortified.

The evening progressed as Viv listened to Barb talk about the Bahamas, the Azores, Fiji, Florida and the Mediterranean like she talked about going to the shops. John kept everyone's glasses filled and the drink flowed. Jerk put away a bottle of Vodka and began to slump, Norma and Bob finished the Bourbon and Barb and John had a decent size pull at the gin and then their schnapps came out. It was dynamite.

There was butterscotch schnapps, cherry schnapps, apple schnapps and something Jerk said had herbs in it and took the hairs from your nostrils. Vivian and Colin were out of their league. They drank. They giggled. They began to recount their near misses with Moonlighting and had the assembled characters in stitches. It was late into the night when the last drop of alcohol was consumed that the party finally broke up. Col and Viv slopped their way to their dinghy and tumbled in.

'Oh look, I found the spring rolls.' Colin giggled and held up the Tupperware. Everyone laughed.

He pulled the outboard into life and it started first time for the first time. The crowd tittered and clapped.

'All in the wrist action.' There was a guffawing from the crowd. He put it into gear and they went to motor off except they were still attached by the rope. Jerk untied the line and there was more laughter and eventually the Tripps made their way back to Moonlighting.

'Viv smiled, 'We promised to always keep in touch.'

'Yeah, and Bob said we could look them up in Canada any time.' It was just your typical end to a typical yachty party full of undying friendship and swapping of business cards with little pictures of boats on them which get lost the minute you step back onboard.

The morning sun peeked over the hills of Hinchinbrook Island, but those anchored at Haycock Island didn't see it. All was still until around 9am when the Tripps were woken by the sound of an anchor chain being pulled. Colin squinted at his wife and then found his glasses. He went to roll over only to discover that his side of the blow-up bed had deflated. He groaned and managed to get on his hands and knees and look out of the porthole. Sassafras was just pulling away and try as he might, he just couldn't remember their names, even though they were his best friends in the world last night. He crawled to the kitchen and put the kettle on as Vivian stirred.

'Morning.' Viv wondered if her eyeballs were still in her head and touched them to be sure.

'I think I've swallowed a fur ball or is it my tongue?' Col picked up the stainless-steel egg spatula and had a look at his tongue. It was still in his head, which he reckoned was a start.

'Coffee honey?' Col busied himself with the makings and Viv closed her eyes. It was a good hour before they finally had their hangovers under control and were sitting in the cockpit.

'We are never going to drink like that again. I can't stand the pace.' said Viv.

She looked around the anchorage. 'Everyone's gone.' Colin nodded slowly.

'We should take a look at getting on too.' He

brought out Cruising the Coral Coast, adjusted his glasses and they looked at their next stop.

'How about Cardwell?' It seemed doable. All they had to do was follow the channel to the end and anchor just off the town.

'We could go shopping for some fresh stuff.' It seemed like a good idea.

 CHAPTER 15

Colin wrestled with the windlass trying to pull up the chain. He cursed, he stomped, he flayed his arms about, but the chain refused to co-operate and kept jumping off the gypsy every 8 metres or so. Through sheer determination he managed to get the anchor up and Viv turned the boat to head north. This time the tide was with them and they held a cracking pace following the markers. The majestic scenery was just the thing their jangled nerves required to recuperate and the boat settled down for an easy ride when Colin said,

'Why don't we try fishing?' The Tripps had, in the mistaken belief that there were fish in the sea, bought a sizeable amount of fishing gear and inherited some from the previous owner. Colin brought out the tangle of lures. These things are designed to catch everything before deployed in the water. He stabbed his finger, he snagged his shirt, he caught his hat and in desperation he threw the jumble down and a colourful fish like lure detached itself from the pack. It was duly rigged and Colin threw it off the back of the boat to trawl.

'Set and forget,' he said slapping his hands

together. The line played out and an hour went by. Snacks were eaten and still there were no fish to be had. Colin checked the rig several times and boiled the kettle, had a snooze, ate a spring roll or two with a spoon and the boast of 'Hinchinbrook is a fisherman's paradise' was wearing thin.

'I don't think there are any fish in the sea.' he said to Viv. She looked at the line and then it happened. The line went taught. The reel began jumping on the deck. There, as they looked, a big fish jumped out of the water, well and truly caught. It was a tossup who squealed the most as the boat was forgotten in their efforts to reel the monster in. Viv grabbed her sailing gloves and pulled the line as Colin wound the reel. The beast thrashed in the water, jumping out and zig-zagging all over. When it dived Viv looked up to see the boat veering to the bank.

'Colin, the boat.' Colin let go the reel and took the wheel.

'Can you do it?' he watched as Viv pulled the fish in close.

'It's enormous Col.' she had it on a short line and it was dragging close to the side of the boat.

'Here, you steer, I'll get it up.' Colin took over. He hauled the exhausted fish aboard and it seemed to gather a new lease on life. It began to flap and jump about.

'Kill it.' Viv shouted, surprising Colin with her blood lust. Colin looked at the 1 metre barramundi. They had bought a fish donger, a thing that looked like a small baseball bat, but it wasn't a job Colin relished.

'You kill it,' he said.

'How can I, when I'm steering? You do it.'

'I can't'

'Well, I'm not going to. They said something about a spike in the top of its head or something.' Viv said.

'You have got to be kidding me.' Colin stepped out of the way of the flapping fish.

' Hang on.' Viv steered and scrabbled around in her memory. 'Get the Scotch.' Colin raced downstairs and came back with the bottle of scotch. He cracked the lid and took a swig thinking he needed fortification if he was going to beat the thing to death or put a spike in its brain.

'Not you. Put it on the gills.' Viv directed the kill. Colin poured some over the gills of the fish. It did a short shudder and lay still.

'Remember Rowdy said about alcohol.' she said.

'Nice one Viv.'

They looked at the catch. It was huge.

'It's a barra isn't it?' Viv asked.

'Yep.'

'Are they in season?' Suddenly their prize catch might cost them more than they expected.

'We better have a look.' Colin went to the computer and Googled the relevant information. He came up with a smile and thumbs up.

'Fish tonight?' Viv did a high five.

Cardwell sits comfortably on the edge of

Rockingham Bay which is a very shallow dirty piece of water at the northern end of Hinchinbrook channel. Moonlighting came into the bay to be greeted with a short chop on the water and a pronounced north wind. She bucked about as they sailed to a spot with suitable depth and then Colin had to go through the shenanigans of putting the anchor down. It was late in the afternoon and over a cup of tea Viv and Col watched the spectacular sun set thinking of fish steaks and salad for dinner.

'This is the life eh?' Col had said it more than once on the trip and now he sat back as Viv busied herself with the BBQ. The BBQ was a briquette type and strapped to the stern rail. It was lit and left to get going as the Tripps relived their fishing experience, the tale getting bigger in the telling. When the BBQ was good and hot Viv put on the fish and they went inside to freshen their beers. A commotion sent them scurrying back outside just in time to see a big sea bird flying away with their dinner, chased by two other greedy birds. The BBQ was empty.

'Just as well it was a big fish.' Viv went for paper towels and another piece of fish and they stood guard over their hard-won delight.

'Do you think we could travel like the pot luck club Colin?' Viv mused on the question as they lay in bed.

'Mmm.'

'We could actually sail anywhere, couldn't we?'

'Mmm.'

'Around the world even.'

'Yeah.' Colin slowly nodded off as Viv thought

everything was possible, they just needed the right boat.

The wind died in the night and the Tripps woke up with the sun sparkling on the water and a calm sea. After a fortifying breakfast of fish and eggs, Colin suggested a trip to shore.

'We can get all the veg you want Viv.' He looked at the town in the distance.

Viv thought it was a good idea.

'You get the dinghy ready and I'll just get a few things.'

Colin lowered the ladder and brought the dinghy along the side of the boat and tided up.

'Viv,' he called. Vivian came out with a beach bag.

'What's in that?' Colin took the bag from his wife.

'Well, I thought we could do some beach things, so there's some sun cream, a couple of towels, a beach mat, a book.'

'Are you sure we need all of it?' Colin asked. Viv frowned like he'd asked if she really needed to breathe.

'Oh, hang on a minute.' She disappeared inside and came back with the small esky. 'Nibbles.' She passed the cool box down. 'Wait a tick.' She went back inside and re-emerged with an umbrella, two folding seats plus cushions. Colin put them in the dinghy.

'And then there is just this.' Vivian passed a length of rope, two sets of extra shoes and a bag of clothes, and sun hats.

'Is that all now?' Colin piled the stuff in the little boat.

'Umm.' Viv thought on the question. 'Do we need to take the radio?'

'NO.'

'Wait.' She went back and fetched a shopping bag and her handbag. 'That's it.' She looked down at the loaded boat. 'Where do I sit?' Colin shook his head and then shuffled things around for Viv to sit.

The dinghy outboard only took three swear words to get started and they began the trip to shore. It didn't look far yesterday, but now they seemed to be putting along forever.

There is a small jetty at Cardwell, but as it was full of sharp barnacles and rusted iron girders the Tripps decided that to pull the boat up the beach would be a better plan. They landed on the white sand and hauled.

'Better get it up quite high I think the tide is coming in.' Colin was thinking ahead. They lugged the boat all the way up the beach and tied it to a tree. When Colin felt satisfied it was safe they walked to the main road and the shops. A few days at sea often puts a different slant on shopping. Now the Tripps felt like they were seeing things for the first time.

'Ooo, bananas,' Viv cooed.

'Look, fresh pineapples.' Colin touched the prickly fruit. They bought a bundle of fresh local produce and hauled it back to the dinghy.

'How about lunch at the pub?' Colin had spied the pub on their shopping trip.

'This is like being on holiday isn't it Col?'

The pub was one of those local watering holes

that highlight the darts night and a chook raffle on Wednesdays. Col walked up to the bar and looked at the blackboard.

'Barra,' he pfffed and jabbed Viv with his elbow. 'We had barra last night, just caught. How big was it darling?' Col said loud enough for the two locals propping up the bar to hear and spread his arms wide in a performance that wouldn't have looked out of place at the Sydney Opera House.

'I'll have a steak sandwich,' Viv said to the barmaid.

'Me too.' Col smiled. They ordered a lemonade, 'I'm having a 'take it easy' day,' he said.

The meal was one of those delicious country serves that could feed a family of four and the Tripps waded through the food.

'This meat is really good.' Viv said as she wiped the last of the lunch from her lips.

'Comes from the local butcher,' the barmaid interjected as she cleared the dishes away. 'Over there.' She pointed to the shop on the main highway and walked away.

'Do you think we should buy some?' Viv asked Colin who sat back with a satisfied smile on his face, shrugged.

'Whatever.'

With two big steaks wrapped in paper under her arm and a warm glow, they made their way back to the boat thinking they could be home for a cup of tea in an hour.

'Oh.' Viv looked at the dinghy, the water and the shoreline...which was a good 600 metres from the sand. Colin looked at the mud flat between them and water.

'No problem. We can just drag it a bit.' He walked down to the water's edge and tried to walk on the mud. He sank up to his shins and retreated with gloopy feet.

'It stinks.' Viv held her nose. What the Tripps had failed to realise was that the water recedes like a balding man's hairline in the northern tropics and this can leave the unsuspecting traveller high and dry.

'What will we do now?'

'We... we could...' Colin tried to figure out how to get back.

'We should get a tide table and find out when it's going to be high tide.' Viv began to walk to the service station.

'I'll wait here.' Colin sat down and began to rub off the sticky mud with sand and palm leaves.

Vivian came back to see Colin had set up their camp. Folding chairs, esky, picnic rug and books were all strewn about on the sand. She plopped down in a chair and shook her head.

'It's not until 7:45 pm. It will be dark.'

'Well, we'll just have to wait.' Colin helped himself to a packet of nuts.

They had drunk all their drinks, eaten all their nibbles, discarded the book as boring and eaten some of their bananas and still had 2 hours to wait before the tide would be over the mud. Colin snoozed and woke up to see an old man watching him.

'Caught eh?'

'Pardon?'

'Caught.' The old seaman pointed to the tide.

'Yes.' Colin giggled.

211

'Won't be 'till late.'

'7:45pm I think.'

'Nope.'

'Pardon.'

'8:05.'

'But the book said...' Colin began, but the man held up his hand.

'Always 20 minutes after here.'

'Oh.' Colin looked over to Viv who had woken up and was listening.

'Do you think the water will come in this far?' Viv asked.

'Nope.'

'Oh.'

'Where then?'

'There.' The man of few words pointed to a log sticking out of the mud.

'Is that all?'

'Yep.' He finished his pronouncement and strode away down the beach. Viv and Colin watched him go and then looked at the log.

'Do you think we should drag the boat a bit?' Viv asked.

Packing up the boat and loading it with their shopping it weighed considerably more than it had when they dragged it up the beach. Now they felt like Egyptian slaves as they hauled their dinghy closer to the water. It snagged on the sand and fell into ruts and holes, but the task was eventually accomplished and they dug the small anchor down into the sand, just in case.

'Now we wait.'

In the tropics the twilight lasts about 10 minutes and just enough time for the sand-flies to have a bit to eat and then it is dark. This night it was very dark, the only night when the moon couldn't be seen. Another thing that couldn't be seen was Moonlighting.

'Did you put the anchor light on?' Colin peered into the night.

'No. Did you?'

'No.'

'Did you bring a torch?'

'No. Did you?'

'No.'

If there was a moon then Viv would have seen Colin glaring at her. She brought everything except the thing they needed most.

'Well, I guess we know where the boat is,' he pointed, 'over there.'

'And I guess we need to buy a torch.' Viv shot back. They traipsed over to the service station and forked out three times the normal price for a torch and the mood swung into sullen.

'What's the time, or didn't you manage to bring a watch.' Colin threw the question at his wife.

'It's 7:30 if you must know.' They sat down on the sand and waited, brooding on the trip ahead. Minute by minute the sea reclaimed the land and when it was just lapping their feet Colin stood up.

'Let's just get going. I'm sick of this.' Vivian rolled up her pants and they began to push. The mud clung to their feet, tried to suck them down to the underworld and stuck to the boat as they laboured to get some depth.

'One big push,' Colin strained and they tumbled

213

into the dinghy and were *just* floating, their feet still hanging over the sides.

'Rinse your feet if you can.' Viv splashed and rubbed on one side and Colin did the same on the other. The mud clung, like a child to its mother's leg.

'Just jump in now.' Colin threw his body into the boat. Viv fell in. Their combined weight made the small boat stick to the bottom with barely enough water underneath.

'Get the oars and push.' Col commanded. With an oar each they poled their way to deeper water. Viv pushed and the oar stuck.

'Col.' She hung on to the oar and the boat as they tried to part company.

'Pull yourself in. Hang on.' Viv strained her stomach muscles as she grappled with her feet to the boat's side.

'That's it. Keep going.' Col sat at the back trying to give the boat a bit of buoyancy. Viv stretched and finally the boat came close enough to pull the oar up.

'Good job Viv.' Now safely aboard, sitting in the dark, stinking of mud they looked at the black expanse of water in front of them.

'Are you worried Colin?'

'Nah.' Col tittered and tried to sound upbeat, but Vivian had been married to him for too many years not to know when he was lying. The small outboard must have taken pity on their predicament, because it behaved itself and started first time.

'You little ripper.' Col bent over and kissed Viv in the excitement. 'Now which way?'

Viv shone the torch out over the sea. It was like black ink. 'I think we were near that bit of hill and opposite that blue light.' Colin headed in the general direction as Viv swept the torch beam across the water.

'No, more over there,' She pointed to the black. Colin swung the boat around and went a little faster. They carried on for a few minutes when Viv looked at the shore and decided they needed to back track.

'Over there now Col.' The boat pointed to shore and they went on. This carried on for a good 40 minutes when Viv finally gave up.

'How about we just go ashore and get a room for the night. We'll never find it in the dark.'

'It's got to be out here somewhere.' Col was loathed to give up. 'I thought we were more over there.' He pointed to the ocean. Viv shone the torch in the general direction and it flicked over a white reflection.

'What was that?' Viv trained the beam as the boat rocked.

'What?' Colin pushed his glasses up his nose and peered into the dark.

'Look.' She steadied the light and caught a reflector. 'I think that is the reflector on the life ring.' Colin adjusted his glasses and gunned the boat and as they came closer he could see the unmistakable round reflector of the life ring on the back rail.

'Yippy.' Viv jumped up and down and kissed Colin.

Moonlighting bobbed at anchor as Colin brought the dinghy around to the ladder. He tied off and the moon came out. A glorious bright moonlit night that in different circumstances might have been romantic. The whole bay was lit up with a silvery glow.

'Will you look at that?' Col shook his head in disbelief. Once onboard they made a pact never to leave the boat without a light on and later at night, in bed, another pact never to talk in company about their stupidity to lose the boat. The first was a rule and easy, the second would be a little harder to keep.

CHAPTER 16

The Tripps sat in the morning sun and sipped their coffee discussing the journey home.

'We could go through *again*,' Col made a face to show that it wasn't his preferred option, 'Or we could do an overnighter and go around the outside to Fantome or even as far as Palm Island.' He smiled and looked at his wife expectantly.

'Can we sail at night?'

'Sure. John and Barb do it all the time.'

'But they are really experienced Col. We haven't had much at all and I think Barb said they had an auto pilot or something. We haven't got one of those, have we?'

'Nope. We will have to steer, but I mean, we gotta start sometime.' He slapped Vivian's knee and it was settled. They looked at the map and on a GPS 5-inch screen Hinchinbrook Island didn't look that big or long and if they stuck to the shipping channel at night they couldn't go wrong.

'Easy, and with that north wind behind us it should be a doddle.'

Colin made ready on the windlass. He gave the

thumbs up to Viv at the helm and she inched the boat forward. Colin pressed the foot-switch and the chain began to rise. It slipped out and so did a swear word. He repositioned the chain and tried again. After the fifth swear word and a hair pulling incident the chain was onboard and Viv turned into the wind to set the sails. Colin came back to the cockpit and sat down.

'That piece of junk is going the minute we get back.'

'Yes dear.' Viv handed the lolly container to Col. 'How about I put the sails up? I should know how to do it, shouldn't I?'

'Well...ok.' Colin took the wheel. Viv put the winch in position and began to haul the main up the mast. Without the benefit of 2:1 winches, the 1:1 pull was a hard slog. She put her back into it and inch by inch the sail rose.

'Just a few feet more.' Colin yelled encouragement. Viv wound as the rope screamed with the friction.

'Now the headsail.'

This one was relatively easy as the wind caught it and it played out on its own. She tightened the triangle and sat back to catch her breath.

'And the first thing we are getting when we get back is proper winches.'

'Put it on the list honey.' Colin said sucking on a humbug.

They sailed out of Rockingham bay and made their way to the east coast of Hinchinbrook Island and the shipping channel. This channel is a super highway for large carriers to get up and down the

218

coast without having to weave in and out of the Great Barrier Reef. It is well marked on the map and used regularly, 24 hours of the day. The north wind gave Moonlighting a great point of sail as they travelled east, and would have been right behind them as they turned to go south, except it died and they were left wallowing on an oily sea.

'Will you look at that?' Colin shook his head and watched the sails flap like little hankies in the hands of damsels in distress. 'Just when we want to go somewhere...' The boat rolled from side to side and was moving at a snail's pace.

'I'm starting the engine.' Col pressed the dunga into service and they picked up some speed.

'Col...I think we have a big problem.' Viv looked to the horizon.

'What now. It's always a big problem with you Viv.'

'Look.' She pointed to the sea ahead of them. There, in the distance was a rolling front of dark cloud stretching east to west for as far as the eye could see.

'It's just rain.'

'What about the wind before the rain?'

'Mmm.' Colin looked at the ominous cloud formation. 'We should reef the sails and get ready.'

'Reef?'

'Make them smaller Viv. I wish you would learn a few nautical terms.' Colin got to work winding in the headsail and pulling down the main. He had seen the little pieces of cord tied to the main and now knew they were for lashing the sail to the boom. The wind picked up from the south as the front gathered pace.

The sea kicked up in front of the rain and it didn't take long for the once smooth surface to start jumping and waves to build with white caps on top. Vivian grabbed tight to the wheel as the boat battled the sea.

An impending storm can bring a lump to the throat of even an experienced sailor. Now as Moonlighting bounced and bucked the Tripps steeled their nerves. A few spots of rain hit the deck, then the squall took a good look at the hapless pair and decided to have some fun. There were big bloppy drops, stinging needles of rain, torrential dumps and everything in between. Viv clung on keeping her head and a steady course as Colin watched their sails. He doubted the strength of the mains lashings and the tractor patch. Every whipping motion brought a wince as he held his breath. It didn't take long for his fears to be realised. First one, then two and it was all over. The lashings gave way and the mainsail began to spill out of its bindings and grabbed by the wind it climbed up the mast by itself.

'Hell's bells.' The Tripps were now in deep trouble. 'Viv, get the thingo, and pull the what's it and I'll go to the thingimy with the doflanger.' Colin shouted.

'What?'

'The thingo.' Colin pointed in his panic.

As a wife, there are certain times when it is wise just to bite your tongue. Vivian had the uncontrollable urge to remind Colin to use nautical terms 'because you just don't know what is required', but she clamped her mouth shut.

'THERE' Colin pointed to the bungy cord bag. She threw the bag at him and went back to steering. Colin climbed up to the boom and acted like a hero, pulling in the escaping sail and tying it up with stretchy cords. When he had tamed the beast, he flopped down in the cockpit and hung on. Viv had by this time sized up the sea and was steering in anticipation of the next wave like an expert.

'Nice one Viv.' Colin sat back and let the rain soak him through. The squall finally petered out and a steady south east wind took its place.

'We did it Viv. Our first storm.' Colin let out a breath.

'You did wonderfully darling.' Viv kissed her husband.

'And you did great honey.' Colin kissed his wife.

'I think we need a new sail, don't you?'

'Put it on the list.'

As the day progressed they fell into an easy rhythm sailing, eating and talking about the things they realised they needed to make Moonlighting a better boat. There was a fair amount of Barb said, John said, Bob told me, Norma showed me and with an optimism that comes with inexperience it all seemed just a matter of ordering what they wanted and

'It can't be *that* expensive, can it?'

Vivian had read about the need for watches at night and so they divided up the night into 4-hour

stints. They went through the navigation at night, checked out the GPS options, and collected the cup of soups and lollies and all those little necessities that can keep you awake and focussed. The sun set and Vivian went to bed and tried to sleep. She closed her eyes and really tried. She tossed, turned and plumped up her pillow. She lay on her back, front, side, but was still awake. She cleaned her teeth and put on a nightie, but it was no good. She lay in the gloom and listened to the boat shooshing through the water. Some say a micro nap is as good as the real thing. Viv dropped off for 5 minutes then woke up refreshed. Her watch was starting in half an hour and so she joined Colin in the cockpit.

'Did you sleep?'

'Sort of. Where are we?' Viv looked at the GPS. They were passing the southern end of the island.

'I decided that the channel was too far out and so we have come back in a bit.' Viv looked at the map.

'What are those?' she pointed to the little dots on the map.

'They are the beacon lights. They flash at a designated rate and so you know which ones you are looking at.'

'Oh.'

'Right, I'm off to bed.' Colin said. He had the unnerving habit of dropping off to sleep in a heartbeat. Sometimes Vivian could be talking to him and he would just nod off. She watched him disappear into the cabin and then was alone with the stars, the moon and the sea. It can be a magical time as the phosphorescence lights up the water and the mind works overtime. Viv imagined what it would be like for Captain Cook and his crew,

222

sailing the waters for the first time. Strange noises from the mainland, dark unfamiliar shapes on the horizon. She imagined the sailors taking their shifts, just like her and looking at exactly the same night sky and the mainland. The sea brings a connection to history, a shared experience. Night sailing is also a time for ghosts. Viv settled in to steer and checked her course. Everything was good. She opened a boiled sweet and a noise startled her. It sounded like a cat crying. She stood up and looked around. She concentrated and waited. Nothing. Her mind began to imagine sailor's souls crying from the deep. Davy Jones taking them to his locker, or maybe people waiting to pay the ferryman to cross the river Styx. All manner of thoughts ran through her head as she sat all alone on the ocean. She began to talk to herself.

'Don't be silly. It's just the wind.' She had made a thermos of soup and now poured a cup and sipped trying to keep busy, lest her mind wander again. The course on the GPS plotter was marked in a blue line and Viv did some mental arithmetic to calculate how long it would take to the next waypoint. She followed the line and then scrolled further down and saw a set of beacons on the map. *Right*, she thought, *I'll look for them.* The sea lulled her into a dreamy state, the gentle rhythm of the boat and the quiet can reset your life compass and make you realise you are just a small part of a bigger picture. Viv watched the water and sighed. Her watch was coming to the end and in the 4 hours she had made a mental list of 'to do' when they arrived back in Townsville. She also rearranged the front garden bed, made a resolution to lose weight and worked out an exercise regime, tried to remember all the car rego numbers she had ever had, then the telephone numbers, figured out what she would do with a million dollars if she won the lottery and wondered why she didn't run for prime minister when she was younger. All in all, it was a busy watch. Colin's waypoint beeped and Vivian stood up to look for the beacons. She saw a flashing light and counted.

'One second on, three seconds off. No, two on, two off. No, three on, one off.' This was getting confusing. She was concentrating when Colin appeared.

'I can see a beacon Col, but I can't figure it out. One on, one off. No, that's three on and one off then two on and one off.' She shook her head and tisked.

'Let me look at the map and you call it.' Colin took up the position in front of the chartplotter.

'One, no two on and one off.'

'Nup.'

'One on, one off, one on three off.'

'You must be making it up.'

'No, look there.' Viv pointed and as Colin stood up a firefly zipped past their faces and was gone.

'Well, will you look at that?' He giggled and Viv joined in.

The steady wind kept up all night as they took their watches and dawn broke just as there was a shift change. The morning sun comes as a soft glow on the horizon, a comforting heliotrope and the promise of another day. The Tripps watched and basked in the sight.

'Amazing.' Vivian wrapped her arms around Colin and they sat watching the day begin. 'Give me a couple of hours and then we will have a slap-up breakfast.' She went to bed. This time there was no mistaking what she was in bed for. Her mind had already done all the lists and she dropped off into the land of nod.

Colin steered a course for Great Palm and enjoyed the command of the boat. He watched the sun rise and marvelled at the feeling of being on the ocean. There were a few niggling things that needed to be fixed on the boat and he had already decided to tackle some of the more pressing jobs as soon as he was back on the berth. One thing that was particularly annoying was the companionway doors. They were ill fitting and banged...and banged...and banged. He looked at them and let them know in no uncertain terms that their days were numbered. The starboard side gave a bang in protest. Next on the list were the winch handles. They were stiff and hard to use. And he would get rid of that snarling handle stuck in the winch. It had caught him in the nether regions for the last time. He gave it a withering stare. He remembered what John and Barb had said.

'Sailing should be fun, not a chore.'

'Fun,' he repeated. A wave caught the boat and she rolled from side to side and the door banged.

'Right. That's it. You're gone.' He left the helm and strode to the door and wrenched it off its hinges and in a mad ecstasy of vengeance threw the door overboard. It speared into the water and then turned back with the wave action and came straight for the hull. Colin heard a loud thud.

'Bastard.' He looked as it sunk out of sight. 'And don't think you can just hang there,' he said to the other door. 'Just you try it.' He went back to the wheel and the winch handle jabbed at his leg with some sort of death wish.

'Oh, want to play rough eh?' Colin looked at the winch handle. He kicked out at the thing and then kept kicking until it came loose. Then he tugged and pulled and swore blue murder and it eventually came out from its hold on the winch.

'HA!' Colin threw the handle over the side and felt like a man in control. Someone watching on the sidelines might disagree. He did a little jig and felt a kind of release, knowing he had just won an important victory. He narrowed his gaze as he took up the steering position again and he figured he saw other equipment, some well past their use by date cower in fear.

'Aw, what the heck.' He spat on his hands and wrenched off the other door and gave it the ol' heave ho.

'Captain Tripp.' He tried out the moniker for size. In his estimation it was a perfect fit.

'Who's next?' He looked around the cockpit. There staring at him was the drink holder. He knew Vivian liked it, but it didn't actually fit a cup, a can or a bottle. Another useless piece of junk. It glared at him and he glared back. He tried to think of something else. He looked at the horizon, fiddled with the GPS, checked their progress, and ate a lollie, but the drink holder, he felt, was mocking him. Vivian would know it was missing. He tried to think of an excuse.

He tried one out for size. 'It was getting in the way.' She would know that was a lie. 'I accidently knocked it off.' That sounded better. 'It was just a useless piece of junk.' This last one was the truth and the truth may hurt, but it was for the best. He gave the holder a good whack with another winch handle and it pulled out, screws and all.

'Sayonara.' He consigned it to the deep. His lust for supreme commander sated, he sucked on a lemon sherbet and sat back to steer and enjoy the day. As far as Colin Tripp was concerned he had done the boat a favour, now he just had to tell his wife that parts of the boat were strewn all over the Coral Sea.

Vivian appeared in the doorway to an effusive Colin.

'Morning darling, did you sleep well. You look rested and everything. It's a lovely day. Do you want me to make breakfast?' Vivian frowned. She knew her husband well enough to know something was up.

'I'll make breakfast Col.' She looked at him and he giggled. He made a show of steering and looking at the compass. Nothing was immediately obvious and so she busied herself downstairs. Presently Viv came up with cheese and mushroom omelettes and coffee and put them on the cockpit table. Colin looked at his wife trying to guess if she would notice. She narrowed her gaze.

'Colin?'

'Yes dear?' Colin said as he hid behind his cup of coffee. 'Nice breakfast Viv. Top notch.'

'Colin?'

'What?'

'Where is the drinks holder?'

'The drinks holder Viv?' Colin said in a lilting voice.

'Yes. The drinks holder.' Viv waited for the explanation.

'Oh, *that* drinks holder.'

'Hmm.' Viv raised her eyebrows in expectation.

'Well it's like this...I was just sitting here and I had the idea that because it didn't actually perform a proper function, and was a bit of a hit and miss thing and that it wasn't actually very good at all and probably wasn't teak or anything and probably came from China or something and well...' Colin took the bull by the horns. 'I threw it away.'

'What?'

'Gone.' He thumbed overboard. Colin, for a moment thought he should come completely clean about the magazine rack, but that was taking honesty a little too far. Vivian looked around and asked,

'And the winch handle?'

'Gone.'

'And...' She looked at the wrenched hinges where the companionway doors had been.

'Gone.' Colin tittered and shrugged his shoulders and tucked into his omelette while steering with his feet. 'Look honey, love, darling. We need to get sensible with the boat. We can't have things that don't work properly. We have to be more canny than that. It's got to be practical.' Colin came out with the homily that he would often repeat. 'Boating is supposed to be fun, not a chore.' Vivian looked at the winch sans handle.

'Remember when Ted copped it.' She pointed and smirked. Colin laughed at the memory.

'And remember when I ripped my trousers.' Viv snickered.

'Good job.' She smiled and gave Col a high five.

'Any more coffee Viv.'

Moonlighting made good progress and the Tripps landed back at Great Palm Island and Casement Bay in the early afternoon. They anchored in the same spot, remembering to put down plenty of chain and felt after an all-nighter they needed to relax. The wind took a breather as well and everything was quiet, peaceful and calm.

'Col.' Viv found him sitting in the cockpit with the binoculars.

'What ya want hon?'

'I was just making a list. A list of things we need. Things we need to go on a trip.' Vivian started.

'Yeah.'

'And we need a lot of things. Things like a holding tank for the toilet, new winches, windlass, sails and who knows what else, and I was just wondering if Moonlighting would be suitable for a trip. You know a big trip and I was just thinking that we would have to do such a lot of work and everything.'

'What are you trying to say?' Col asked.

'Well...it seems to me that we would be better getting a different boat. One that is a cruiser. A blue water cruiser.'

'You mean sell Moonlighting?'

'Well...it's just a thought.' Viv shrugged her shoulders.

The thought was there and the seed had been planted. Viv looked at Colin and waited.

'I was reading there is a boat show coming up and I think it would be a good idea to just see what we need.' Viv said.

'Shopping?'

'Well, we can just go and look. No harm in looking is there? And there're any amount of experts too. Barb said they never miss a boat show 'cause they have all the new gear and stuff.'

'Stuff?' Colin could see there might be big bucks involved.

'Oh, you know. Wet weather gear, shoes, waterproof map bags, telephone bags and then there's all the big stuff. Engines, GPS stuff and other stuff like toilets.'

'Mmmm.'

'And binoculars Col. Really nice binoculars.' Vivian added trying to sweeten the deal.

They drank a beer at the end of the day and disappeared into their own daydreams. Viv was sailing the seas in matching wet weather gear and Colin was eating steak, chips and eggs.

A little experience goes a long way and the sail back to the marina might have been into the wind, but to the Tripps it was a magical journey. They had seen things, done things and experiences things that whetted their appetite for more. Their confidence grew with each nautical mile and as they rounded Orchid rocks on the edge of Magnetic Island they felt like real sea faring folk. A pod of dolphins cruised in their bow wave and Vivian squealed as she took photos. The dolphins were having fun and then they peeled off and began feeding on a shoal of fish. Birds came into the mix and the sea boiled with frenetic energy as the Tripps looked on.

'Wow, look at that.' Col pointed to a very large bird circling above the crowd below.

'Is it an albatross?' Viv asked.

'Don't know.' They watched the bird soar and dive, soar and dive for fish and then it came in close and was going to land on the rigging.

'It's going to sit on the spreader. Quick Viv take a photo, this is amazing.' Col pointed. The sea bird with big feet came in and in a clumsy attempt to land slipped and its foot wedged in the rigging and it was stuck. It squawked and flapped and shat all over the deck.

'What are we going to do?' Viv could see the bird was frantic. It was getting exhausted as it tried to free itself. She began to yell and wave her arms about which made the bird even more frightened and it regurgitated its dinner. A shower of pre-digested fish hit the deck.

'Aw, that's not nice.' Viv screwed up her nose at the smell. 'Col, any suggestions'

'I don't know.' Col said trying to look up and steer at the same time. The bird gave up and dangled, swaying from side to side as the boat sailed on.

'I think it's dead.' Viv peered through the binoculars as the mess began to stink of fish.

'I bet it's a bad omen or something.' Col said.

'Not a good look coming into the marina with a dead bird stuck on the rigging and stinking fish all over the boat.' They looked at the hitchhiker. It was dead.

The remainder of the trip Viv sluiced the deck trying to get rid of the smell and then as they neared Hope Basin Marina she took over the helm and Colin made ready with the fenders and lines.

'I just want to turn around and go back out, don't you?' Col stood next to Viv and sighed.

'I don't want it to end.' They looked at the breakwater coming up fast.

'It was magic, wasn't it?'

'Sure was.'

The Tripps had fallen in love with the sea.

 CHAPTER 17

With the holiday over, the boat scrubbed, the extra spam donated to the local charity, the bird unhooked and given a burial at sea and the sunburn healed, the Tripps felt deflated. Oh, there were plenty of jobs to do, but nothing excited them like talking about travelling to exotic locations. They dreamed about adventure. Vivian hunted out books from the library on women who had downsized their Tupperware and swapped sensible shoes for a sarong. Colin read cruising guides and studied maps of prevailing winds and they made plans.

'We need a whole lot of things Colin.' Vivian was reading a sailing magazine. 'And you know, the boat show is in a few weeks. We could go for the long weekend.'

'Is it expensive?'

'Not really, considering all the things we can see in the one spot.'

'Hmmm.'

'So...?'

'Ok.' Colin said. Vivian jumped up and kissed her husband. If she was going to a boat show she needed some advice from her girlfriends on the dock so as to maximize her time.

'I'll be going down to the boat tomorrow Col, anything you want me to do?'

'Can't think of anything.' Colin picked up the magazine and began reading about anodes.

Vivian strolled down the dock and knocked on Connie's boat.

'Yoohoo,' she called.

'Hi luv, what's up?'

'Colin and I are going to the boat show and I was just wondering if you knew much about them?'

'Step aboard honey.' Connie smiled and ushered Vivian inside. When she emerged two hours later she had the lowdown on boat show specials, freebies and how to grind the stall holders down. All in all, it had been a productive morning and Viv felt ready to tackle her first boat show.

'Over there,' Viv pointed to the sign for designated parking.

'$5.00 for parking. I'm not paying that.' Colin balked at highway robbery.

'Well, we are here now, so just pay up.' Viv handed over a $5.00 dollar note. They joined a growing gaggle of people all heading for the turnstile.

'I didn't think there would be so many people.' Colin joined the queue.

'Oh yes. These things are mega popular.' Viv had the voice of someone who knows everything
234

about boat shows. Colin grumped at the admission price and then they entered boating heaven. Vivian consulted the map of stall holders.

'Shall we do the hall first?' Colin was led like a lamb to the slaughter.

The hall had all the electronic gadgets. Viv and Col pushed their way in the door and were assaulted by radar, GPS, radio and fish finders all blinking and winking. They walked up to the first stall and browsed the latest fish finders pressing buttons and marvelling at the 3D clarity.

'Looking to buy something today?' the salesman slid up to the pair. Viv smiled and let the man do his spiel. They came away with a small show bag and a key ring each. As they moved down the line there were more key rings, hats, badges and vouchers. Colin began to get into the groove and instead of looking at the wares on offer he was on the lookout for freebies.

'Over here Viv, they have pencils.' He pretended to be interested in a timeshare for a mega-yacht, eyeing off the pencils. They did the rounds of the hall and then went to sit down and consolidate their booty.

'Five key rings, two hats, a few drink coasters, a stubby cooler and a pencil.' Colin looked at his loot.

'Three stubby coolers, a bottle opener, a tube of glue and two key rings.' Viv added. 'Plus, all the reading material on the latest and greatest.'

'Did you see that radar?' Col pointed to the picture in his magazine. 'Amazing stuff.'

'And did you know that they have those new radios on show specials. You actually save heaps of money by coming to the show.' The day was shaping up nicely. On the way out Vivian found herself squashed next to a stall selling toilets.

Sanitation Hygiene Instillation Technician the banner read. She pulled Colin from the throng and the Tripps were collared by,

'Max Blenheim at your service.'

'Oh, hello.' Viv smiled.

'Looking for a solution to your problem?' Max asked.

'Well...' Colin looked at the apparatus on the stall table. 'What is that?'

'Glad you asked my friend.' Max began to explain the intricacies of his unit 'The Super Pooper. There were plungers, plugs, through valves, one-way valves and syphons. Colin nodded a couple of times and let out a titter.

'Er. Mr Blenheim, we need a holding tank.' Viv said.

'Not really Madam. If you have our product it processes the poo and passes through.

'Really?'

'Yes. And I know you're going to ask if it is regulation. Well let me assure you it has all the documentation you will need.' Max then went into overdrive on the poo situation. He gabbled on about bacteria, types of diseases, different types of systems to deal with it, how to neutralize it, how to capture it, and how to dispose of it.

'Oh.' Viv looked at the contraption. Colin fingered the dials and buttons. Max showed the Tripps how easy it was to install, how simple it was to use and how friendly it would make the boat smell. The last bit won Vivian and she gave Colin 'the look'. Colin had seen 'the look' before and knew his wife well enough to know she was sold. He looked at the banner and it occurred to him that the first letters spelt something not wholly unrelated to the product on sale.

'*S*anitation *H*ygiene *I*nstillation *T*echnician.' he giggled and nudged Vivian. His wife was bargaining like she was buying a Turkish rug at the souk. The price went up, down, up, down and then Max started to throw in some extras. Viv was a hard woman when it came to price and she wheedled some chlorine tabs, some toilet paper and some electrical wiring before she was finished. The deal was done and the Tripps walked away with a new holding and processing facility. It was heavy and so Colin suggested they leave it at the stall and pick it up later. Max, at this stage, would have agreed to throwing in a leprechaun to get rid of the woman. Vivian took Colin's arm,

'Ask me anything Col. Anything at all about poo, 'cause I think I know it all now.' The Tripps moved on glowing in the knowledge that their poo was taken care of and stopped at the back of a crowd. Colin tried to see what everyone was looking at. He muscled to the front to see a sand pit with tiny little anchors in it and people having a go at setting them.

'It's anchors Viv,' he threw the comment back to Viv who was still stuck in the rear. Viv squeezed to the front and saw Colin pick up a dinky anchor and drag it through the sand pit. It just ploughed a furrow.

'That's a plough, or a CQR.' The salesman said as Col tried to get the anchor to dig in.

Colin thought on his anchor. He huffed and puffed and then opened his eyes wide in a sort of epiphany.

'CQR, CQR. That means secure doesn't it. Viv it really means se-cu-re. Do you get it?'

'Oh, I see.' Viv looked at the salesman and smiled.' I think we have one of those.' Viv pointed.

'Chances are Madam. Ever dragged?' Sam the salesman whispered as if talking about underwear stains in mixed company. Vivian nodded and frowned.

'Well they are just about the worst anchors around. Cheap.' Sam shook his head and saw the Tripps hanging off his every word. 'What you need is this.' He steered the Tripps to the display and showed them the latest in ground tackle. The anchor looked like a stealth jet, all wings and sharp bits and was black.

'Oh, it looks great.' Colin felt his life wouldn't be complete without one, but when he found out the price he changed his mind.

'Er, anything in the grotty yachty range?' Colin asked. Sam took a step back like he'd just stepped in something a bit smelly and needed to get as far away as possible.

'No.'

'Anything that is...foolproof.' Viv asked. Sam looked at the Tripps and thought the last description was an apt one.

'This.' He pointed out an anchor that was set and forget. 'The Manson Supreme will do you.'

'How much?' Viv looked at the monster. 'Oh, that much!' Viv nudged Colin who couldn't believe something so ordinary as an anchor could cost that much. The Tripps started to back away.

'Look,' Sam came in for the kill. 'Do you

want to feel safe? Do you want to go to bed and not worry? Do you want to keep your boat or see it on the rocks? It's a simple equation. Buy now and save yourself salvage fees later.' Sam raised his eye brows and smirked. He had the Tripps hook, line and sinker.

'Well...' Colin fiddled with the anchor. 'I guess...'

'So, listen,' Sam came in close. 'How about I give you my card. You are coming tomorrow, right? Well, I'll let you sleep on it. Come and see me for a show special tomorrow. We might be able to do a deal.' At the mention of a deal Viv's ears pricked up.

'Ok.' Colin took the card. Sam knew they'd be back.

Next they hit the apparel and home-ware pavilion.

Women outnumbered men two to one as the Tripps pushed through the crowds. They tried on lifelines and life vests and jackets, very expensive jackets.

'Col, this one has a life vest in it.' Viv did a twirl in a red jacket.'

'And I like all the zips and pockets on this one.' Col put his hands all over the place. The saleswoman hovered as the Tripps looked like they were going to buy.

'These are show specials,' the woman said trying to ease Vivian out of the one thousand dollar sailing jacket.

'Hmm.' Viv hung on for another look in the mirror. 'It's very comfortable isn't it?' she smiled. The woman, who had more than a few boat shows on her résumé, knew the Tripps were just lightweights and whipped the jacket off Vivian like a Marx Brother pulling a tablecloth from a dinner service.

'Oh,' Viv giggled and moved on.

'Look Col, shoes!' If there was one thing Vivian knew about, it was shoes. She loved shoes, but Colin put a cap on her shoe wardrobe at six. Viv pranced around in sailing boots, loafers, cut sole deck shoes, slip-on non-slips and crocs. Colin tried on sailing shoes, reef shoes and lifetime guarantee sandals. They each came away with sandals in their own little zip bag. The hat stand took a particularly savage going over as Colin became a Greek fisherman, a stockman, a sea dog, a trawler skipper and a deep-sea marlin fisherman. He found a cap that had Galley Slave and one for himself that said Captain and handed over his money. Vivian fancied herself in a sailing hat that was waterproof, floated and had a rather nifty string arrangement. They bought two and wore them straight away.

Then Viv saw a cooking demonstration about to begin. They floated over to the stand and were mesmerized by the patter. The patented slow cooker, they were told, was a time saver, a fuel saver, and a lifesaver. It could cook, boil, broil, bake, had a rack and could stack. Vivian squeezed Colin's arm as she was sucked in by the versatility of the pot, for when it all boiled down, it was just a pot.

'Oh, Col.' Viv bit her lip and put on her puppy in distress look. She waited for Col to respond. Nothing. 'I could do roast pork. Beef stew. Meatballs.' She waited and watched the women line up to buy.

'I guess...' That was all Viv needed as she

scooted to the end of the queue.

With her purchase under her arm, her show bags hanging off her elbow and her hat on her head she moved along to crockery and gadgets.

'How about lunch?' Colin could feel his stomach grumbling. Viv felt her life wouldn't be complete without looking at crockery, but could see Colin was flagging.

'Alright.' They pushed their way to the outside and gasped for air. 'What would you like?' Viv knew that the way to a man's wallet is through his stomach. There was a fair size line up for Texas Ribs, but they were worth the wait. Now the Tripps sat on a couple of steps in the shade and enjoyed.

'Over there,' Viv consulted her map, 'is the water exhibits. You can go on the boats and see how they look, straight from the factory.' She wiped her mouth and it watered in anticipation of seeing what a real blue-water set up should look like.

'Shall we go?' Viv stood up.

'I just want to see the engines Viv. How about we meet back here in an hour?' It was a sound plan and they split up their bank balance. Viv went to crockery and gadgets and Colin went to the big fella's end of town. He talked engines, gearboxes and soon realised he shouldn't mention his Lister two cylinder if he didn't want to be laughed at. He also collected a few more hats. If he didn't actually have a Mercedes or a CAT, he could still look the part. Col let the MTU man take his particulars just to get a t-shirt and promised he would be in touch when he needed to re-power.

Viv came back to their designated spot with a few small purchases.

'And this one is for the grab bag.' She showed the flip-o-matic.

'What does it do?'

'Well...it's an essential tool. Prising oysters, opening lids, that sort of thing.'

'Wouldn't a screw driver so the same.'

'Well...yes, technically, but this has a plastic handle.' She popped it in her goody bag. 'And this thing.'

'What is it?'

'It's for opening things.'

'But I thought we just went through this.'

'No. This is for other things.' Viv could see she wasn't getting much support and left her other bits and pieces for later.

'Oh, and I found a drink holder. One size that fits all. I tried it and it really does.'

'Nice one Viv.'

'And I found a stall that you really must see.'

'What is it?'

'Wait, just wait Colin Tripp.' Vivian led her husband by the hand through the crowds and they ended up in front of a stand selling binoculars, monoculars, telescopes and the like. She smiled at the salesman and pushed Colin forward. The salesman took a breath. He extolled the virtues of a decent set of binoculars. Colin listened and then the acid test came. The man handed Colin a cheap pair and asked him to look. Colin took the challenge.

'Not bad.' He handed the pair back.

'Now try these.'

'WOW.' Colin staggered back and took another look.

'See the difference?' The salesman asked.

'Sure can. Viv you should look.' He handed the instruments over to his wife.

'Crikey.' Viv couldn't believe it. She had budgeted for a nice pair, but these were too good to put down. Colin looked at the price tag and coughed.

'Lifetime guarantee.' The man said.

'Colin, I really want these for you. They will *just* last a lifetime.' Viv enthused. The man nodded.

'But Viv the price.'

'I have put some away. We can afford it.' She nudged Colin who had the binoculars around his neck in the first step of ownership.

'We'll take them.' The salesman eased the binos away from Colin and packed them in a case.

'You won't regret it.'

'Thanks darling.' Colin carried his expensive present like a young father with a newborn baby.

'Now we need go to the toilet.'

'Nah, I'm right.' Colin said.

'No, to pick it up.'

'Oh, right.' They traipsed back to the S.H.I.T. stand and collected their Super Pooper.

'What about the anchor Colin?' Colin pursed his lips. He hated the thought of sailing with something inferior, something that would give them trouble and endless sleepless nights. *But the money, oh the money.*

'Well?' Viv was ripe for a bit of bargaining.

'Do you really think we need a new one?' Col asked his wife. She nodded.

'Foolproof Colin.'

Sam saw them coming.

Loaded up, pushing a boat show courtesy

trolley and heading for the car park, Colin stopped, applied his binoculars to the vast parking area and spotted the car.

'Over there.' he pointed. 'You should take a look Viv.' And Vivian would have, had Colin actually let go of his Nitrogen filled, actualized prism, German made, lifetime guarantee binoculars which were firmly strung around his neck.

Back at their hotel room, for the Tripps had decided to make the boat show a two-day excursion, they spread their booty on the bed.

'Not bad for one day.'

'And tomorrow we can do the water.'

The second day at the boat show is always the biggest as it usually falls on a Saturday. Col and Viv lined up to get in the two-day pass gate and felt like boat show experts. They walked the alleyways past the kayaks, dinghies, small sailboats and runabouts looking at cool boxes, eskies and fishing gear. Colin took a liking to a mackerel reel that was the size of a hubcap and bolted onto the back rail.

'Fish do you?' The salesman came in on Colin's musings.

'Well, we try.' Col looked at the reel and then tittered as he was put on the spot.

'This is a sure winner. The Gladiator 350 has...' and the man went on for a good ten minutes describing the reel.

'So, what sort of craft do you have?'

'Well, it's a yacht actually.' The Salesman took a step back like Colin has just spat at him.

'The Gladiator trolls at 7- 15 knots buster.'

'Oh.' Colin backed away.

'You grotty yachties. You come in here like you know something. Wasting my time. Asking questions. Why don't you just shove it?' The Tripps hot footed it out of earshot and ducked behind a stall selling t-shirts. Vivian giggled and Col tittered. They stood up when the coast was clear and looked at the t-shirts.

'Grotty Yachty,' we gotta have one of those.' Viv purchased two.

The water display is a Mecca for dreamers. The Tripps climbed aboard a 44-foot Beneteau leaving their shoes on the dock, which had as many shoes as Friday prayers at a Mosque. They stepped into another world. Modular furniture, leather seats, all mod cons crowded their senses. Viv touched everything and came out onto the deck with a frown.

The next boat was a Swedish design and was brimming over with wood grain. It had fancy cupboards, a walk-in wardrobe and a bathroom to die for. Viv began to feel dissatisfied with her lot.

'Colin, we need to talk.'

'Huh?' Colin was looking at the hydraulic back swimming platform with the remote control. They moved on down the dock looking at what half a million dollars can get you, or in some cases three quarters of a mil.

The motor boats had even more luxury and Vivian stopped trying to compare apples and oranges.

'Don't forget Viv, we *own* our boat.'

'Oh, I know Colin, but I would like a bit of a makeover. Perhaps just a few things here and there.' They stepped off a 50ft yacht that had a bath and a bar.

'Let's go and get a drink.' Colin led Viv to the beer tent. Over a cold one they gushed about the possibilities on Moonlighting. The things they could do with what they had. Vivian was all for ripping out the guts and starting afresh, Colin could see they needed to start with a new engine.

'But you know Viv, what we really should be doing is looking for a different boat.' Suddenly the kernel of the idea Viv had planted just a few weeks ago showed promise, only now it was Colin's idea.

'But it would have to fulfil our criteria Colin. We would need something that can take us where we want to go.'

'Yeah.' Colin drank his beer and wondered if the beer would be as cold and delicious in Thailand.

After water world the Tripps took one last look at the halls and Vivian steered Colin towards the windlass counter.

'We are just looking Col.' They walked around the display and an old salesman came up.

'Looking for a new one? Jim's the name.'

'Maybe.' Colin fiddled with the controls on a shiny new machine.

'What have you got?'

'A yacht, 10mm chain and the blasted thing keeps slipping off.'

'Mmm. Old chain.'

'No actually it's brand new chain.'

'Mmm. What's your windlass?'

246

'An American thing. Florida Engine Co.'

'Mmm.' Jim pondered as the Tripps waited. 'Well, there is your problem. I bet you have 10mm chain on a 3/8th gypsy.'

'I was told it was the same.' Colin remembered Rowdy saying exactly that.

'Nope.' Jim shook his head. 'Slight difference. 3/8th is 9.5mm not 10mm. Jumping off every 10 metres or so is it?' Colin nodded and sighed.

'That's what it is then.' The Tripps looked at one another as they remembered the trouble they had had with the chain. It was an experience they would rather not repeat.

'So, what's the solution Jim?'

'Get yourself a new gypsy or some 3/8th chain. Or a new windlass, but really by the sound of it you have already forked out a heap of money on the chain. I would suggest you find a 10mm gypsy.'

'Thanks Jim.'

'No worries.'

Colin hovered. 'Ah, Jim...' he began.' You look like a man who knows a thing or two.'

'Well you might say that.'

'Well we,' and Colin introduced Vivian to the conversation. 'We were trying to decide what to do.' and Col went on to outline their thinking. Do they get another boat or try to fix Moonlighting?

'How old are you Colin?' Jim asked and then went on. 'Now what do you want to do with your life? Fix a boat or use it. Just think what you could be doing if you already had a boat that could take you where you want to go.' Jim smiled and stepped back.

'He's right you know.' Viv said as they walked

back to the car. The drive home gave them plenty of opportunity to mull over their predicament. They loved Moonlighting. It was their first boat, but one boat show and one long sailing holiday and their goals had changed, they had matured. There would be a heap of work to do to get Moonlighting into a saleable condition. They realised that they had been duped by the broker Mr Lightfoot, but as Viv put it,

'We climbed a steep learning curve with Moonlighting, now at the top of the curve we can see the horizon and beyond.

'What?' Colin couldn't quite see the analogy, but knew one thing. Whatever it was, it was going to cost money.

FIG. 133.—Matthew Walker
(complete).

CHAPTER 18

Back on the dock the Tripps looked at Moonlighting and felt like they had won the booby prize. Their eyes were still sparkling from the boat show and nothing they saw in their ferro boat came close to what they wished for.

One of the first jobs was to rouse out Rowdy about the chain. Colin marched up to the chandlery and pushed the door open expecting to see Rowdy behind the counter picking something off his body or out of an orifice. A young girl popped up from behind the counter instead.

'Where's Rowdy,' Colin asked a little taken aback.

'He's in hospital.'

'What?'

'Yep, he's got a hernia. Tried to lift something and poof. Hernia. I'm Summer.' She held out her hand. 'What can I do for you?' Colin wasn't quite sure what a slip of a girl could know or do, but tried to explain his story to her. She nodded and listened.

'So, have you tried the internet yet?' Colin shook his head. 'Here let's take a look.' She swung the computer screen around so Colin could see and started to search. It took all of 10 seconds to find Colin's windlass and the spare parts list.

'Amazing.'

'See, a 10mm gypsy. If you want to order it, I can have it delivered to the shop. That way there is less freight and stuff.'

'Ok.' Colin was captivated by this young girl.

'Do you want to go ahead?' He nodded and smiled. 'Anything else?' Summer asked.

'Well, I was thinking about slipping. We have a skin fitting that's a bit wobbly and we just thought that we might do the job out of the water. Where do you think I should go?' Colin knew of the boat yard where they did their antifouling, but there was another one around about the place. Summer considered the question.

'Well, depends on how much you want to spend.' The conversation ranged over the various options with Summer adding her considerable knowledge. She looked up the rates on the internet and even rang to ascertain if there were available spaces. It was service Colin wasn't used to and he was completely under her spell.

He came back to the boat and gushed to Viv.

'Summer said this, Summer said that, Summer suggested something else.' Viv held up her hand for Colin to stop and draw breath.

'So where is Rowdy?'

'Hospital, hernia. Summer said he might be away for some time.'

'Oh, I hope it's not serious.'

'Summer doesn't seem to think so.'

'Oh. 'Did you ask about the gypsy Col?'

'It's sorted. Summer ordered a new part. Just

like that.' He clicked his fingers.

'I see.'

'And I asked about slipping. If we want to make Moonlighting presentable...*if* we are going to sell her, we need to take a look at that wobbly skin fitting.'

'I agree...*if* we want to sell, we need to do a few things.' The Tripps were circling the acorn of an idea, but in reality the seed had grown and now the sapling was taking hold. No-one wanted to be the first to say 'let's do it', but they were thinking it all the same.

The slipway could take Moonlighting on the high tide on the 20th. It was ringed on the calendar in the kitchen. Whereas the boatyard had a travel lift with slings, the slipway had a cradle and railway tracks. Colin had stipulated that he only wanted to be out for a few days and so it was decided they could stay in the cradle and not have to be craned to a spot in the yard.

'It's cheaper that way,' he said to Viv. Colin forgot to mention to the slipway owner that he wasn't the Sultan of Brunei nor did he have a share portfolio to match the Big Four Banks.

Ted knocked on the back door and let himself in,

'What's cheaper?' he asked as he came in on the tail end of the conversation.

'We are going on the slipway next week and it's cheaper than the other boatyard.' Colin pointed to

251

the calendar.

'Well, don't you worry about that Col. I've seen how these things operate and I can give you a hand.'

'Well...thanks Ted, but...'

'That's settled then.' Ted slapped Colin on the back as Viv rolled her eyes.

'Look Ted, thanks for the offer and all that, but I think we can cope.' Colin grew a bit of a backbone in relation to his pesky neighbour, Ted Gunn.

'And we have to go to sea first Ted. Wasn't the weather a bit bleak for that day Col?' Viv tried to scare Ted off with sea sickness.'

'At sea?'

'Mmm, that's right.'

'You mean in the ocean.'

'Yes.'

'The 20th you say? Too bad.' Viv smirked and winked at Colin.

'Well, won't keep you. Sorry and all that. Darn shame really, cause I've seen these things and well... don't you worry about that.' And with that Ted shot out of the back door over the grass, through the adjoining gate and was gone.

Vivian cracked and began to giggle, then laugh and by the time Col had joined in they were wiping the tears from their eyes.

'Don't you worry about that!' Viv mimicked Ted and they fell into another bout of laughter.

With a week before they needed to slip, Vivian pressed Colin to install the super pooper. They laid out all the necessary bits on the saloon table and Vivian read the instructions. It all seemed quite simple as far as marine toilets go.

252

Vivian read the pamphlet out aloud step by step. They did a mental run through and then Colin went to the head as only one person could fit in the small room at a time. Vivian hovered with tools like an assisting nurse to the surgeon.

'Screwdriver,' Colin held out his hand.

'Darling, I think that hose is below the waterline. Should we close it off maybe?' Viv pointed to a hose that used to be white. Colin tried the skin fitting lever and it wouldn't budge. He leaned into it and it was stuck fast.

'What about a wrench?' Viv tried to see if she could help. Colin put an adjustable spanner on the handle and with the extra leverage he gave it a tug. It moved and so he gave it a good pull. The whole skin fitting ripped off in one action and water began pouring into the boat.

'Ahhhh.' Colin put his hand over the hole and tried to stop the flow.

'What?' Viv tried to see what was going on. 'Has it moved?'

'It's off. It's off.'

'That's good.'

'NO. It's come off. We're sinking.' Colin looked up from his cramped position. 'I need to put something in the hole.' Water was gushing from around Colin's hand as he tried to plug the hole with his palm.

'How big is the hole?' Viv hopped from one foot to the other.

'Get something NOWooowowwwooo.' Colin's back went into a spasm and he let out a yelp.

'Something, something.' Vivian searched around for something to plug a hole of indeterminate size. Nothing sprang to mind. She pulled out the cutlery drawer, looked in the fridge and there looking up at her was a big salami. She grabbed the meat and gave it to Colin.

'What the...' He looked at the sausage and shook his head.

'Just shove it down.' Viv could see the water rising now and began to panic.

'Call the fire brigade Viv. We need a pump.'

'Right.' Viv grabbed the mobile phone and rang triple zero as Colin tried to fit the salami into the hole. It was way too big and kept coming out.

'Which service?' The operator asked.

'We need the fire brigade to bring a big pump.'

'Fire. Is there any danger to life?'

'No, we are sinking.' Vivian didn't want to panic, but the calm attitude of the operator made her feel like the telephonist wasn't taking the emergency seriously enough.

'We need a big pump, NOW!' Viv gave the address and then offered to take over from Colin as his back went into contortions. They swapped places, Vivian holding the salami in place as Colin hobbled up the stairs and onto the dock. He could hear a siren in the distance and struggled, clutching his back to the locked gate to let the emergency services people in. A police car rolled up.

'Hi, do you have a pump?' Colin asked expectantly. The policeman and policewoman took it in turns to squeeze through the gate as their utility belts made it impossible to go side by side. Colin hovered as they asked his name, his boats name, the rego number, his telephone number and did he have email.

'Look, we really need a pump.' The police proceeded to walk down the dock like they were on a Sunday stroll. Colin tried to instil an air of panic in the emergency services personnel. He saw a fire engine roll up. He opened the gate and let the men in.

'Do you have a pump?' he asked. The fireman asked his name, his boats name, the rego number, his telephone number and did he have a fire.

'We need a pump; the boat is sinking.' The firemen, all six, walked down the dock to Moonlighting and joined the police in 'hey there, hi, how's it going, what's up and no way - you here again. Colin hopped about like a man on steroids and said he really needed to go and see his wife who was keeping the water at bay.

'Viv,' Colin jumped onboard and three firemen followed, boots and all.

'Col, the salami is nearly gone.' Viv had been pushing the sausage through the hole and it was disintegrating in the water. Now there was only a nub left and she couldn't stem the flow for much longer. The water was rising fast.

'Step aside sir.' A burly fireman came in and took a look.

'Hello,' He smiled at Vivian who was scrunched up like a pretzel that hadn't quite made the grade.

'Hello,' Viv replied and smiled. 'Do you have a pump?' The fireman looked at the new super pooper which was sitting on the table.

'Good are they?' He pointed to the contraption. Colin was tearing his hair out and ran outside to see a crowd of people watching. He yelled,

'Anyone got a pump?' Max, from Maxamillion

shot off and came back with a big mother of a pump with a lay flat hose. Connie came up with an extension cord and the pump was plugged in, the hose directed to the outside and then put into action. It sucked like its life depended on it and when the water was at a level to see the skin fitting once more Mr Ashcroft came up with a bung. He gave it to Colin and told him to thump it in good and hard. Colin nearly kissed him. As the firemen watched Colin swapped places with Vivian and on the count of three he thumped the wooden bung in. The Tripps emerged and gave the thumbs up. There was a small cheer and then the fireman asked for a blow by blow account of the incident and when they had finished the police came in and went over the whole thing again, scribbling little notes in their books. Colin's address was taken, his occupation, he supplied them with details of when he bought the boat, who sold it to him, where he intended to take it and in a fit of pique Colin asked,

'Do you want to know what I had for tea last night?' The officers, who didn't have a humorous bone in their body, had ticked all the boxes and packed their pencils away.

'Well good luck with that,' the policewoman said and the emergency services dispersed. The dock crowd stayed, as there is nothing like a crisis to bring out the other near misses people have had. The stakes grew ever higher as the stories went from near misses, nearly sinking, sinking, near drownings, complete right offs and a gas explosion. The pump was doing a stirling job and so Colin brought out some beer as a thank you and it was inevitable that the gathering turn into a bit of a dock party. Now the Tripps also had stories to tell including losing the boat in the dark. Colin brought out their boat show purchases, the binoculars were paraded, the super pooper discussed, the anchor was goggled at and Vivian gave the women a quick demo with her pot. Viv and Col felt they had done really well and considered their very smart purchases when someone mentioned the dirty word in boat reno's and repairs.

'Do you think you've overcapitalised?' It was as if someone had farted in a lift. The crowd went quiet and there was a lot of shuffling of feet. It is like an AA meeting. Everyone knows they do it, but no one wants to admit to doing it. Hello, *I'm Colin Tripp and I overcapitalize.* Viv pulled Colin aside,

'Colin, do you think we have overcapitalised?' It was a question Colin didn't want to think about too hard, because he might come up with an answer he didn't like. He coughed and giggled.

'Sheesh, I think we need more beer.' That statement was greeted with a rousing cheer and it turned into a very entertaining afternoon. As Vivian cleaned away the empty beer cans she had decided they needed a pump. A good, sturdy pump and said as much to Colin.

'Put it on the list Viv.'

The pump was returned as the bung was doing its job and the 20th came around. High tide was early in the morning and so Moonlighting was made ready just as the sun came up. Vivian eased the boat from the dock and pulled out into the channel. They had to go around the breakwater and down the creek to the slip to be there at the top of the tide. There had been a reconnoitre the day before, just to make sure, and now Vivian steered to the slipway helped by the incoming tide. They had been told to ring as they rounded the last bend and so Colin followed instructions and rang. There was no answer. He tried again. Nothing.

'No-one is answering Viv.' All the Tripps could do was carry on regardless. They could see the slip in the distance and it looked deserted. No grinding dust, no noise from the compressors, no people mooching about.

'Shall I blow our horn?' Viv steered for the cradle.

'Hang on.' Colin raced downstairs and produced his binoculars. With ocular clarity he could almost see as well as Superman. He scanned the work area and saw a fellow coming out of the toilet. 'These are great Viv. I can see the buttons on his shirt.'

'So someone is there then?'

'Yup.'

Moonlighting eased its bulk into the cradle, which had been lowered into the water. The slipway rouse about waved his arms like a semaphore signalman on heroin. The drug of choice not too far from the truth. Vivian wasn't quite sure if his name was Dougie or Druggie. She tried her best to get the boat in the middle as Frank/owner/manager looked like he was signalling how to make fried rice while umpiring football. Finally Moonlighting came to a stop and then the carpeted arms were wound tight to her sides and as the Tripps watched, the whole contraption was winched along the railway line, one agonising inch at a time. A ladder was produced and the Tripps were on the ground just in time to see the last of Dougie for the duration.

'Well, that was fairly painless.' Colin said. It would be the last time he would utter those words while on the slip.

The Tripps knew the drill and got to work on the hull with scourers and brushes. They inspected the skin fittings and to the untrained eye it just looked like a matter of popping the old ones out and putting new ones in. Frank/owner/manager/chandlery operator, said he could source two new ones asap. What he didn't mention was *asap* actually meant, as savings all purloined.

Colin went to work pulling out the old fittings, which the previous owner had decided to epoxy into the hull with some sort of glue that could have put the ten commandment tablets back together. They refused to move no matter how he chipped, pulled, swore, heated, cooled and thumped. Frank/owner/manager/chandlery operator/shipwright came over and suggested that the only way was to make a bigger hole.

'Never shift that stuff.' He poked around Colin's workings. It seemed a logical solution so Viv was dispatched home to Colin's shed to bring back the hole saws. While he waited, Colin asked Frank/owner/manager/chandlery operator/ shipwright/ paint expert about antifoul. Frank's recommendation was a cheaper option than the other boat yard, so Colin ordered a couple of tins.

Vivian arrived back at the site and Colin went to work. By the time he had finished he had two very neat holes in the hull and stood back to look at his handy work. Frank, who knew a bit about boats, took a look at Colin's work, having no work of his own to occupy him.

'What size is that?' Frank pointed to the hole.

'Er, it's a 42mm hole saw, around about.'

'Mmm.' Frank frowned and Vivian began to think they had made a mistake.

'What is it Frank?'

'Well, what skin fitting did you have in mind?' Viv visibly slumped. She could see the problem straight away.

'You don't have a skin fitting to match, do you?' Viv said.

'Nope.' Frank answered. Colin, who was a bit slower on the uptake, said,

'What?'

'Well darling...' Viv then explained what they had done by making a hole bigger than any skin fitting on the market. 'Nothing will fit.'

'Oh.'

Frank, who added boat builder to his skills said he could fix it.

'What about El Nino?' Viv said under her breath and nudged Colin. Frank coughed and waited.

'So, Frank, what will it cost?' Frank screwed up his nose, stuck his hands in his pockets, sucked in his breath and blew it out again. The Tripps waited. Frank bit his bottom lip and looked at the holes. He pursed his lips and rubbed his chin.

'Frank?' Viv wasn't quite sure Frank was going to say anything, or anything that could come back and bite him.

'One day's work.' Viv and Col did a quick calculation at $100 an hour.

260

'What if I help?' Colin asked.

'Two days.' Frank had dealt with boat owners and knew the pitfalls. He was of the opinion that near enough was good enough and what the eye doesn't see the heart doesn't grieve. Boat owners were fussy individuals who just had no idea on how to get a job done.

'Oh.' The Tripps felt the shackles of expert advice tighten around their wallet. They looked at one another, the hole, Frank/expert repairer and slid uncomfortably to the conclusion that they need to pay.

'Alright.' Colin nearly choked on the word. Frank smiled and walked away, the Tripps assuming he was going to get the wherewithal to start the job. When he didn't return after a decent interval they made all sorts of excuses for him.

'He must be ordering the stuff.'

'Perhaps he's gone to get some special tool.'

'Well, we are not the only ones that need stuff done. We will just have to wait our turn.'

'You don't think he gone home, do you?' Colin just shrugged his shoulders. They waited and when nothing was forthcoming Viv decided they should go for lunch and then come back to tackle the Super Pooper instillation.

Hard standing, or having the boat out of the water and paying through the nose for the privilege, is a fraught business. You know you should be utilising your time, getting value for money, doing everything, but as none of the jobs are that appealing, it is so easy to do as little as possible. The Tripps fell into a malaise while they ate. They talked about the job, discussed the possibilities of

261

the job, wondered on Franks methods, and made lists, but still sat at the table and pushed the crumbs around the plate.

'We should get back and do something.' Colin felt pangs of guilt. They packed up and drove back to the slipway. Frank/pub patron with a lifetime membership, was nowhere to be seen and none of his handy work was in evidence.

'Probably at lunch.' Viv climbed the ladder followed by Colin. They looked over the instructions for the Super Pooper and it wasn't long before heads were down, bums up, installing, what the salesman described as *the most trouble-free system in the world.* It was just a pity the pre-drilled holes didn't quite fit the screws supplied, if there had been enough of them in the first place. Nor did the hose connection come in a proprietary size, but something the inventor had dreamed up while taking medication. By the time the Tripps had finished, Viv had been to the chandlery four times for different bits and pieces. Now the Super pooper nestled down in the bilge waiting for its first offering.

The Tripps stood looking at the little box as if it was their first child.

'It's nice isn't it?'

'Marvellous.'

'A miracle.'

'Absolutely.' Colin felt his chest swelling with pride. He had yet to discover the terrible twos, not to mention the teenage years. Toilet systems on boats are about as family friendly as a Hell's Angel and just as much trouble as if the whole gang were living next door.

Frank hadn't reappeared as the Tripps made to go home. The holes in the hull stood like two blank eyes.

'Well, there is always tomorrow.' Colin giggled. Viv thought on the bank balance. At the price of hard standing that might make polite company blush plus all the trips to the chandlery those two little holes were turning into black holes.

CHAPTER 19

Day two dawned with the chance of rain. Frank walked over to Colin as he looked at his holes.

'Too wet today. Won't work.'

'Oh.' Colin wasn't sure if Frank didn't work in the rain or what.

'Er, Frank, what is it you are actually going to do?' Colin just had to get to the nub of it.

'Well, see here. It's like this. This is the thing.' Frank beat around the bush.

'Yes?' Colin put on his 'I'm listening' look.

'I figure we can...' Frank's phone rang and he walked off. Viv shook her head.

'I think he is keeping us hostage Colin. I'm getting Nino.'

'Viv.' Colin didn't like to upset the fragile relationship he was cultivating with Frank. Vivian held up her hand and then took the car keys and was gone. Col stood about for a bit then decided to get started on the antifoul. He assembled all the equipment. Looked over the job. He put his equipment in a neat pile. Rearranged the pile several times and went out to the car park to look for Viv. He saw the car turning the corner and scooted back to the boat and pretended to look busy. Viv came up.

'He says he can do it tomorrow. Apparently,' and here Vivian whispered, 'Nino has no qualms about working in the rain.'

'Oh.' Colin said. 'I started the antifoul,' Colin pointed to his pile of things. 'This is one job I know we can do ourselves.'

Antifoul is a paint that prevents things growing on the hull. The main ingredient is not lead, as the weight of the tins might suggest, but copper. Colin lugged the tins to the boat and then when the tins were prized open he realised they had settled. Six inches of goo had congealed on the bottom. The small paint stirrer he had purchased from Frank / paint stirrer expert, couldn't even make a dent.

'We need a bigger stirrer.' Viv went to the shop. She came back with something that would do the job. Colin attached it to an electric drill and stuck it in the tin. Physics wasn't a strong point with Colin at school. The centrifugal force of the paint stirrer threw the paint into a water spout and it climbed up the side of the tin at an alarming rate and then threw itself on the ground. In his haste to stop the action, Colin pulled the paint stirrer out. Someone should have reminded him to take his finger off the trigger. The paint flew 360° coating the Tripps, the boat, the boat next door and a pile of rope.

'Ahhhh.' Viv ran for cover. Colin put the drill down.

'You really should spray it. Goes further.' A man walked up to the catastrophe.

'Pardon?' Colin looked at the small man who resembled a very wrinkly raisin.

'Don,' he held out his hand. 'Spay it, easier in the long run.' Don looked over the paint splats on Colin's face and Vivian came back to the group.

Colin did the intro's. 'Don, Viv, Viv, Don. Don was saying we should spray it.'

'Spray.' Viv said.

'Spray.' Don said. The conversation lacked depth, but when Colin said it was cheaper in the long run, Viv's ears pricked up.

'Cheaper?'

'Cheaper.' Don repeated. Vivian then went into twenty questions about the spraying of antifouling. Don was a fount of knowledge. By the time he had left the Tripps wondered why they ever thought to do it themselves, realised it was cheaper and easier in the long run. A Jehovah's Witness could only wish for such a quick convert. Viv found Frank/ spray painter and arranged to have the job done. He pencilled it in the book.

Now with nothing left to do, but pay, the Tripps made a plan that the next day would be full on. They hadn't actually achieved very much, but 'organising everyone is a necessary part of the job too'.

CHAPTER 20

Day three promised to be a fine day. Nino turned up early with all the necessary tools. He stripped off to the waist, gave a winning smile to Vivian who blushed, and surveyed the job, as Colin hovered.

'No problemo.' Frank came up with the skin fittings and nodded as he watched Nino work. Anyone who could do the job, so he didn't have to, was a bonus. Nino worked all day reinstating the hull and putting the skin fittings back. Col and Viv began to think this hard standing wasn't so hard after all...all it takes is money.

'It-a will take a day to get hard si?' Nino pointed to the new matrix and the skin fittings. 'Then we-a paint si?'

'Si.' Colin nodded. Nino packed up and left, but not before giving Vivian an air kiss, which made her go all girly.

'Better tell Frank.' Colin said as he narrowed his eyes at the tanned, muscle bound back of the Italian. Viv nodded and went in search of the elusive Frank. He seemed to be nowhere in sight when you wanted work done, but had a sixth sense when you opened your wallet. Now he was in the office eating the remnants of his lunch off his shirt. Vivian relayed the information that they would be one more day and Frank wrote it in the book.

 CHAPTER 21

Day four came with the promise of a touch up. Nino arrived and went to work as Colin paced and watched the clock ticking. He kept mumbling, 'by the hour, by the hour,' as Nino worked.

'Now we wait for the drying, si?'

'Si.' Colin had already dipped into his long service leave for the haul out and now was spending his time watching paint dry. It was going to be a long afternoon.

CHAPTER 22

Day five and the Tripps were informed that the massive winch that was needed to put them in the water had to be repaired and it was raining - again. Colin began to pace and discovered he had a nervous twitch when anyone mentioned money.

CHAPTER 23

Day six and he confronted Frank about the wait. Frank/wasn't born yesterday, produced a signed document stating that inclement weather was not the responsibility of the owner/manager and the customer was liable for any fees occurring because of the above.

'Who uses the word inclement anyway,' Colin railed to Vivian. 'Pphhhffff.'

CHAPTER 24

Day seven and with the black holes plugged and costing more that Colin made in a month, the antifouling sprayed and the Super Pooper ready to go, so were the Tripps. Frank/accountant came over with the bill.

'No cash, no splash.' He reiterated the ol' hard stand chestnut and retreated back to the office. People, Frank found, like a bit of privacy when they have hysterics.

Vivian opened the bill. She read the bottom line and handed it to Colin. He steeled himself and looked at the number.

'That's not the telephone number is it?'

'No.'

They stood in silence for a minute or two and then looked at Moonlighting. She was clean, fresh, and ready for more sailing adventures. The reality gap was jumped.

'Well, it's a good job, a specialized job.'

'And the paint job will last longer too.'

'We couldn't have done it in the water.'

'We really needed an expert to do those fittings. It makes all the difference.' The justification-o-metre went to the red line. Viv took the bank card to the office and paid up. Frank swiped the card and knew daylight robbery was the easiest thing in the world when you had a boatyard.

Back on the dock Moonlighting stood ready. Vivian and Colin sat in the cockpit and felt a deep longing for the sea. They watched a couple mooch up the dock looking at the boats. The couple stopped next to moonlighting.

'Nice boat.'

'Thanks.' Colin smiled. 'You have one?'

'No, we are looking for a boat.' The couple smiled.

'Really' Colin jabbed Viv in the ribs with his elbow.

'Is this...?'

'For sale?' Colin offered.

'Well, yes.'

'Could be.'

'Wife's not too keen on boats.' The man said. Viv smiled and Colin nodded.

'Just think of it this way. You're not buying a boat, you're buying a lifestyle.'

Herman Melville,

*There never was a very
great man yet
who
spent all his life
inland*

Lightning Source UK Ltd.
Milton Keynes UK
UKHW020636080520
362982UK00009B/236